"How many?" Janeway whispered, her eyes riveted to the viewscreen. . . .

"Twenty-three vessels, Captain, all heavily armored, with shields raised and weapons ready," Tuvok said in a calm, grave tone.

Janeway patted Tom Paris on the shoulder. "All stop."

The engine whine died to a dull hum, and the silence of the bridge chewed at the captain.

"Accept the hail, Mr. Kim."

"Yes, ma'am."

A humanoid face appeared.

Captain Janeway stepped forward. "What do you want?" No sense wasting time with an introduction. Her initial hails had identified the *Voyager,* its mission, and its intentions. This new enemy knew all that and didn't care.

"My apologies, Captain," the alien said, "but what I want . . . is your ship. . . ."

STAR TREK® VOYAGER™

BATTLE LINES

Dave Galanter
and
Greg Brodeur

POCKET BOOKS
New York London Toronto Sydney Tokyo Singapore

An *Original* Publication of POCKET BOOKS

POCKET BOOKS, a division of Simon & Schuster Inc.
1230 Avenue of the Americas, New York, NY 10020

This book is published by Pocket Books, a division of
Simon & Schuster Inc., under exclusive license from
Paramount Pictures.

ISBN: 0-671-00259-7

First Pocket Books printing May 1999

10 9 8 7 6 5 4 3 2 1

POCKET and colophon are registered trademarks of
Simon & Schuster Inc.

Printed in the U.S.A.

For our parents

Sarah and Max
&
Barbara and Donald

ACKNOWLEDGMENTS

Just some words of thanks . . .

Greg Brodeur has his name on this book and gets half the money, so I see no need to thank him. Except maybe to say, I couldn't write the words without his plotting, his editing, and his good humor. I don't really consider *myself* a writer. I consider *us* a writer.

Thanks to Carol Greenburg for finding things I wouldn't have seen for a few years (if ever) and would have wanted to change. Her suggestions were golden.

A standing O for Trek Novel Senior Editor John Ordover, who always deserves one. He makes it fun.

Dr. Pino Colone was a fountain of valuable medical information. If the Doctor in this book sounds like a real doctor, I owe it all to Dr. Colone. Thanks, Pino!

Thanks to Lyn Scharf for knowledge of all things military and naval, and for her comments throughout.

And I'd also like to thank any friends and family who accepted that I needed to work on this book and couldn't always "come out to play": Len and Wendy Spampinato, my cousin Howard Weingarten and his family, Peggy Eaton and her brood, my parents, just to name the ones I can think of as I write this. Thanks to them for being understanding.

ACKNOWLEDGMENTS

Finally, a writer's thanks to authors Diane Carey and Robert B. Parker. When I try to achieve a style in my writing, I work for a mix of Diane's well-crafted and talented wordsmithing and Robert B. Parker's straightforward, no-nonsense tone. Thanks to them for their respective bodies of work. They never cease to awe me with their prose.

Cheers,
Dave Galanter
DHGalanter@aol.com

"I object to you. I object to intellect without discipline. I object to power without constructive purpose."

—Spock of Vulcan
"The Squire of Gothos"

BATTLE LINES

CHAPTER
1

"YELLOW ALERT!"

Captain Janeway wedged her rigid shoulders into the command chair as the ship took on an acute hum. Like her captain, the *Voyager* tensed as she approached the unknown.

"Defense fields energized. All decks report ready." Lieutenant Tuvok's voice was a calm baritone. Vulcan-calm.

"Intensify scans. I want to know what we're dealing with." Janeway let her glare lock on the rushing starscape of the forward viewscreen, as if human eyes alone could watch ships that sensors only saw as shadows.

The captain pushed herself up and over toward the Ops station, where Harry Kim leaned into his console, shaking his head, frustrated.

"Ensign?" the captain prodded.

"It's there, Captain, all over the sector. Heavy subspace activity."

She frowned. "But not the burst you saw before."

There was no question in the captain's voice, but the young man answered anyway. "No."

The tension in Janeway's shoulders worked its way up her neck and down her back as she pivoted toward the tactical station. "Tuvok?"

"Scanners still indicate two slight subspace signatures which *may* be warp vessels, at extreme range."

May be. May not be.

"Find out."

Tuvok nodded once, and silently returned to his tactical sensors.

Janeway pulled in a deep, unsatisfying breath. She dragged her fingers along the rail on the upper bridge as she stepped down to the command deck. Fresh, uncharted space was what she'd always wanted, *still* wanted . . . but now a Federation Starbase wasn't only a month or two away—it was decades distant. Starbases didn't exist for her or for the *Voyager*'s crew, and that had to figure into her reasoning, her tactics.

But no matter how far she was from port, Starfleet's mission was to seek out new life . . . and these ships were unknown.

"Mr. Paris, maintain course but reduce speed by one-quarter. Mr. Kim, narrow sensor frequency to focus on Mr. Tuvok's vessel shadows. Tie in to his console."

"Unrepaired damage from our last encounter with the Aakteians has left the sensor array weak," Tuvok said. "A narrow-band focus will reduce long-range sensors."

She nodded. "Then hurry."

Risk was an albatross around every explorer's neck, from Magellan to Byrd, from Cochrane to Kirk. They all knew home for them was months away, and if they were stranded, hope could be counted in years. They had dealt with it. So would *Voyager* and her crew.

"Scanning. . . ." Tuvok said suddenly. "Definitely two space-faring vessels with warp signatures, bearing one-one-nine mark seventeen. A parallel course."

Janeway pivoted toward tactical again. "Identification?"

Would they be friend or foe? *Voyager* had found plenty of both in the Delta quadrant.

"These data *are* from extreme range—"

"Noted. Report."

"Both ships are of a class heretofore unseen. Class five warp signatures, no detectable weapons, and a class fifteen shield."

"Class fifteen shields?" Lieutenant Tom Paris angled

around from the helm. "We could snap through those pretty quick."

Tuvok cocked his head so that he could see past the Captain and into Paris's eyes. "I also register thick armor, construct unknown, class unknown, but more dense than any Alpha quadrant vessels on file."

"Oh." The helmsman turned back to his console.

"Captain, we're being scanned," Ensign Kim called.

Tuvok confirmed with a nod. "Verified."

Janeway took the center seat again. "All right. We're looking at them, they're looking at us."

Hope and apprehension rode the same wave of emotion across the bridge. Many new races had greeted the *Voyager* with friendship: the Talaxians, the Raduk, the Baadalian. But many they'd left behind had become enemies: the Vidians, the Kazon sects, the Aakteians.

Where would this new race fit?

"They're changing course," Tuvok said, a slightly surprised edge to his voice. "An intercept vector."

Lieutenant Paris held his fingers just above the helm console, apparently ready to make a course correction if ordered.

Janeway noticed. "Hold your course, Lieutenant."

"Aye, Captain."

"Hailing frequencies, Mr. Kim. Let them know we're not a threat. Mr. Tuvok, revert to a full sector scan."

Giving orders held a satisfaction of its own—the feeling that any situation could be controlled, tamed.

And an ensign as young as Kim needed his captain to be fully in control. Janeway gauged the ship's tension through his young voice, and from the way it cut now, she knew she had to be *Voyager's* anchor. "Captain," he said, "they're receiving the hail, but not responding."

Not a good sign. "I don't like this," Janeway said. "Come about, Mr. Paris. I want a course that curves away from the intercept point. One-one-five, mark two-zero. Z plus point-two light days. They want to intercept us before we see them, and I don't like that."

Paris dabbed at his console. "Aye, Captain. One fifteen, mark twenty. Z plus point two L.D."

"Captain, they're matching our course and speed," Tuvok reported. "Correcting for our change in trajectory."

Janeway nodded, as if she'd expected that, and allowed no surprise to show in her eyes. She palmed a control on the arm of her command chair. "Commander Chakotay, report to the bridge."

Immediately the turbolift doors slid open and Chakotay marched forward.

The captain allowed herself a brief smile.

"I was on my way when I saw the Yellow Alert." He lowered himself into the seat next to the command chair and activated his status viewer.

Janeway pointed to the tactical screen at her left. "We've got two ships on an intercept course, refusing to answer hails."

"And two more," Tuvok added, "now on sensors at extreme range."

"Kim?"

"Still no response to our hails."

"Raise shields." Janeway shared a moment's glance with Chakotay, then looked toward the tactical display. "Let's hope they realize we lack armor only because we have other defenses."

"All four vessels have increased speed. Intercept in forty-three seconds."

"I'm reading power surges on those ships, Captain. Could be a weapons charge."

"I don't like these odds. Edge away, Mr. Paris. Get us some safe distance."

"I'll try, Captain, but the other two are zig-zagging around as they come in."

"They're trying to box us in," Chakotay said.

Janeway nodded agreement. "Red Alert."

"Battle stations. Battle stations. All hands, battle stations!"

The bridge lights flickered to a red hue, cutting the glare from white accent lights. Janeway could feel power surging through the ship, vibrating up the deck plates from Engineering, deep below. The small *Voyager* crew took to their alert stations, and she imagined she could feel their energy too—boots rushing down corridors, staccato voices chopping out orders and routines.

"Locking phasers," Tuvok said.

"Belay that." Janeway rose and took a few steps toward tactical. "If they can scan us, they'll see we're targeting them."

"Indeed," Tuvok said. "Wouldn't that be advisable?"

"Are we *sure* they have armed their weapons?"

The Vulcan checked his scanner. "I cannot be sure until we have positively identified their weapon type—presuming they have armaments that can be identified by our sensors."

New encounters were always a tightrope walk between too much caution and too much risk.

"Captain." Chakotay rose too. "Boxing us in *is* an aggressive act."

Janeway nodded slowly. "No argument. But we have a reputation in this quadrant now, Commander. A bad one, as far as some are concerned. They may have scanned us, recognized our design from rumors, and now see *us* as the threat."

"Captain, they're trying to herd us. I can't keep out of range." Paris was annoyed. The starscape on the viewscreen wheeled by as he tried to maneuver *Voyager* between the approaching ships.

Now visible on the main screen, the alien vessels looked large, bulky, and rocket-shaped, with dark hulls that nearly blended into the blackness of space.

"I want a few phaser shots across their bows, Mr. Tuvok." The captain came up behind the conn station. Paris was grappling with the control panel, twisting the ship as she readied herself to fire. Janeway had an urge to sit in that seat herself. Every job on the starship was ultimately her job, and she would have felt better with her own hand on the helm.

"Phasers . . ." Tuvok droned. "Firing."

Voyager spat a few phaser slices into space, just missing the mild shields of the approaching ships.

"All targets changing course. Attack vectors."

"They're firing, Captain. Point-blank!"

As Kim spoke, blue tendrils of electric flame whipped around the ship, slapping the shields.

"Disruptor-like weapons, Captain," Tuvok called. "Shields, aft and fore, down to ninety-three percent."

Janeway gripped Paris's chair as the vessel shook around her. "Return fire! Full phasers. Evasive substarboard."

"They're firing again!"

Lightning crashed against the shields.

"Damage—decks five and six, aft sections."

"Damage control, Chakotay."

"En route."

Again, blue rods of flame shot from one of the enemy vessels and raked *Voyager* back.

"Aft phasers. Ready torpedoes just in case." Janeway forced herself back into the command chair. On the tactical screen, four alien vessels kept swooping down, firing, then withdrawing. "Protect our flank, Mr. Paris."

"Aye, aye."

"Kim, do what you can to get an answer to our hails." Janeway looked up toward Tuvok. "What could this be about? Why?"

The Vulcan had no answer.

"Captain, one of them is damaged and retreating."

"The lead ship has released a solid object." Kim's voice, not panicked, but charged. "Simple propulsion—twenty-four seconds to contact."

Before Janeway could glance back up to Tuvok, he was acting on her unspoken order. "Checking . . ."

Only a moment of silence, as Paris spun the ship this way and that, before Tuvok spoke again.

"A nuclear device," he said matter-of-factly. "Armed for impact against our shields."

"You've got to be kidding," Chakotay said, incredulous.

"They're still ignoring all hails."

"Keep trying," Janeway ordered, then quickly spun back to Tuvok. "They don't want to talk? Let's give them some incentive." She glared at the screen, at one of the alien vessels as it retreated. "That ship is moving away—the nuclear device is a danger to them."

"Without proper shielding, it may disrupt their subspace and impulse systems."

"Seven seconds to impact," Kim said.

"Tractor beam," Janeway ordered. "Swing the warhead back at them."

Tuvok nodded appreciatively. "Aye, Captain."

A quiet bridge . . . in battle, that meant a bridge stoked with tension.

Tuvok jabbed at his control panel. A moment—

The warhead swung around as if pitched from an invisible sling-shot. The enemy vessel tried to increase speed. Tried—

And failed.

Space before them bubbled white hot, then cooled and expanded outward in all directions—an explosion basic in physics and power.

"Shockwave," Kim reported.

Voyager shuddered slightly, and only for a moment, as the energy from the chain reaction washed over them.

"The alien vessel," Tuvok said, "has been destroyed."

Janeway and Chakotay shared a bewildered look.

"I surmise that the impact created an internal explosion in their warp propulsion system." Tuvok slid from one screen to another on his console. "Three more ships have arrived. Different configurations but similar armaments."

"From three-to-one to six-to-one." Janeway tugged at the collar of her tunic and leaned forward toward Paris. "Evasive pattern omega three-four, warp one."

"Engaging."

"Tuvok, even those odds. Fire phasers at will. Kim, tell them this ends when they end it."

Voyager lashed out. Orange sabers of energy punctured the weak shields of the alien ships and sliced into their armor. Molten lines of damage quickly cooled in the vacuum of space.

"Direct hits. We've damaged one severely, the other has lost propulsion," Tuvok said. "Two enemy vessels limping back, reserve three coming in."

Enemy vessels. *Enemy.* Janeway had no idea who they suddenly had as enemies. There had to be a reason . . . she needed to have one.

She'd find out before this was over—she promised herself that.

The largest of the next three alien vessels ascended across the forward viewscreen.

Paris punched at his naviconsole. "This one's a biggun', Captain. I'm trying to stay out of its way."

"Mass of this vessel is twenty-three times our own, Captain," Kim said.

Tuvok bowed over his sensors. "Weapons status unknown. Dense armor. High subspace output."

A flash on the screen, and a thousand small projectiles appeared, speeding toward *Voyager*.

Chakotay motioned to the tactical screen. "They've called in the big guns."

"Metallic alloy objects, Captain. Unknown propellant," Tuvok called. "Meant to disrupt our shields."

Armor rather than shields . . . mechanical *and* energy weapons. Whoever they were, they lacked some of the technology the Federation had in abundance. Janeway could use that.

"Launch countermeasures, Mr. Tuvok. Let's show them that bigger isn't better."

Tuvok dabbed at his board and *Voyager* launched a torpedo that shot forward, hovered a moment, then exploded into a million small flares. Space ignited as each flare found one of the enemy shells, and both died in a fiery struggle.

"The two smaller vessels are firing disruptors again. Aft dorsal shield weakened."

"I need our flank protected, Mr. Paris."

"Trying, Captain. They're targeting our aft."

Janeway hit a button on the arm of her chair. "Janeway to Engineering."

"Torres here."

"We're losing dorsal shields." Neither statement nor question—the captain wanted a solution.

"I'm switching to secondary generators, Captain, but circuits are overloading."

Every sentence punctuated with an explosion of power that raked *Voyager's* shields, Janeway leaned down to the chair-arm comm. "Reroute wherever you have to, Lieutenant. I don't want to lose shields. We don't have the armor these people have."

"Aye, Captain."

Janeway thumbed the comm off. "Bridge out."

"Captain—" Paris called her attention and pointed at the forward viewscreen.

"What are they doing?"

Tuvok answered, as the largest ship sped toward *Voyager.* "Pursuing a collision course," he said calmly.

"They're going to ram us," Janeway whispered.

"We cannot cope with a warp-speed ram from a vessel of such mass," Tuvok said.

Janeway jabbed at a safe coordinate on the tactical board. "Warp evasive! Get us out of here!"

"No room to maneuver, Captain."

"Warn them off, Tuvok. Tell them we'll cripple them if they attempt to ram this vessel." She wanted Tuvok to handle the hail. He'd word it better than Kim.

"Aye."

"They're coming around to the aft," Kim said, his tone calmer than Janeway might have guessed it would be.

"Become a corkscrew, Mr. Paris. Don't let them in."

Paris shook his head. "This is fun," he said dryly, and *Voyager* began a spinning course upward as the two other enemy vessels continued to direct fire at her aft shields.

"Aft dorsal shield collapsing, Captain."

Voyager lashed out in its spin, spitting hot phaser beams at the three attacking ships.

The enemy lashed back.

"Impact with lead ship in fifteen seconds!"

They'd been warned. . . .

"Photon torpedoes," Janeway said. "Fire all bays. Aim strategically, Tuvok. I want that vessel stopped. Target their engines. Fire at will."

Phasers still lighting up the hulls of her enemies, *Voyager* hissed out a spread of torpedoes, point blank into the approaching vessel.

The most forward vessel erupted into molten debris as its hull collapsed and its engines imploded. *Voyager* was pushed back by the force, tossed aside by a wash of energy and wreckage. She rolled, end-over-end, riding the wave of debris that exploded too close to her hull.

Janeway pitched from the command chair and onto the

hard deck. Balance restored itself, and she quickly pushed herself up, giving Chakotay a hand as well.

"Status!"

"Continuing to fire." How Tuvok managed to hold onto his station when everyone else lost theirs . . . "We have a shield breach at aft dorsal. Damage to decks five, six, and ten. Warp power is offline."

"Auxiliary power to the shields." Janeway returned to the command chair but didn't sit. Without her aft defensive shield, *Voyager* could be carved up like Christmas ham. "I want that screen up. Mr. Paris, best speed evasive. Get us out—"

"They've ceased fire," Tuvok said.

All looked up as four loud *thunks* vibrated through the ship.

A physical hit, on the ship's hull.

Not the sound of a weapon, but the sound of debris hitting the hull plates.

Janeway spun toward Chakotay. "What was that?"

He shrugged, more with his eyes than his shoulders, and leaned into his status screen.

"The vessels are backing off on their own," Tuvok said, just a hint of surprise in his tone.

"Engineering says warp is still offline, and now warp power levels are fluctuating!" Paris pounded on his board.

"We have a hull breach." Kim was incredulous. "I think."

"You *think?*" Janeway jumped up to the upper deck. She leaned over Kim's console. "Tuvok, verify this." She pecked at Ensign Kim's control panel.

The captain waited a moment, then met the Vulcan's eyes. "A mine?" she asked.

"Negative."

His voice was too passive at times like these.

"Then what?"

"A device of some kind, producing a warp-dampening field. They've launched it through the hole they blasted open in our shields."

"Captain, we're being hailed."

She looked up at Ensign Kim, then down to his console and the communications display which showed an incoming message.

Straightening, Janeway strode down to her command chair. "Ignore the hail. Mr. Paris, warp speed or not, get us out of here."

Paris shook his head once. "Aye, Captain."

"Chakotay, I want that thing off my ship." She crooked a thumb over her shoulder. "Get it off."

He nodded and was into the turbolift before she sat down.

Under Paris's prodding, *Voyager* tensed, gathered herself, and twisted out toward open space.

A moment further into the maneuver, and the ship was violently wrenched back, the air on the bridge cracking with the sound of stressed bulkheads.

"Tractor beams, class four," Tuvok said. "One from each enemy vessel."

Enemy. Why?

Janeway dug her fingers into the armrests of the command chair. Alien vessels had a tight grip on her ship. She should have a tighter one. "Full impulse, Mr. Paris. Push her."

Laboring against the energy that seized her, *Voyager* inched forward on her course. The engines whined.

"Torres to Janeway. We've got a bad coolant leak. Impulse overheating."

"Do what you can," Janeway said. "Push, Mr. Paris," she rasped. "Tuvok, reroute phasers through impulse power. Disable those tractors."

"Aye, Captain."

Voyager fired, and even with impulse phasers she cut fire into their alien hulls. Explosions racked one ship, and it fell away.

The loss of its pull on the *Voyager* pushed the ship forward and took some moan from the engines' whine.

"One vessel has been disabled, Captain."

"Three on one again. We might never have a better advantage. Disable these and we've earned our pay."

Before Tuvok could respond, the viewscreen filled—a multitude of ships falling out of warp. Janeway pushed herself up and toward the viewer, making sure she kept her jaw from gaping. "How many?" she whispered.

Tuvok's answer did not come immediately. He'd probably double-checked the sensors.

"Twenty-three vessels, Captain. Not all the same class or design, but all heavily armored, with shields raised and weapons armed." This time his voice was not as neutral. Vulcans had a grave tone, too, and this was Tuvok's.

Janeway patted Tom Paris on the shoulder. "All stop."

The engine whine died to a dull hum, and the silence of the bridge chewed at the captain. What order could she give? What could they do—without reinforcements, without a Federation—surrounded by two dozen ships?

The tension was too thick to cut.

"Accept the hail, Mr. Kim."

"Yes, ma'am."

A flicker of the forward screen, and an alien face filled the viewer. Humanoid, with angled features that could pass for Vulcan or Romulan, except the ears were more Okampan, long and close to the skull, with many ridges.

Captain Janeway stepped forward. "What do you want?" No sense wasting time with an introduction. Her initial hails had identified the *Voyager,* its mission, and its intentions. This new enemy knew all that and didn't care.

"My apologies, Captain," the alien said, the Universal Translator interpreting his tone as flatly as his real voice sounded. "But what I want . . . is your ship."

CHAPTER

2

CAPTAIN JANEWAY LOOKED AT TUVOK, THEN TURNED TOWARD Kim so the alien on the forward viewer could not see her face. "When I turn back, cut me with static and lose the signal."

Kim gave the slightest of nods.

"We should discuss this," Janeway told the alien as she slowly turned back around. "Perhaps we can—"

Static scratched the screen back to a starscape view.

"Simple code only," Janeway ordered, pivoting back to Kim. "Tell them we're having comm trouble." She marched toward the tactical station, stepping quickly to the upper deck. "Tuvok, have hand phasers issued to all crew members. Security will carry phaser rifles. They want a fistfight? They'll get one."

"Aye, Captain."

"General Quarters. Intruder alert status." She slapped at her combadge. "Janeway to Chakotay. Tell me you've got a way to get that thing off the ship."

"Wish I could, Captain. We can't even get close enough to tell. It's emitting high-level radiation right through the bulkhead. Seven-of-nine and I are rigging some special suits now, for a closer look."

The captain looked toward the turbolift and stifled the urge to go down there herself. "Danger to the crew?"

"Not after we evacuate this section."

"Do it, and let me know something—fast. You have five minutes. Janeway out." She crisply jabbed the comm off and pushed herself toward Harry Kim's Ops station. "Mr. Kim, tell them we have audio now and are working on visual communications." She rested her hand on his shoulder a moment, then left it with a pat. "We want to sound like we're working, but make sure they get the idea we're having a lot of problems."

"Aren't we?" Paris asked.

Stepping back down toward her command chair, Janeway glared at the tactical board and nodded grimly. "Twenty-six problems, to be exact, Mr. Paris."

"Twenty-four. Two ships have retreated." Tuvok stepped down to the lower deck and handed Janeway a hand phaser and a holster. "Auxiliary power circuits are overloaded on three decks. Battery power is at ninety-three percent. Warp power can be restored, but with their warp dampener, we will not be able to create a subspace field. The impulse engine coolant leak is under control, but as Lieutenant Torres puts it, 'Band-aids don't fix broken arms.'"

"Repair time?" Janeway attached the holster to the waistband of her uniform and snapped the phaser into place. The sound and feel of that was comforting. She'd defend her ship to the last ounce of energy in her sidearm, the last thought in her mind, and the last bit of strength in her body.

"Three hours for optimal repair." Tuvok leaned toward the helm and held out a phaser and holster for Paris.

"We're not getting out of here on impulse drive," Paris said, taking the weapon. As he turned around, Janeway noticed he was sweating. The bridge was hot, partly with tension, partly because of circuits that had burned in battle. It was a dry heat, though, and the perspiration evaporated quickly, leaving everyone's forehead shiny rather than drenched.

Everyone but Tuvok. He looked almost content, as if nothing had happened, as if the *Voyager* weren't teetering on the edge of a cliff. Only his tone told a different story, and probably only to Janeway.

"I am forced to agree with Mr. Paris," he said. "Twenty-four vessels is a major force. We cannot escape on impulse power."

For a moment too long, Janeway said nothing. Too much silence from a captain could worry a crew, so she turned her silence into a determined march and stalked forward toward the viewscreen.

"Maybe we won't need to escape." She motioned toward the viewscreen. "Clear up our communications, Mr. Kim."

A crackle of static, and the alien visage they'd seen a few minutes ago reappeared.

"Who are you?" Janeway asked, without banality.

"Dahlyar Lekket," the alien said, his tone very neutral. *"Commodore of the Edesian Fleet."*

Leaning forward, balancing one arm on the back of Tom Paris's chair, Janeway almost rasped her hard question. *"Why?"*

She needn't say more. Lekket knew what she wanted to know. Any ship captain would.

"It is complicated, Captain," Lekket said, sounding almost penitent.

Janeway nodded and stared hard at Lekket. "I'm listening."

Lekket glanced to someone off screen. *"I would rather speak to you in person."*

Janeway looked back to Tuvok, *her* someone off screen.

"I assure you, Captain, we mean you no great harm," Lekket said.

No *great* harm. Interesting phrasing. If that was a lie, why not completely lie? If it was the truth, why nearly destroy the *Voyager?*

"Your vessels refuse to answer peaceful hails, attack us, and now you train twenty-four banks of deadly weapons on my ship. Am I really supposed to believe you mean us 'no great harm'?"

"As I said, Captain . . . the situation is complicated. I have a shuttle and am prepared to dock—"

Janeway shook her head. "We'll not be opening our bay

doors for your party just yet, Commodore. This is *not* your ship, and an attempt to board will leave all parties . . . unhappy."

Lekket nodded his assent. *"I understand."*

"We'll send a shuttle to receive you," Janeway said. "And then, we will indeed have a long conversation."

"I look forward to it." With that pleasantry, spoken still rather flatly, the communication ended.

Paris turned and looked up at Janeway. "I'll take that shuttle, Captain."

Allowing herself a slight smile, Janeway said, "I wouldn't think of sending anyone else, Tom."

"We have fifteen minutes until the commodore of these Edesians is aboard, and I want to be able to trump him when he gets here." Janeway had one hand on her holstered phaser. She leaned a little on the lip of Tuvok's station console, allowing the ship to give her support as she tried to protect it from further attack.

"Unfortunately," Tuvok said, pointing to the monitor above his tactical station, "he holds most of the cards."

Janeway pushed herself erect and looked intently at the screen.

"Commander Chakotay and Seven's tricorder data confirm our initial scans," the Vulcan continued. "The warp-dampener will flood the ship with radiation if we attempt to deactivate it. It will flood the ship with radiation if we attempt to carve it off the hull. If we initiate a strong warp field, it will flood the ship with radiation."

"You're being redundant, Mr. Tuvok."

"I am being factual, Captain. Any action we take will kill the crew within minutes, while leaving the vessel intact."

"They have a fleet . . ." She narrowed her gaze and leveled it at the alien ships on the forward viewscreen. "Why do they want our one ship?"

"I do not know," Tuvok answered. "But Commander Chakotay and his team are in sickbay with mild radiation sickness. Unable to even further study the device on our hull, we will have to wait for Commodore Lekket's explanation."

The turbolift doors opened, and her First Officer stepped onto the upper bridge deck.

"You're fit for duty?" Janeway asked.

"I'm fine," Chakotay said, "but I did get a sermon from the Doctor on the medicinal use of radiation and how I was going about it the wrong way."

The captain smiled, briefly, and Tuvok . . . remained Vulcan.

"Has the doctor finished my little project with the subcutaneous transponders?" Janeway asked Chakotay.

He patted his arm. "Everyone."

"All right," Janeway said. "This is what I want. All transporter rooms are to be sealed, their doors made to look like bulkheads. All records of transporter technology are to be hidden. That means hiding the command processes, even in the computer."

Tuvok nodded.

"Replicators too. We'll eat rations and the products from Mr. Neelix's gardens."

"Docking bay to the bridge."

Janeway pushed a panel on Tuvok's tactical console. "Bridge here."

"Lieutenant Paris's shuttle has returned."

Less than the fifteen minutes in which Janeway had hoped she could find a miracle to answer their predicament.

Thumbing the comm off, she nodded to Tuvok. "You're with me. I have a few other special arrangements I want made. We'll stop in Engineering and handle them from there."

Tuvok rose and they marched toward the lift doors.

"You have the conn, Commander."

Chakotay nodded. "Aye, Captain."

Either Commodore Lekket and his companion were flashy dressers, or they were in high-occasion military garb. Their uniforms, if that's what they were, weren't the same as she'd seen over the comm. What Lekket wore now was more elaborate, more colorful, and had what could have been citation medals around his neck.

They approached Janeway with a brisk march, apparently

undaunted by the three guards with phaser rifles that stood against the bulkhead opposite the shuttle.

Tuvok at her side, Paris at Lekket's side, they met in the middle of the shuttle bay. The wide open space above them made the setting almost ceremonial.

"Commodore," Janeway greeted, reluctantly holding out her hand.

When he was close enough, Lekket placed a thin pouch in Janeway's outstretched palm. It was as if he'd handed her his wallet.

Then he spoke: "Captain Kathryn Janeway, of the Federation *Starship Voyager* . . ."

She almost replied, then realized that he was making a formal presentation, memorized and blandly read.

"I am Commodore Dahlyar Lekket, Edesian Fifth Fleet Command."

"I am Lieutenant Azil Bolis, Edesian Intelligence Command," said his companion.

"By order of his honor and highness Leader of the Fifth Fleet," Lekket continued, "I am authorized, with all just powers and rights, to impress this ship and her crew to one rotation in the Edesian Fifth Fleet."

Janeway said nothing, and with a quick shake of her head, quieted a possible comment from Paris.

She wanted Lekket to speak, and no one else. She wanted to hear his words, not those written for him.

After an awkward silence, Lekket finally spoke again. "I'm sorry, Captain. I understand that this is difficult to grasp, but *all* aligned and nonaligned vessels in this area are now under martial command, no matter what their affiliation."

His words finally, but still Janeway could tell he'd said them before, perhaps many times.

"Of course," he continued, obviously uncomfortable with the silence Janeway wielded, her expression unchanged, "If the *Voyager* has nonessential crew they will be transported to safety, but the rest of the crew must run the ship as they have been trained. It is Edesian law."

Still Janeway said nothing. She continued to hold out her arm, Lekket's pouch in her hand. Probably official orders.

Orders from an alien fleet, about her ship and her crew, in a language she didn't know.

"I *am* sorry, Captain. When the crisis is over, if you survive, the *Voyager* and her crew will be allowed to go on their way."

Janeway nodded once, then dropped the pouch he'd handed her. The sound of it slapping against the deck startled him and his head drew back as if he'd been struck.

"Why?" she demanded.

Lekket didn't answer a moment. He shared a brief glance with Bolis, then looked back to Janeway. Either he was surprised by her question, or the insistant tone in which she asked.

"The survival of countless starsystems depends on such drastic measures, Captain. We have no choice."

"And if I do not agree to your terms?"

"Then we are all dead."

CHAPTER

3

"THIS SHIP WILL NOT BE BOARDED." JANEWAY BROUGHT UP HER own phaser and leveled it at Lekket and Bolis. "I am in command here, no one else."

Lekket frowned, as if only disappointed in Janeway's actions, but not dissuaded from his own. "We don't intend to remove you from command, Captain. We seek only to enlist your help in our time of need."

Political cow-cookies.

Captain Janeway kept her phaser up. Paris had stepped away from Lekket and Bolis, and had his phaser raised as well. The only people without weapons drawn were the two Edesians.

"I'm sorry," Janeway said. "But we can't help you."

Races that closely resembled humans often had similar body language, and when Lekket sighed, Janeway sensed regret—possibly sorrow—that *Voyager's* capture wasn't as easy as planned.

"We are not offering a choice, Captain. We intend to treat you well, but these are difficult times . . ."

"That's not 'seeking to enlist our help,'" Janeway said harshly. "That's a death threat."

With a slight nod, Lekket accepted that. "As you wish. But many lives have been lost, and many more are sure to pass from us. If threatening you is but one brick in a new foundation of Edesian hope—if together we can save just a few more lives—then I will proudly hold the knife at your throat."

Janeway squared her shoulders as if she might have to lunge forward and knock some sense into him. She wouldn't, but tensing her body was somehow an emotional release and it helped to clear her mind. "You can't force us to fight if we refuse."

"No, I cannot," Lekket said, hands at his sides, an oak of calm and dispassion. "But we do not *have* to treat you with respect, Captain. We'd like to, but we need not. We now grapple for our own survival, and if you choose to fight us, rather than join us, we will kill you and your crew, and take your ship for our own."

The shuttle bay plunged into silence. Her arm bent, Janeway continued to level her phaser evenly, at mid-chest level.

"Or," she said finally, "I could destroy my ship now, and you with it." She let that thought weigh on the Edesians a moment, then she cocked her head toward Tuvok without taking her eyes, or her weapon, off the aliens. "How many ships could we maintain tractor beams on while we initiated a self-destruct countdown?"

"Fifteen," the Vulcan said.

"And how much damage would the shockwave from our warp-core breach cause those ships?"

Tuvok was matter-of-fact, and took no time for calculation. "Taking into account the inherent instability I've monitored in their various types of warp drive, I believe they would all be destroyed in a chain reaction subspace explosion."

Captain Janeway allowed herself the slightest of "checkmate" smiles. "Maybe we're worth one or two of your ships," she said. "But are we worth fifteen or twenty?"

Lekket shook his head, and looked to Bolis. "Proceed."

His fingers on a pendant around his neck, Bolis pressed a button and spoke. "Begin."

Janeway felt her brow furrow. *Begin what?*

A moment later, the computer alert system explained:

"Warning, level one radiation contamination. Warning. Dangerous levels of radiation detected. Warning . . ."

The captain shared a glance with her tactical officer.

"Apparently, they can control the radiation output of their warp-dampening device," Tuvok said, punctuating the obvious with his cool explanation.

Janeway outstretched her arm, leveling her weapon at Lekket's head. "Tell them to stop."

"Warning, level one radiation contamination. Warning. Dangerous levels of radiation detected. Warning . . ."

"In three minutes," Lekket said flatly, "every living being on this ship will be dead. If you stand down from a defensive posture, your life and the lives of your crew will be spared. If you attempt to destroy your ship, we will increase the contamination, and all will be dead in a matter of moments."

Edging her words around the angry lump in her throat, Janeway ground out a demand. "Tell me how you can claim not to want to harm anyone, and still do this?"

Lekket gave an elaborate shrug. "The same way you can threaten to do such a thing to your own ship and people, Captain. We are all animals." He gestured to her phaser, then motioned his hand about to include the entire ship. "Our teeth are sharper, of course. Our muscles are stronger as we cloak our physical weakness in technology, but we are still just brutes, fighting for survival. Sometimes we forget that, because we're not always so raw as in war . . ." His voice was thick with self-pity and perhaps even disgust. "But captains like us would be wise to remember, there is no such thing as civilization. We play at civilization, Captain, like children who put on their parents' clothes and pretend to be adults. Like an ugly monster might delude himself into imagining a mirror reflection of unique beauty." His jaw tensed, and he looked as if he might spit his own words onto the deck. "Lies, Captain. All lies. We are beasts, and must live our lives as such."

"Warning, level one radiation contamination. Warning. Dangerous levels of radiation detected. Warning . . ."

"You'll die with us in any case," Janeway rasped.

"Yes," he said.

She lowered her phaser and let it dangle useless at her side. "Tell them to stop," she whispered.

Lekket nodded, and Bolis spoke. "Cease."

"Warning, level one radiation contamination—Radiation level dropping. Condition yellow."

"Some of your crew will need to undergo decontamination. Perhaps even ourselves," Lekket said.

Janeway nodded. She'd been outbluffed. But she'd taken steps for even this contingency, and while this round was lost, the fight would go on.

Lekket stooped and retrieved the packet Janeway had dropped. He handed it back to her, and when she refused to accept it, he held it close to his tunic. "Lieutenant Bolis here will need to review your computer record banks, your crew roster, your ship's status reports, and so on."

Janeway nodded, holstered her phaser.

"We will shuttle over several guards, but your crew will be allowed to man their usual stations, with some guidance."

"My crew won't be loyal to you." Janeway had to keep herself from nearly growling her words.

"You will remain in command of your vessel, Captain, and I will make this my flagship, commanding the battle from here. Your crew will follow your orders, and you will follow mine."

She could stun them both now, put them in the brig . . . and then what?

She'd promised to see her crew home. This was now a major, perhaps final, detour.

Captain Janeway nodded very slowly. For now, she would do as asked. Only for now.

"You have a fine ship here, Captain," Lekket said. "It is not my intention to lose it. We've sacrificed much to add your vessel to our force . . . I *will* act to keep it safe."

Janeway hammered Lekket with an angry glare and stepped toward him. "Oh, so will I. You have my word on it."

The bridge. Intruders here were a violation, and somehow the situation felt more desperate than it had an hour earlier. Janeway had allowed Lekket to shuttle his soldiers aboard, and now the ship seemed farther from home than ever before.

Bolis, obviously Lekket's right-hand man, hovered over Tuvok's console. The Vulcan stood by and watched the alien's doings.

Breaking her from thought, Ensign Kim handed Janeway an information padd. She thought his tight frame broadcast the entire crew's anxiety. Or perhaps she was just reading her own burden into his posture.

She took the computer display board from him, glanced over the information, and gave him an encouraging nod. *This isn't over,* she thought. *We're not done fighting.*

Lekket pulled the padd from Janeway's hand. He placed one of the pendants that hung around his neck on the computer board, then handed the padd back and looked at his necklace as if it were a stopwatch.

"Our secondary power is restored," Janeway told Lekket. He nodded. "So I see."

"Then you also see that we can't get warp power online with your warp-dampening device active."

Lekket's lips were cold slices that arched upward. A chilling, emotionless smile. "Lieutenant Bolis?" He prompted.

Bolis turned from Tuvok's tactical station and stood at attention. "The warp dampener will not hamper warp power from being restored, only from the creation of a warp field. You can restore power with the dampening process in effect by using matter/antimatter intermix settings previously calculated."

Nodding, Lekket took one step closer to Janeway. "Yours is a brave lie, Captain, but your engineers no doubt are aware of that process. You must employ it quite often, in fact, during battle. Unless you calculate an intermix ratio every time you increase warp speed."

He knew a lot. Maybe not about the *Voyager,* but about warp vessels and battleships.

She wanted him off her bridge. Off her ship.

Not likely to happen anytime soon—there was an Edesian guard at every turbolift, not only on the bridge, but throughout *Voyager.* All phasers had been confiscated from the crew. Those crewmen not on duty were confined to quarters. Bolis stood next to Tuvok, and Lekket stood next to Janeway. Their every move was watched. No whisper was safe, no action unguarded.

Chakotay was in Engineering, and had reported even more Edesians down there. Janeway had covertly ordered him and Torres to delay repairs as long as they could. The way repair reports were coming in, they weren't having much luck.

The Edesians had a knack for alien technology. They were learning the ship . . . and eventually Janeway and her crew would become expendable.

Tuvok stepped down to the command deck and faced Janeway. "Captain, all but four of the other Edesian vessels have retreated to positions off our long-range scanners."

Janeway looked to Lekket, who was glancing toward the forward viewer. He nodded, his expression as stoic and distant as the starscape at which he stared. "Five ships in a battle squadron," he said. "You are now the lead ship. If you attempt escape, radiation levels will again reach critical." He turned, looked down at her. "I assure you, Captain . . . there is no chance of your flight from this matter."

At that, Janeway frowned. *Hope springs eternal,* she thought, but there was a bitter rock in her stomach which pressed down on any confidence she might be able to muster. The command chair was her only comfort, and even that was slight. She gripped onto the arms and told herself there was still much to be tried, much to be done, before things were truly hopeless. Her deep regret was that she couldn't communicate that to her crew.

"What if you die in battle, and with you the control of the radiation?" she asked.

Again, Lekket's flat expression, seemingly without feeling at all. "If I die, Captain, the radiation will trigger instantly, and you will all die. It is within your best interests to protect me, Captain."

The Edesians had done this before, and planned for every alternative. "Have the other ships been shanghaied too? Is that your hold on them as well?"

Lekket frowned, his lips becoming a drooping line. "You will know things when they are important for you to know."

"Know thy enemy," Janeway said, "is a saying from my homeworld. We need to know what we're supposed to fight."

"You will eventually," Lekket said grimly. "You'll know, and like me you'll wish you didn't."

"Shields."

"Raising shields."

"Charge phasers."

"All banks charged."

"Warp power?"

"Still at seventy percent, but stable."

Captain Janeway nodded. Lekket was sitting where Chakotay normally would, and as she spoke she realized how much she missed the first officer's presence. "This is a patch job. We're not running at full steam."

Lekket's brow furrowed. The phrase must not have translated well.

"We're not ready to go into battle," she said.

The Edesian commodore's alter-ego, Bolis, spoke from across the bridge. Apparently he was always to share Tuvok's tactical station. "They are ready."

"He doesn't know this ship like we do," Janeway said, attempting to appeal to Lekket's military sensibility. "We've been through two heavy battles in the last five days, without sufficient time to repair."

Again, Lekket looked to Bolis, who nodded and replied. "Yes, there is evidence of previous damage and repair to offensive and defensive systems."

"Are they ready for battle?" Lekket asked.

"Yes."

"We're not," Janeway said. And that wasn't such a lie. She wouldn't normally make an offensive strike in this condition. On some systems, they were running on backup circuits to backup circuits. Warp power was stable for now, but had fluctuated spastically for twenty minutes before Chakotay and Torres were able to balance the system.

Lekket leaned back in his chair, but somehow maintained his stiffness. "I trust Lieutenant Bolis much more than I trust you, Captain."

Janeway felt her lips purse, and finally she nodded. Either the man was stupid . . . or desperate.

"This course," Lekket said, pointing at the graphic on Janeway's monitor, "will take us just round the edge of the Tagal'sincha Nebula." He pointed to a spot just within the nebula as he continued. "Intelligence reports tell us that the enemy is just within, hiding themselves from our sensors and energy weapons. We will send in two of our smaller ships, in an attempt to draw them out."

"Draw them out how?"

"That is not your concern."

Janeway was silent a moment, then rubbed her palms together a bit anxiously. "You're not giving me what I need to fight this battle." She pushed herself up from the command chair and paced toward the helm and back. "I need to know what your strengths are, and what your weaknesses are, and what the enemy's strengths and weaknesses are."

"I understand," Lekket said evenly. "But I need you to approach this without prejudice. I need you to fight for your life, not to a draw. You will know our weakness when we are dead, and you will know the enemy's weakness when you find it, and take advantage of it. Remember, you are in command of this ship, but I am in command of this battle and this war."

What is he hiding? Janeway asked herself, then figured the question was a fair one.

"You're hiding a lot. Things I have to know. Tell me."

One corner of Lekket's mouth turned upward. "I appreciate your concern. I will tell you what you must know, but the rest you will learn only as necessary. Ask me again, and I will have you relieved of duty."

Leaning down, Janeway flattened her palms on the arms of Lekket's chair. She placed her face close to his, and talked just above a whisper. "I am in command of this ship, a vessel which you obviously need. If I don't remain in command, I will destroy this vessel, and you with it. You've given me some choices, Lekket, and I don't care for them one bit. But I'm willing to wait until my options are better . . . unless you force me to take a course neither of us would really want."

27

So very little behind his eyes, Janeway wasn't sure what effect she'd had on him.

"Of course," Lekket said quietly. "I understand fully."

Janeway nodded slowly and pushed herself up.

"Do you see why I say we are still but beasts, Captain?" he asked bitterly. "Do you hear the thick sound of murder in your own voice? How well you speak the words of war."

"We're approaching the nebula," Paris called from the helm.

Lekket and Bolis exchanged a cast-iron glance.

"We need no longer pretend about our respective civilizations, Captain." Lekket returned his vacant gaze toward the forward viewer, and the dark nebula in the distance. "That is at least one lie we will not have." He turned his head slightly, but looked more at the deck than at Janeway. "Prepare for battle. You have proven it is what you do best."

CHAPTER
4

"Evasive astern! Back off!"

"Shields are at maximum."

"Phasers!"

"I can't get a phaser lock—interference from the nebula."

"Manual override."

"They're still not accepting hails."

"Cancel communications. Leave a channel open if they decide to talk."

"Minor damage to aft shield array."

"Cover the flank, Mr. Paris."

"Aye, Captain."

The once dark nebula flashed with internal explosion—cold blue dust backlit by the lightning of blindly fired weapons. Disruptor fire lanced into open space. Two new ships—*Gimlon* ships, Lekket had called them—swooped out from behind their cloudy cloak. Their torpedoes spat forward as *Voyager* fell back.

Enemy ships.

Enemy. Yet another one. But who was the real enemy? The *Gimlon* ships firing at Janeway now, or the Edesian vessels that would force her to stay and fight?

Voyager took the brunt of one shot, then another—and

another—white-hot blobs of plasma pounding against her shields.

Janeway gripped onto one arm of the command chair with both hands. Knuckles white, she tried to bolster herself as the ship trembled from bow to aft.

"Tuvok, target those new vessels."

"Targeting."

Voyager's phasers pierced space and punctured first one ship's armor, then another's, toward the rear of each ship. Explosions rocked the enemy and they fell off their course.

Other vessels replaced them, darting out of the nebula, firing freely, rapidly.

"Three more ships, Captain," Kim said. Tuvok confirmed, as Janeway ordered the ship around to a better firing position.

Disruptor fire lit up space as one ship crossed *Voyager's* bow, then another.

"Damage to primary navigator/deflector array."

"Bypass to secondary systems. Keep damage control parties on the aft shield generators."

Static cut the forward viewer. Janeway glared through to the new enemies that attacked her ship at the exclusion of the two Edesian vessels that tried to guard *Voyager*.

Pallbearers, protecting the ship they had dragged to war.

There had been four Edesian ships when the battle began. Two had gone into the nebula—and hadn't returned.

Around her, all phaser banks were alive and hissing fire.

"Have the squadron fight back the two enemy ships," Lekket ordered Bolis. "Secure the *Voyager*."

Lekket's plan had failed. He'd ordered in two of his convoy in the hopes of forcing his enemy out from the nebula. All he'd driven out were the enemy's own escorts.

"All about full. New course, two-five-five, mark seventeen." Janeway wanted out of this battle—out of this war. Would Lekket agree to the retreat?

His enemy didn't. They'd obviously scanned her ship, and knew it was more formidable than the various Edesian craft they were used to. They charged at her and fired point-blank.

"Distance, Mr. Paris. Get us distance."

"Aye, aye," Paris huffed, wrestling with his naviconsole.

"Two more runabout-sized craft have emerged from the nebula," Tuvok reported. "They are armed and heavily armored."

Back and forth across the forward viewer, small Gimlon craft sped around *Voyager*, firing disruptors and small torpedoes at close range.

"We're being swarmed," Paris said. "I can't get a clear course."

Bolis nodded grimly. "Kasakta-class intercepts. Small, maneuverable at sublight. Many of these were left disabled after the war. The Gimlon have obviously refit them, *against* our signed treaties."

"Armor and weapons are comparable to the Edesian vessels," Tuvok said.

"Yes," Lekket admitted acerbically. "After we won the last war, we were foolish enough to rebuild their factories— their economy. The technology we shared with them is now used against us."

Janeway listened, wondering if any of what they said was true, but her gaze was on the tactical board and the incoming torpedo. "Phasers," she ordered. "Detonate incoming."

"We still don't have a phaser lock."

"You'll have to eye it, Tuvok."

Two red spears stabbed from *Voyager* and sliced the approaching torpedo into nothingness—Tuvok didn't often need a phaser lock. The shockwave shook the ship a little, but it was nothing like the tossing about they would have gotten from an impact.

A strand of hair fell over Janeway's eyes and she waved it back over her ear.

On the forward viewer, Edesian and Gimlon fighters sped one way and another, firing at each other, tangling like angry bees with fatal stings. Curving around *Voyager*, the Gimlon ships took potshots at the larger Federation vessel when they could.

"Return fire," Janeway ordered, and knew Tuvok would continue to target engines and weapons centers only. This wasn't their war, and *Voyager* and her crew would not become a tool of death for Lekket.

"Aft shield generators weakening. They are focusing on aft dorsal," Tuvok said.

Lekket leaned close to Janeway, to be heard over the din of an active bridge in battle. "The small ships will try to weaken you so that their flagship can take you easily. You cannot limit yourself to secondary targets. You *must* destroy them."

"This is my battle, Commodore," Janeway said. "I'll fight it as I see fit."

Lekket shook his head and his voice raised loudly above the din of the battle. "No, Captain!" He pointed to the forward viewer. "You do not merely clip the wings of birds of prey. The enemy will annihilate us if we do not destroy them."

Adamant, Janeway ground her voice low. "I have no intention of being annihilated . . . but I also have no intention of being forced to annihilate those I don't know to be my enemy."

"They *are* your enemy, Captain," Lekket said, passion cutting his voice for the first time. "They are enemies of all free peoples—of all living things."

Captain Janeway leaned toward Lekket and let her low voice rend the distance between them. "I'm not feeling very free right now, Commodore, and my conqueror isn't on a Gimlon ship—he's sitting right here, wearing your death threats."

Lekket turned away. "We will not discuss this now! You will do as I say!"

Janeway shook her head. "No, I won't."

"Our shields are at eighty-seven percent," Tuvok said, breaking one tension with another. "One of the Edesian vessels and two of the Gimlon interceptors are disabled and adrift."

Lekket turned back to Janeway, his eyes dark and hard, but he spoke to his Lieutenant. "Bolis, take care."

Bolis nodded and spoke into his compendant. "Destroy disabled Gimlon attack ships," he ordered.

Jolted out of the command chair, Janeway pivoted toward Commodore Lekket. "They're helpless. Harmless. We've disabled them—that's all that's necessary."

Lekket shook his head. "They are the enemy."

She was aghast. "Board their ships and take them prisoner. Take their vessels for your own."

"No," he said. "Boarding their ships would mean death to our people. This may be your battle, but it is our war, and I will not temper mercy again, only to have the merciless later invade!"

In space before her, Janeway watched the last Edesian vessel descend, fire charges at the drifting Gimlon ships, then retreat as explosions pushed out, rupturing the edge of the nebula and sending a subspace shockwave out into the starsystem.

Bubbles of energy washed across the remaining ships, rocking them all back. Janeway was bounced into the command chair, a chair that was not completely hers anymore.

The dark dust of the nebula ignited and pulled back into a rolling chemical inferno. Crimson-orange spikes of gas flared in all directions. Pockets of white explosions—probably hidden Gimlon ships—burst from the quickly disappearing nebula.

A master stroke—and a turning point. Lekket had ordered the death of helpless ships, knowing their destruction would inflame the nebula and expose or destroy those Gimlon vessels concealed by the cloud.

Janeway looked back to Tuvok, only to find Bolis hovering over the Vulcan's tactical console. He'd pushed Tuvok aside.

"Four of five remaining Gimlon intercepts in the nebula were destroyed, but their *Marauder* is intact," Bolis reported in monotone.

Lekket nodded, unimpressed with his own tactic, unsorrowful for his own deeds. "Status of the other enemy ships?"

Like his commander, Bolis also sounded . . . almost tired. "They retreat, Commodore."

Lekket told Janeway, "When they retreat, the *Marauder* is ready for battle."

The *Marauder*. Janeway wondered if such a name was a Gimlon invention, or an Edesian attempt to paint their enemies in shadow.

Distant on the forward viewscreen, a dark ship, larger than *Voyager*, on the scale of a Federation Galaxy-class starship, moved forward.

As if these people, Edesian and Gimlon alike, lacked imagination, their ships were painted dark, without banner, without stripe. The *Marauder* looked as murky as its name. Cylindrical, no nacelles, shaped more like a missile than the sleek vessels from the Alpha quadrant.

Janeway twisted toward tactical and hit Bolis with a glare that could ignite driftwood. "Get out of my officer's way or I'll have you removed from the bridge."

The Edesian man looked to Lekket, who shrugged slightly. Bolis moved back and Tuvok stepped up.

"Report."

Tuvok scanned his console. "Our shields are at seventy-six percent. Aft phasers damaged but functional. Three casualties from a coolant leak has Engineering under-staffed."

Janeway nodded. "The nebula?"

"Ninety-three percent of the nebula was ignited in the shockwave. Residual radiation is hampering sensors. The Gimlon interceptors that remain are highly damaged and heading out of this section." He paused. "One Edesian escort is disabled, two are still severely damaged, and the other has fared slightly better than we." Tuvok tapped at his console, pulled up a screen. "The Gimlon 'Marauder' . . . is on an intercept course."

Lines of static traced the forward viewscreen. The *Marauder* grew closer, a zombie-like monster plodding toward its prey.

The situation was surreal. Here Janeway was pitted against someone's worst enemy—not hers—in a battle that felt almost choreographed. The little ships fought each other, and now the big guns would square off. Unlike most battles she'd fought, the two warring parties seemed to know one another too well.

"Open up our course," Janeway ordered. "I want room.

Pull them out of the radiation and get some solid sensor readings."

Paris nodded and his hands jabbed at his console. "Z axis plus seven light days, two-ten mark fourteen."

She didn't want to be in this fight—it wasn't hers. But the Gimlon didn't know that. Or didn't care. There was no way of telling if Lekket had been honest about them or not. In any case, to the *Marauder, Voyager* was just another enemy ship.

What if she surrendered to them?

Not a real option, since Lekket controlled the warp-dampener on her ship and could irradiate the crew in minutes if she crossed him.

"Tell me about this *'Marauder,'* " Janeway demanded of Lekket. "I need to know all you know."

"It is strong, and without mercy," Lekket said, "and we cannot defeat it. But you have new tactics, Captain. Tactics they have never seen. You are alien to this space. That is your advantage."

Janeway tilted her head to one side, realization dawning on her. "That's what this is about. You think we can win this for you because we're unknown to them."

"No, Captain. In fact, I don't think you can win. I don't really think it is possible to conquer their vessel."

At that Janeway scoffed. "Your lies are catching up with you. On the one hand you have hope, on the other you have none? Just hours ago, by outnumbering us, *you* bettered *us*. By your own account, you should be able to better them as well."

Lekket shook his head. "What you witnessed when we 'bettered' you, as you say, was every vessel left in our fleet together capturing a ship caught by surprise in unfamiliar space. What you witnessed, Captain, was the last grasp for salvation by a people that will die if the *Marauder* isn't stopped."

The captain cast an unbelieving glance. "One ship?"

He nodded. *"One* ship. And if we do not stop it . . . if you don't have the means to destroy our enemy here and now . . . then there is no salvation for us."

Janeway let her gaze flow from Lekket beside her to the *Marauder* on the screen, then back to Lekket.

"You have to tell me," Janeway said quietly, her anger at him coiled around the burden of the moment. "What is so special about this one ship?"

"Something I would not have believed had I not seen it with my very eyes, and barely escaped with my life."

Pausing, Lekket glared at the viewscreen a few moments.

"Tell me," Janeway prodded, now worried more about *Voyager*'s chances with the Gimlon. "Why is this ship so special?"

The Edesian Commodore shook his head. "You must promise me, Captain, you *will* destroy the *Marauder* if you can. You must!"

She shook her head. "I will not murder people solely because you wish it. I can fight a battle for you, when you threaten the lives of my crew, but I will not take the lives of people whom, for all I know, are guilty of nothing but self-defense against your empire." The captain continued to shake her head. "No. Some battle lines I will not cross."

"You will destroy the *Marauder* if you can, Captain," Lekket said. "Or I will kill you and all your crew."

"Why?" Janeway almost growled. *"Why is this ship so important?"*

There was a long pause as Lekket seemed to lose his gaze on the forward viewer and the approaching *Marauder*. "In all battles it has been . . . invincible," he said darkly, his gape unmoving. "There has been no way to win . . . against what surely must be magic."

"Incoming—disruptor fire, Captain."

"Evasive twist. Be random, Mr. Paris. Return fire!"

"Forward starboard and aft dorsal shields weakening."

"Transfer power procedures. E.P.C. backflow, initiate!"

"I don't have the power, Captain."

"Find it!"

Unilluminated and unforgiving, the *Marauder* rose toward *Voyager*. The ship loomed large across the forward viewer, as if reminding any enemy that speed was unnecessary where raw power reigned.

Then the Marauder spat out that raw power—in weapons fire nearly as nasty as *Voyager*'s.

Only her shields saved her, and they were weakened.

"I'm having trouble penetrating their hull with sensors," Tuvok said.

"Kim?"

"They're not putting out *any* signals, Captain. Not even a standard hailing carrier."

"You cannot talk to them," Lekket said. "They do not talk."

"Evasive pattern beta-epsilon," Janeway ordered, then turned toward the Edesian commodore. "Everyone talks. No one listens, but everyone talks."

Paris jabbed at the helm and *Voyager* spun around the *Marauder* until the image of the alien vessel appeared to retreat. Now the Gimlon ship had to turn back toward them, and as it slowly did, disruptor fire glanced off *Voyager's* shields and rocked Janeway's bridge.

"Maintain phaser fire," Janeway ordered, and the ship's weapons whined across space until they sliced into a layer of the *Marauder's* slick armor.

"Barely glazed, Captain," Tuvok said, and Lekket's shoulders slumped a bit.

The commodore was a liar, Janeway thought. Lekket *did* hope that *Voyager* would be a savior. She saw that in his body language, in his eyes, and even heard a grain of it in his bitter voice. "You're not trying, Captain. You *will* try, or you'll die. There is no retreat from this battle. Not for you."

Kill or be killed. He'd made it clear, and was overplaying it as he kept brandishing the threat.

Janeway said nothing yet.

Another shudder rolled the ship, bouncing the captain back into the command chair as she tried to rise.

"Pull back, Mr. Paris. Prepare for warp speed. Maximum warp."

Lekket lurched forward and grabbed her wrist. "What are you ordering?"

"A full retreat." Janeway pulled her hand rather easily away.

"You cannot! I order you not to!" Lekket's eyes widened and he looked more full of life than ever before.

"Choices, Commodore. It's all about choices. I don't have

to choose to fight—even when the alternative you threaten is death."

Commodore Lekket's body was tense and he clenched his fists at his sides. "You are foolish, Captain. There will be nothing to stop the Gimlon if *we* do not! Your people will die eventually anyway!"

Janeway leveled her voice. She was angry, but calmed her tone as it broke onto the bridge. "You want me to kill the crew of the *Marauder*—"

"As they are trying to kill you!"

"They don't know I'm not part of this war."

"You *are* part of this war."

She shook her head. "Not any more. Not if it means killing people I don't know to be guilty of crimes. If you want me in this war, you'll have to agree to *Voyager* disabling the *Marauder,* not destroying it."

Lekket and Bolis shared a glance, the commodore shaking his head continuously.

"It would serve the same purpose, Commodore, and would enable us to examine their new technology."

"An evil technology—"

"Nonetheless," Bolis offered, more rationally, it would suit our purpose for now, Commodore."

Janeway stood and took two steps toward Paris and the navigational console. "How soon until the *Marauder* reaches us?"

"Thirty-three seconds."

She nodded. "Shields down."

"Captain!" Lekket rose.

"Aye," Tuvok said.

"Slow to half impulse," Janeway ordered, then turned to Lekket. "You don't have much time. You will agree that we will not destroy that ship. We will disable it, and its crew will be left on a neutral planet."

"There are no neutral planets," Lekket spat, his thin fingers clenched around his pendants.

"You have twenty seconds to decide," she said. "We can all die here now, or you can vote for a fighting chance. The choice is yours."

Lekket began a protest. "Captain—"

"Don't waste time, Lekket. You've only got fifteen more seconds . . ."

"I will order our men to kill your crew! You will die and I will take your ship."

Janeway nodded. "Ten seconds," she said. "I hope you can learn to run this vessel in the moments you have left."

A moment—but not a long one. The Edesian commodore huffed out an angry breath. "I agree. Now—do as you said."

"I want your personal assurance, Commodore. This is a promise you will not break."

"Yes, yes, I agree! Now, please raise your shields!"

The captain pivoted back toward her command chair and lowered herself quickly into the center seat. "Shields! Restore multiphasing. Evasive!"

Under Janeway's command, *Voyager* came alive. She'd been holding her stallion of a ship back, making it trot when it could run faster than the wind.

Now the ship hummed with fresh power, and Janeway basked in that a moment.

She smirked at Lekket's solemn and surprised expression. He wasn't as in charge as he'd thought.

And that center seat felt a bit more like Janeway's own.

"Full impulse. I want that distance."

"Aye, aye."

"Mr. Tuvok . . ."

The Vulcan nodded. "Captain?"

"Reroute phasers back through the warp engines."

Lekket gripped Janeway's wrist and wrenched it tightly toward him. "You can do that?"

Janeway pulled her arm back with a fast tug. "Commodore, I can do a great many things. You'd be wise to remember that." She gestured to the forward viewer. "Call off your other ship. I don't want it swooping in to destroy what we disable."

Nodding reluctantly, Lekket grabbed his compendant and spat into it. "Retreat. *Voyager* will act alone." Bubbles of sweat over his lip, he looked so very young. His features were smooth, his dark hair thick. Was he younger than Janeway? Kes, an Ocampa, had been only a year old when they met, and looked twenty-two. Lekket and his race looked Ocampa, and so he might be a two-year-old for all Janeway knew.

Yet, with his threats, hardly a toddler.

Rejuvenated by her new bargain, the captain pushed herself up from the command chair and bounded up to the tactical station. She glanced at Bolis a moment, who was poring over one of the back consoles, then looked to her officer.

"What's our real status?"

"Minimal damage." Tuvok proclaimed. "Shields at ninety-three percent."

"Tuvok, give me *something* about that ship. Anything I can use."

His charcoal eyes a bit narrowed, his lips only slightly turned down, Vulcan grimness played across Tuvok's features. "Only what you already know. We have the advantage of speed and shields. They have size, armor, and—apparently—magic."

This last Tuvok said with a hint of disdain, and Lekket turned and rose.

"We will wait, Mr. Tuvok," the Edesian commodore said, "and I will not laugh when I see fear in your eyes."

"You will not see fear in my eyes," Tuvok said evenly. "I neither act on nor show fear."

"A man without fear is a man without sense," Lekket scoffed.

Tuvok shook his head. "I did not say I do not *have* fear. I said I do not act on the emotion, nor do I display it. Neither would serve to aid me in any task."

Janeway put up a stiff hand. "This isn't the time."

"The Gimlon ship is pursuing the Edesian vessel," Tuvok said. "They are increasing speed."

"I'm reading an energy buildup on the Gimlon ship," Kim said, dabbing at his control panel. "Subspace frequency."

Tuvok shook his head. "I am not scanning an energy signature."

From the front of the large Gimlon ship, a port opened. A maw with teeth of energy.

Kim jabbed at his control panel. "I'm reading a high-energy jump on all subspace bandwidths."

With a bright flash, a rod of white energy stabbed forward and struck the last remaining Edesian vessel squarely.

Lekket spun toward the viewscreen. "No!"

A brief moment . . . the Edesian ship glowed red, then exploded in all directions.

Large slabs of wreckage smashed into *Voyager*'s underbelly.

Janeway held on to a handrail to keep her legs beneath her. "Debris? From this far out?"

Tuvok nodded. "Incredible force, Captain! Debris is riding a subspace shockwave. Had it been a phaser blast, the Edesian ship would have been vaporized."

Tom Paris looked back to the Vulcan. "You gotta be kidding. Vaporize an entire ship?"

On the viewer, the *Marauder* turned, then bit into *Voyager*'s shields as well: a thick arm of energy slamming into the ship and wrenching it back.

Voyager heaved to one side under the force of the punch and Janeway was tossed to the deck. Sparks flew, and for a moment the hisses and sputters of exposed high-energy cables flashed the only light. A ceiling strut clattered to the deck, and Janeway felt a piece of its metal slice into her hand.

She pulled herself up, noticed Lekket was having to do the same, and turned to see Tuvok helping Bolis to his feet.

"Report!"

Tuvok turned away from Bolis quickly. "Shields down another twelve percent." He jabbed at the controls on his console. "Damage to decks fifteen, sixteen, and Engineering."

Scooping a rope of hair from her eyes, Janeway noticed the back of her hand was bleeding. She wiped the blood on her tunic and clasped one hand in another to stop the flow.

"Get us out of here, Mr. Paris. Best speed."

"They're turning away too, Captain."

Janeway glared at the screen. They *were* turning. They'd dealt *Voyager* the most serious blow yet—and they were turning away. "Powerful, but limited."

"They may have to recharge before using it again," Tuvok agreed.

The captain looked to Lekket.

"No one has survived to be hit twice, Captain."

"Just what was that weapon?" Kim asked. "Subspace is active off the scale."

"Mr. Tuvok?" Janeway came around to stand next to the Vulcan.

He pointed out a graph, Janeway and Bolis both watching over his shoulder. "High-energy subspace disruptorlike weapon. Impact with the Edesian scout caused debris to spread outward at warp one point zero three five."

"Amazing," Janeway breathed.

"Yes," Tuvok said. "But sensors indicate the second use of the weapon was markedly reduced in output to the first."

"Like I said, powerful but limited."

Tuvok brought up a display of *Voyager*'s deflector strength. "Even our multiphasic shields may not survive a full-charge attack from this weapon."

"Can you estimate its range?"

The Vulcan shook his head. "Not without more intensive study of the sensor data. But its range is probably greater than our effective phaser radius."

Not good. Janeway chewed on her lip a moment and weighed her options. She wanted to save her finite number of photon torpedoes, which had longer range. But she couldn't let herself be hit again with the Gimlon's major weapon. Not if she wanted to survive.

"Captain." Lekket stood and Janeway turned toward him. "No ship has been able to withstand what yours has."

A wave of pride washed across Janeway, but she didn't savor it as she might. "My ship shouldn't even be here."

"I beg you, Captain," Lekket said. "If the Gimlon now must recharge themselves, now is the time to attack."

"We don't know how long it takes them to recharge," Janeway said. "And we don't know if we can take a full blast from that thing."

"If you don't act now, the *Marauder* will escape, and it will come back to destroy you. You are its greatest enemy . . . and the Gimlon will not want your technology to survive in our hands."

Neither will I, Janeway thought. She nodded to Tuvok's console. "Arm torpedoes."

He nodded as she stepped back down to the command deck.

"Set an intercept course, Tom."

The helmsman nodded and turned back to his panel.

"You cannot simply target this beast's eyes and claws, Captain," Lekket said. "You must hit at its black heart and destroy it. I gave you my promise that I would not—but now I beg you to reconsider. If you don't, I know we will be destroyed!"

The captain shrugged, attempting to be as cold as she thought Lekket was about death. "Then you will have been right about us. We wouldn't have been able to defeat them."

His posture defeated, his tone low, Lekket said, "I do not wish to be right, but fate was never in my hands."

Janeway frowned and turned away from the forward viewer for a moment. She tried to take in his eyes, cool them with hers. "Fate isn't something you wait and hope will fall into your hands. You have to take charge of it."

He turned away, unwilling to meet her gaze. He watched the Gimlon ship on the viewscreen, and ground out his biting words. "Only one side can have fate, Captain, and we've never had it to take."

"Captain," Tuvok called, "the Gimlon ship is slowing. They are angling into a return trajectory."

Janeway leaned forward. "Could they have fully recharged so quickly?"

"Unknown."

"Are we within range of it?"

Tom Paris shook his head and shrugged. "I don't know either, Captain."

"We're receiving a hail," Kim reported, incredulous.

The captain shared a glance with Lekket a moment. "Put it on screen."

Kim shook his head. "It's audio only, Captain."

Janeway nodded. A standard tactic—keep the opponent guessing, even wondering what you look like. The Romulans did that to their enemies when they could—they'd done it years ago, in the war with the Federation.

"Let's hear it."

"This is Gimlon Sakalat. I am Dasna. You are vanquished. Surrender."

Lekket huffed out an angry breath. "Gimlon negotiation."

"How very Borg. Patch me in, Ensign," Janeway ordered.

They're not accepting the comm channel, Captain."

Talk, but no listening.

"Ready torpedoes."

"Torpedoes ready."

"Mr. Tuvok, fire on my mark."

"Captain," Paris said, "the *Marauder* is increasing speed."

"Mr. Paris, a change of plans." Janeway came right up behind her navigator. "Angled intercept vector. Full impulse."

"Captain?" Paris was surprised.

"Get as close to them as you can, Tom."

"We may not withstand a direct hit with their heavy weapon if it is fully charged," Tuvok said.

Janeway nodded. "I'm gambling that it's not. Engage."

Voyager swooped around and surged forward. The *Marauder* swelled in the forward viewer.

"They're firing!"

The Gimlon ship plunged toward *Voyager,* and *Voyager* toward it. The enemy's main mauler of a weapon came to bear—a smashing fist of hot white power.

"All decks! Brace for impact!"

Electrical flame sheeted off *Voyager*'s shields. Crackles of power sparked over every console and across every monitor.

"Power overload!" Kim yelled above the din. "We're being forced into warp!"

"Compensate! Warp one!" Janeway braced herself against Tom Paris's chair. "Torpedoes! Fire all bays!"

Voyager dove forward against the plasma blockade, as screaming torpedoes hurled themselves into the *Marauder*'s armor.

Explosion after explosion, space detonated into fire.

CHAPTER
5

"Again! Fire!"

Quaking, the *Marauder* twisted away—spasms of electrical fire clutching its hull—raw molten wounds pocking its armor.

Voyager rose, turned, her aft phasers stinging shots into the Gimlon vessel's midships. Phaser flame walloped into holes blasted apart by photon torpedoes. The enemy limped, bleeding.

What must the Gimlon be making of the torpedoes? A weapon which their first taste of is at point-blank range.

"Their heavy weapon has drained our shields by another thirty-seven percent," Tuvok said. "Probably not a full charge. Apparently they are not used to being pursued."

Captain Janeway nodded encouragingly. "Keep on them, Mr. Paris."

"Aye, Captain." Paris's hands waltzed over the naviconsole. "Ride 'n' hide."

Her muscles still knotted along the strains of the battle, the captain allowed a part of her mind to relax. There was a different feeling to the bridge now. It was her bridge again, and she had control of the engagement. Maybe it wasn't a war she'd wanted to fight, but if she could end the conflict quickly, at least long enough for *Voyager* to gain her freedom . . . Janeway meant to be out of the sector before any vessel, Edesian or Gimlon, would be able to follow. Even if she had to carve that warp-dampener off her hull.

Lekket was more tense than Janeway. His tunic stretched over his rigid shoulders. Shaking with anticipation, he held his fists in his lap and leaned stiffly toward the forward viewscreen.

The captain pivoted toward Tuvok. She felt a slight smile tugging at her lips. "I think we've impressed the good commodore."

"One good impressment deserves another," Paris said dryly.

"I want the dynamics on that weapon, Tuvok. Anything that can push a starship into warp . . ."

Tuvok nodded agreement, but continued to run a tactical battle with his fingertips. "There is a similarity to early Romulan plasma weapons, but on a subspace level—" A blast from the Gimlon's disruptors cut him off.

"A subspace weapon," Janeway said to herself. "They can't detonate it too close or it would damage them, wouldn't it?"

"That is my theory," Tuvok said.

"We'll keep testing that theory. Get even closer, Tom."

The *Marauder* was an angry, wounded bull—and *Voyager* was the cowboy, riding the animal's back. The Gimlon ship lacked speed and grace, and Janeway ordered her vessel to spin close, then far, to twist in, then out. Phaser shots stabbed at one side of the *Marauder*, and as the large vessel turned to fight, *Voyager* was suddenly on the other side, striking blows there.

"We are significantly damaging their armor, Captain," Tuvok said, no more in his voice than when the *Voyager* was taking a pounding. Perhaps there was a slight rise in his tone, she couldn't tell. A little pride for his ship? "If I read this correctly, their engines are pushing their weapons to overload. And at this close distance," he continued, "due to their lack of shielding, energy from their own disruptors damages their armor."

"How is that possible?" Bolis asked, incredulous. The lines on his face and the red alert lights painted his sharp expressions in demonic strokes. He was as anxious as

Lekket, and also seemed not to believe that *Voyager* could pummel a ship so many times its size.

"At this range the blasts from their disruptors are dispersing off our shields and onto their armor," Tuvok said.

Another crack of weapons fire sliced toward *Voyager*, skewing off her shields. The charge raked both vessels and sent shudders through bulkheads and crew. The captain could feel when her ship was dealt a harsh blow, and this was one of those wallops.

Lekket almost slipped from his seat, and Janeway had to lean over and steady him. She turned to her tactical officer as soon as the Edesian commodore was stable.

"Shields?"

"Holding." Now more intent on his console, Tuvok shook his head. "They are targeting our shield generators whenever possible."

"How would they know where to fire?" Kim asked.

Janeway glared at the main viewer and the clumsy *Marauder* as it turned slowly away. "They might be able to tell from scans." She shared a glance with Ensign Kim, and a nod of encouragement as well. "See what you can do to jam those sensors of theirs, Harry."

He nodded, his black hair looking orange in the crimson accent lights. "Aye, Captain."

"Their engines are off-line, Captain," Tuvok said. "They have switched to chemical thrusters."

"Now, Captain! Now is the time!" Lekket turned to Janeway suddenly and gripped her wrist again, this time more pleading than mandating. "They will destroy you— they know they must. They know you are all that we have now."

With more effort than before, Janeway wrenched her arm from his grasp. "They meant to destroy me before," she said. "Nothing has changed."

"You *must* destroy them, Captain. Stop targeting their engines and annihilate their bridge! Cut off the serpent's head and its body withers!"

"No," Janeway ground out in a bark. "I have nothing but your word to convince me that the Gimlon are acting on anything more than self-defense—and your word isn't nearly enough."

Lekket began a retort but Janeway pushed it away with a wave of her hand.

"Stow it, Commodore," she snapped. "Or I'll have you hauled off my bridge."

She turned away from him. "Tom, can't we get out of the way of their close-range weapons—even closer to their hull? I want their weapons off-line or out of range."

Paris shook his head and kept guiding the *Voyager* on a random course close around the *Marauder*'s underbelly. "Captain, we're in so close now that when my shift ends I was going to try *their* mess hall."

A slash of the *Marauder*'s weak disruptor fire glanced off the shields. The vibration shook some ceiling insulation free, and small fiber particles fell into Janeway's bleeding gash. She ignored the pain as best she could and ordered that the high-voltage cable that sparked above her be terminated.

"Casualty count?" the Captain asked. Inwardly she chastised herself for not asking sooner, before her own injury had reminded her that crewmen might be hurt.

"The Doctor reports light casualties," Kim said. "Minor injuries, radiation burns, nothing too serious if he's allowed to, and I quote, 'return to his duties without further distraction.'"

Janeway nodded and turned her attention toward the tactical screen.

"No engines, half their weapons turrets are dead, and they're still fighting."

"Tenacious," Tuvok said, "if not foolhardy."

"Mr. Paris, keep sticking close." She spun toward the tactical station. "Tuvok, I want that ship hog-tied. Disable its weapons before we have to destroy the entire ship. They think we're out to destroy them, let's prove we're not."

"Ready," Tuvok said.

One nod, and Janeway returned to the command chair. The adrenaline was pumping, and she didn't even bother to glance at Lekket, who'd returned to his seat. He was probably scowling at her, and that thought felt good. "Full power to the phasers—narrow beam."

Tom Paris jabbed at the navigational console and the starscape sped away. The Gimlon vessel filled the screen at point-blank range. "Coming up on mark."

Janeway inched forward—
"Fire!"

Voyager punched a thin phaser beam down into the base of the *Marauder*'s engines. Orange explosions erupted over the enemy's hull and electrical flame spread across the aft armor.

The *Marauder* lumbered forward, plodding at first as its thrusters sputtered out, then listing at an angle. Sparkles of chemical and electrical flame cloaked her aft as she slowed to a slither.

The enemy's weapons were cold, its disruptor banks dark.

Janeway wasn't ready to celebrate. "Tuvok?"

Both he and Bolis were bending over the sensor console. "Scanning," the Vulcan said. "Minimal power readings. Null weapons output." He looked up and met Janeway's gaze. "The Gimlon ship is disabled and drifting."

Captain Janeway nodded and rose. "Mr. Kim, hail that vessel. Mr. Paris, all stop."

"No!" Lekket leapt up. "Destroy it now! It is our only chance! You must!"

"You gave me your word, Commodore," Janeway said.

His face creased in rage and fear, Lekket looked as if he might himself explode. "No! You must! I—"

A smash, and space electrified.

The forward viewer shined such an intense white that it blinded the *Voyager*'s own sensors and the screen had to go dark.

Janeway and the bridge crew shielded their eyes for a moment, then the captain turned to Tuvok, questions flooding her mind as the deck flew from under her.

The universe lost itself.

Tossed to the ceiling, then the deck, Janeway grunted with pain. Slammed into her seat hard, she felt like a toy in the grip of an angry child. She clutched the command chair as the universe pulled her back to the ceiling.

Voyager groaned under the strain and creaked eerily, bulkheads straining against whatever was tearing her ship apart.

There were no commands for such a storm. People were yelping and moaning in pain, but no one listed damage or gave a station report.

Janeway knew why. They were being killed—torn apart with the force of a hundred suns. All her muscles spasmed, then she felt the thrust from her torso outward, a pulling not only on her limbs but on her every cell. Space was playing a tug of war with her body, and she would lose.

One moment crushed, then another light as helium, Janeway rolled agony into nausea and back to agony.

Finally she fell to the deck, bloodless and pained. She heard thuds around her, as the other people on the bridge collapsed.

The numbness left, replaced by an ache, and every muscle cried. Her eyes hurt, her ears . . . she had the metallic taste of blood in her mouth. *What happened?*

"Tuvok?" Her voice croaked over a dry throat. "S-status—" She pulled herself up, slowly, and saw Tuvok already standing at his console. His lip was bleeding and a spot of dark green blood made its way down his jaw.

"Unknown energy wave, Captain. The ship is intact. Shields are holding."

Janeway stumbled up toward his station. "That was through our shields?"

The Vulcan nodded once. "Affirmative. External sensors are overloaded. I'm bypassing damaged systems."

She nodded. "Did they destroy themselves? What the devil was that?"

Tuvok shook his head, and if it hurt him to do so, he didn't show it. "Unknown."

"Captain—" Paris called from the helm.

Janeway turned toward him, her bones sore from the marrow outward. "Lieutenant?"

"It's gone!"

Janeway looked from the forward viewer to the helm's sensor readout, then up to Tuvok. "Self-destructed?"

"I read no debris," Tuvok said.

Skeptical, the captain looked to Harry Kim at Ops.

Kim shrugged. "Same reading."

As Bolis rose behind him, Tuvok checked one readout, then another, and a last screen just to be sure.

"The Gimlon ship," he said, "has vanished."

Janeway pivoted to Lekket, who was just now scraping himself off the floor.

"A cloaking device?" Janeway demanded, stomping down toward him. "That's not magic, Commodore."

From the corner of her eye, she saw Harry Kim shaking his head. "No, Captain . . . it can't be a cloak. They had no propulsion—they'd still be *there* if it was a cloak."

Janeway nodded. "Sweep the area with a neutrino beam. Or use solar wind patterns from the nearest star. Any evidence of a cloak?"

Kim worked a moment. She could tell he was weak too, but his voice was excited and he was very serious. "Nothing, Captain. They're just *gone.*"

The captain now twisted full toward the young ensign. "Are you telling me that in a flash of power that nearly turned us to rubble, that massive ship just disappeared?"

Half shrugging, half nodding, Kim could only answer, "I don't know."

Lekket placed his hand lightly on Janeway's arm and turned her toward him. Even the weightless touch made her muscles ache worse.

His eyes were dark and his expression more death-mask than living face.

"Magic, Captain," he mumbled almost unintelligibly. "I warned you, and you wouldn't listen."

"Warned me of what?" Janeway demanded. "Where are they? Tell us what you know!"

Lekket lowered his gaze. "They have escaped," he said. "And when they return . . . they will destroy us. This ship, and our civilization." Despondently, he lowered himself awkwardly to his seat. "I warned you . . . and now we are all dead."

CHAPTER

6

"Captain's Log, supplemental.

Met by two Edesian escorts, we are slowly leaving the sector where the Gimlon Marauder disappeared. In an effort to determine the Gimlon's method of cloak, Ensign Kim and Lieutenant Commander Tuvok continue to scan the area for evidence of the enemy ship. So far, there's no sign at all. Such a complete cloak is unheard of in our technology. Commendations: Commander Chakotay, Lieutenant Torres, Seven-of-Nine, Crewman Chen, Crewman Lothridge, Crewman Rossi, Damage Control Teams One and Three, and the on-duty bridge crew."

"Scan it again." Janeway massaged her left shoulder. She'd fallen hard—a half-dozen times it seemed—but didn't want to take the time to zip down to sickbay. "It's there—somewhere."

"Scanning . . ." Ensign Kim had swept for the *Marauder* fourteen times, and all searches had been fruitless. "Nothing, Captain. And we're getting too distant for short-range scans."

Where? Where had the ship gone? *No* cloak was that good. There had always been some flaw in the Romulan and

Klingon cloaks Janeway was used to. The problem was usually not having time to see the flaw.

Captain Janeway glared at the stars on the forward viewer, as if she might see the *Marauder* as *Voyager* sped away from the now empty system. "Their propulsion was damaged," she said. "We should at least see radiation and plasma residue."

"We should," Tuvok said. "However, the substantial gravimetric disruptions rendered our sensors useless for a short time. Once we lost the trail, and with sensors in their current state . . ."

Disheartened, Janeway nodded. "Cancel scanning. Log the data we have and pore over it. How sure are we of our current sensor readings?"

"Not very," Kim said, obviously disappointed in his own answer. "A lot of circuits are burned out. We've had to reroute to systems that have nothing to do with sensors. I can't be sure of our accuracy."

"What *are* we sure of?"

Kim wouldn't say. He looked to Tuvok, whose eyes widened a bit as he spoke. "The Gimlon ship has disappeared in a manner our science cannot at this time determine."

"Magic," Paris said corrosively, pecking at his console with one hand, cradling his other arm in his lap.

Janeway pursed her lips and turned to Lekket. "How do we know we didn't destroy it, then?" No one thought that was the case, for there was no debris, but it was a notion that had to be considered.

Down in Janeway's stomach, however, she was building a base for understanding Lekket's fear. How could anyone fight an invisible monster? If the *Marauder* could disappear . . . then later reappear . . .

Lekket was silent. He continued to look at the main viewer, and the empty space on which Janeway had focused a moment before.

They both wanted to see that Gimlon warship. If they could see it, they could defeat it.

Lekket had known the *Marauder* would disappear. He'd known, and he hadn't wanted to tell Janeway.

Why?

"We'd better talk." Janeway grabbed Lekket at the elbow and motioned him toward her office.

The commodore nodded lightly, and they stepped up the bridge and through the sliding door to the captain's ready-room.

Neither of them sat. Janeway stood behind her desk, and Lekket took on a defeated posture before her. His shoulders were slumped, his features sharp and dark. She realized he needed a shave.

"I couldn't tell you," he admitted suddenly, without prompt.

Janeway listened, asking nothing more. She'd hear him out, then continue.

Commodore Lekket stroked his chin stubble nervously, then groped for a chair behind him and sat clumsily down. "We needed to see you fight the Gimlon on your own terms, with more or less your own tactics, just as you did. We have lost too many impressed vessels by confiscating technology only. We needed you in whole. Not just your ship, but your experience."

"You'd said that." Janeway leaned down across her desk, flattening her palms over its surface. "Now explain why we couldn't know what we were up against."

Lekket was slow to answer. Was he looking for the right words, or was he looking for the right lie?

"Captain," he began, "never in our history have we been defeated so . . ."

Janeway looked away and pulled herself into an upright position. Her neck and shoulder still ached, as did almost every muscle, but she refrained from showing any kind of weakness by rubbing her soreness.

She was sore in a less physical manner, too, and the last thing she wanted to hear was an imperial sob-story about how tough the conquering game had become. "Is this about arrogance? Revenge?"

"No, Captain, it's not."

She turned back to look at him and slapped him with a disbelieving glare.

"I assure you," Lekket said, "this has nothing to do with personal *or* cultural ego. When I say that we have never been defeated so, I mean so completely, and by such a weapon as the Gimlon have—"

"You seem to be faring better than you say."

Lekket shook his head. "Captain Janeway, the ships that stopped you are all that is left of a fleet of 373 vessels. We have been reduced from a space fleet to a band of weak ships, in just over a month."

At this Janeway was taken aback, and a slight chill ran her spine. A fleet of nearly four hundred—cut down to less than thirty in a month . . . not since the Borg attack at Wolf 359 had she heard of such force . . . *if* it were true.

Her mind's eye lingered on the scenes of destruction hers and other ships had found at Wolf 359—starships sliced in half, blown into three or four chunks of debris that floated eerily together . . . not a ship's graveyard, but a death-filled morgue.

"Staggering, isn't it, Captain?" Lekket asked, his voice dry and low.

"Why couldn't you tell us about this . . . cloak of theirs?"

"You think it's a cloak," Lekket said. "I wish I could believe that. In any case . . . last time we told an impressed ship of this, they refused to fight it. The time before, they panicked in battle and were quickly destroyed."

Janeway swiveled the desktop computer screen toward her and punched up the small amount of data *Voyager* had on the Gimlon *Marauder*. "It's not magic."

His eyes red, Lekket rubbed his temples with both hands. "If you have a better term, Captain, I'd like to hear it. We can't even tell you any more than you know because many of our scientists think the *Marauder* doesn't actually disappear—that it's some form of mind control. We can't risk tainting your thoughts."

"Mind control?" Janeway made no attempt to disguise her skeptical tone. "If you can question whether mind control is happening, chances are you can either prove that it isn't—or end it."

"Then I ask you to explain it, Captain," Lekket snapped, his anger boiling over his mental exhaustion for a moment. "Scanners show *nothing,* no debris, no unusual radiation—"

"Your sensors must have been as overloaded as ours—"

"Yes, more so. *When* an Edesian vessel has survived, which is not often."

Voyager had been a match for the *Marauder* . . . if it hadn't had the "magic" to disappear. "You told me it would return," Janeway said. "How soon?"

"Soon. We never know when."

"Will they have repaired themselves?"

Lekket chuckled softly, bitterly. "We've never done much damage to it, Captain."

"And now my ship has."

Looking almost encouraged, Lekket glanced up at her, as if he'd forgotten that point. "Yes. And we are grateful—"

Janeway dismissed that notion with a harsh look. "Please, Commodore, I don't need the superfluous platitudes. We did this for you because we were forced to. You would've had us destroy the ship—"

"You should have, Captain. It would all be over if you had."

She shook her head. "Yes, it would all be over. And as I said before, I don't just kill people without provocation."

Lekket straightened. "Neither do I," he said indignantly. "I am provoked by Gimlon atrocities: mass murder, tearing children from families and killing them all. Rumor of medical experiments, suffering beyond imagination. . . ."

"So you say, Commodore. And I'm supposed to take it all based on faith." She felt her face flush as a ball of anger caught in her throat. "I don't have faith in a man who has threatened the lives of my crew and still holds an ax over my head. We've done what we could, and now I demand you release us."

The commodore shook his head. "I cannot."

No, Janeway didn't think he would. She looked at him, stared him down some, and tried to focus her pique into a battle against her muscle aches. She needed a better strategy than "sit and wait."

"Where are we headed?" she asked.

Perhaps caught off guard by the question, Lekket looked startled and he leaned back in his chair. "The Rasilian system. One of our few colony worlds. Rasilian Two has a docking port, where your ship will be repaired."

And studied, Janeway thought.

"As I said, you'll be treated well, Captain . . . but there is yet a role for your vessel in our struggle."

Janeway's door chime sounded, and she responded. "Enter."

Tuvok stepped in. "I have casualty and repair reports, Captain."

"I leave you the dignity to discuss these matters in private," Lekket said, gathering himself rather majestically as he rose and exited the room.

The office door slid closed, and Janeway expressed her surprise in a glance to Tuvok.

"Apparently he believes we cannot plot an escape," offered the Vulcan.

She nodded a half shrug. "Or he's listening with some device."

Tuvok slid easily into one of the chairs in front of Janeway's desk and swiveled her computer toward him. His fingers worked quickly on the keypad and the console bleeped in happy response.

"Now," he said, "we should be relatively safe from any electronic 'listening ears.'"

Janeway widened her eyes. "Only relatively?"

"I cannot anticipate a technology dissimilar to ours. If they have a method with which I'm unfamiliar . . ."

She nodded. "Of course."

"Casualties were light," Tuvok began. "Minor injuries on most decks. One crewman is refusing to report to sickbay, however."

The captain allowed a slight smile. "I'll go when I'm ready."

The Vulcan shook his head. "While I could certainly be referring to you, I did not think it my place to counsel you on such a personal action, rather I leave tending of your minor injuries to your discretion. I was speaking of Lieutenant Paris. He insists that he should finish his shift. I did not press the matter with him, but he is holding his wrist at an odd angle. It might be broken."

She nodded again. "He and I will see the doctor together."

"Very well." Tuvok handed a padd to Janeway and

continued. "A list of damaged systems and repair esti-
mates."

Janeway took the padd, skimmed its contents, then laid it
flat on her desktop. She looked back to Tuvok's calm
expression. He was an anchor at times like this, his visage
not much changed from when they might play cribbage in
the officers' lounge.

"This isn't a cribbage game," she said suddenly.

His eyebrows rose. "No, indeed not. Cribbage is a rather
simple game. I still fail to see why you enjoy such low-
skilled diversion."

She smiled again. He probably just didn't like the game
because there was so much luck involved, skill didn't often
determine the winner. "It's the company, not the cards."

He gestured his acceptance of that. "If I may extend the
metaphor, I believe we are 'ahead on points,' even though it
may not seem that is the case."

"I agree," Janeway said, rubbing at the scabbed gash on
her hand as it began to itch. "But how far do we want to take
this? If we let them repair our vessel, if they learn too much
about the ship and how she runs . . . we risk them simply
killing us and using our technology."

"That was always an option to them, but they are more
desperate, I think. I don't believe they have the time to train
a crew for a ship of our technological level."

"Maybe."

"And," Tuvok added, "they don't know about the command codes. Or our self-destruct procedure. Or . . . many
things."

Janeway put up her hand. "Self-destruct is our last
option, and I won't honestly consider it at this point."

Tuvok nodded very slightly. Janeway had come to learn
that with him such was an expression of respectful disagree-
ment.

"You'd destruct now?"

"No," he said. "But I suggest we also cannot dismiss the
option so quickly that we don't consider it at all. This vessel
is being used as a weapon by a warring culture. That is not a
situation we can morally allow to continue."

"People—and ships—have been drafted into military

service in almost every culture, including my own. Starfleet even has a reserve activation clause."

"As I recall, the oath we took with Starfleet includes the possibility that reserve activation might be necessitated. I submit there is a distinct moral difference between coercing an innocent to participate in forceful action, and requiring that someone fulfill a previously agreed-upon, consensual contract."

"Hmmm." Janeway gestured her agreement and massaged her shoulder.

"Of course, one might also suggest that the law of this space applies to us so long as we are within its boundaries."

The captain cocked her head to one side. "Playing Devil's advocate, Mr. Tuvok?"

"I would not advocate any position but reasoned debate. Logic suggests that if we abide by one culture's laws while in their jurisdiction, we must abide by every culture's laws while in their respective jurisdictions."

"No, that's not logical at all."

Tuvok's expression was one of sincere and respectful surprise. "How so?"

"We can't be expected to change our value system every time we cross a border. If the murder of innocents is wrong in one place, it's wrong in every place."

"The definition of innocence, and indeed values, changes from culture to culture."

"That's not relevant. You can call the sun cold, but that doesn't lower its temperature. Look at your logic, Tuvok," Janeway said. "Is it logical to change your values based merely on your location and the conclusions of others?"

The Vulcan thought a moment. "No. Logic is simply the act of noncontradictory concept formation—reason applied to base perceptions. One's location cannot change one's moral values, if those values were logically chosen." He nodded his assent. "Your point is well made."

Janeway took that as the highest possible compliment. "I think you ended up making it for me, but thank you."

Rising, Janeway looked out the porthole window and the stars flying by. "We need a plan, Mr. Tuvok."

"I concur."

She pinned her attention on one star, and followed it away until it disappeared in the distance. "But I also want to know if we've acted on behalf of an evil empire . . . or a defending homeworld. If we've caused the deaths of innocents—" Captain Janeway looked down at her hand and the blood-caked scab of her injury. "Whose blood is on my hands? I need to know that."

"Our hands," Tuvok said. "And I must know as well."

The captain turned and gave him an encouraging nod, even though he didn't need it. "If we've been fighting for the wrong side, and I think it's possible, Commodore Lekket will have more problems than he *ever* bargained for."

CHAPTER

7

"WHAT HAVE WE HERE?"

In response, Janeway held out her hand, palm down, and showed the doctor her gash.

Tom Paris had accompanied the captain to Sickbay and was attempting to mend his own broken wrist with some gadget Janeway didn't recognize.

Most of the beds in Sickbay were now empty, but Janeway had first visited the two injured crewmen who still required treatment before she sought out the doctor for herself.

"You should have come to me with this sooner," the doctor sneered, scanning Janeway's hand with a medical tricorder.

Not in a smiling mood, the captain simply nodded once.

"Nice bedside manner, Doc," Paris said. "I thought you were going to work on that."

"I'm a doctor, not a toastmaster." He snapped his tricorder closed and took another appliance off a tray to his left. It hummed to life and he ran it over her injured skin. "I'm not trying to win a popularity contest."

Paris smirked. "No, you seem to be trying to lose one."

The doctor turned abruptly toward Paris. "My programming," he said matter-of-factly, "is for healing, not for

61

yucking it up with patients who are slow to report to sickbay."

Shrugging off the comment, Paris put down the healing device and picked up a medical tricorder. He scanned his hand and glanced at the captain. "Have you ever noticed that whenever anyone criticizes him, he blames it on his programming?"

The Doctor finished erasing Janeway's gash. "Pity you can't say the same, Mr. Paris."

"That'll be enough," Janeway ordered. "How's Ensign Chen?"

His expression shifting from annoyance to concern, the doctor moved a fair distance from Rob Chen's bio-bed, and Janeway followed. "Ensign Chen inhaled a great deal of coolant steam before Seven was able to bring him to Sickbay. We've filtered the toxins from his blood, but he is weak and I recommend at least two days' rest."

Janeway sighed. She didn't like the fact that a crewman of hers was injured, but she liked less the possibility that he'd be seen as a liability by the Edesians. Of what worth to them was a crewman who couldn't perform? Bed rest itself could be putting Chen's life at risk. "Get him up sooner if you can, Doctor."

The doctor lowered his voice and added an annoyed edge. "Captain, I'm not an engineer. As I've said, I don't give you one estimate when I actually have another in mind. Ensign Chen spent too long repairing a coolant leak behind Holo-deck Three. His healing will take time."

"I'd rather have these men sick and on duty than dead because the Edesians see them as unfit to live because they can't perform," Janeway snapped. "Pump them with drugs until he and Rossi can stand, and get them back to work. Understood?"

"I will have to log an official protest—"

Janeway puffed out an angry breath. "Fine. Log it, Doctor. But *after* you follow my order."

She looked from Ensign Chen to Crewman Rossi, and hoped she'd helped to save their lives, not shorten them.

"Monitor them closely, but help me make sure this crew is fit for duty."

The Doctor nodded, and Janeway wondered how, if *Voyager* ever returned home, she'd explain the ship's computer logging a complaint against her.

"Keep me informed," she ordered, and left the Doctor and sickbay behind.

A blue planet, speckled with gray mountains and brownish planes, peppered with green expanses of life, and aqua lines of river-flow.

Class "M." Earth/Mars conditions. Rasilian II was more like Earth.

Voyager fell into orbit around the planet, sliding from the day-side to the night. Janeway watched the lights of cities twinkle up through the clouds, and then the spaceport of an orbital docking station appeared over the horizon.

Again, the architecture was crude. Starfleet ships were sleek, smooth monuments to man's understanding of physics and appreciation for beauty and imagination. The Edesian and Gimlon ships Janeway had seen were utilities, not works of art. They were warships, not starships. Yes, *Voyager* was meter-for-meter more powerful than any of the Edesian or Gimlon cruisers, but her purpose wasn't as a weapon. Theirs was.

"A beautiful planet," Lekket mused, stepping down to the left of Janeway's command chair. He sounded more at peace with himself than he had six hours ago. Six hours— that's how long it had taken them to travel to the Rasilian system—at Edesian maximum warp. *Voyager* could have traversed the same distance in thirty minutes, had she been allowed.

"Just a planet," Janeway said. "Round and blue." She didn't want to share his appreciation at such a wonder of nature, even though it would have been easy to do so. She'd seen so many star systems with barren planets—more commonplace than class "M" systems—and was never able to shake the semi-sad feeling of that dead space.

Empty rocks circling a ball of hot gas could be scientifically fascinating, but worlds that supported life, that had *grown* life . . . Well, that was truly spectacular. So many life forms, so different and yet all so similar. Nature is consistent on the whole. That had been proven to Janeway again and again. A flower on Earth and a flower on Rasilian II were probably very similar, in structure if not appearance.

The planet below made her homesick . . . for just such a planet . . . round and blue.

Bolis joined Janeway and Lekket on the lower deck. "The station is ready to receive the *Voyager*," he said.

Lekket gestured toward the docking structure that now filled the forward viewscreen. "Proper moorings have been constructed from the technical schematics found in your computer banks."

Nodding slowly, Janeway ordered her vessel to dock in the alien work station.

When the procedure was complete and the mooring clamps had been locked, Janeway suddenly felt trapped. She had a few tricks up her sleeve yet, but what if she never got the chance to use them? She'd taken an oath . . . made a promise to her crew, to get *Voyager* safely home.

They were far from home.

"Your ship needs repair," Lekket said. "Time is short, and we will not waste hours stumbling over a ship we do not know.

"Your people will request the materials they need, and will service your damage with all possible haste."

Janeway nodded.

"I should like to give you a tour of our facilities, Captain," Lekket said. "You *are* a guest here."

Said the spider to the fly.

Guards lined the corridors, each of them carrying weapons and marching robotically. Janeway wasn't in a spider's web, she was in an alien prison. Or so she felt.

Lekket was treated with respect by the guards. They saluted him as he passed and didn't give Janeway a second look. Or oft times even a first.

"What do you think of our little station, Captain?" Lekket asked with some pride.

She stroked the nearby bulkhead with a finger and checked for dust. "It's very clean," she said caustically.

He smiled a thin sad smile. "I understand. I will give you what you want—"

"I want my ship's freedom."

"So we've established, Captain. I meant answers."

She stopped short and he spun around to her.

"Commodore, what if you give my ship her freedom, and keep me as your consultant. I'll fight your battles for you, and order the *Voyager* away."

Lekket shook his head. "A valiant attempt, Captain, and most virtuous. But the situation is as I have stated, and cannot change."

He motioned her forward, and they continued walking up the spartan corridor. Like the Edesians' ships and other constructs, the hall was without decoration. A stark metallic floor touched a stark metallic bulkhead, which stretched to a stark metallic ceiling. Bright white illumination panels washed the walkway in bleak light and made even the red in Janeway's uniform seem bland.

She hadn't been impressed with the space station, perhaps because humans tend to gauge even the most utilitarian facilities at an aesthetic as well as a functional level. People needed bright colors to remind them they were alive and not part of the machinery.

Guiding her toward a sliding door, Lekket gestured Janeway into a slightly dimmer room. She entered, and saw that this was a cabin with a viewing port. Out the window, she could see *Voyager* moored to the other side of the station.

"Dine with me, please," Lekket said motioning toward the table in the center of the room.

There were place settings with bowls and cups, but no food except for pale-brown doughy wafers that looked like they might be a type of bread.

Janeway didn't want to break bread with this man. He was trying to put her at ease, but there was no ease in this situation.

Nonetheless, she sat at the table, as did he.

Lekket pounded on the table once with the flat of his palm, and a young man arrived from a side room. The waiter poured a clear liquid into the cups on the table, and said he would be back with food.

Janeway picked up her cup. She smelled the liquid, then took a sip.

Ice water. Not bad tasting, either, she thought.

Well, at least he wasn't trying to get her drunk.

"Answers," she said.

The commodore nodded. "As many as I can, in the time we have."

She took another sip from the wooden cup, then held it up, admiring the craftsmanship. An actual hint of an artistic culture.

"You're assuming," she began, "that I even want answers at this point. Maybe I know all I need to."

The waiter came in again, carrying a small pot. He ladled both Janeway's and Lekket's bowls full of a stew. The meal gave off no steam, and she wondered how warm or cold it was.

Lekket picked up a wafer of the bread, broke it in half, then scooped up a mass of stew on the half he kept. "You have nothing you want to ask me?" He took a bite of his meal.

"What next?" Janeway left her stew untouched.

Lekket nodded, perhaps assuming that would be her first question. "Your ship will be repaired as promised. Most of your crew will be left intact—"

"Most?" She felt her muscles tense.

Apparently unmoved by the change in Janeway's tone, Lekket continued to slurp stew off his bread spoon. "We find it necessary to remove at least one shift of crew off an impressed vessel with such different technology as *Voyager*. If many of the current crew are injured, we'll have replacements."

Janeway abruptly stood. "No. I won't allow it. You're not taking my people off that ship."

"Captain—"

"I won't have it. I told you—I can be pushed only so far—"

Lekket dropped his bread in his bowl and stood as well. "Captain, I assure you—"

"The only thing of which I want you to assure me is that my crew is intact."

The Commodore shook his head. "It's already done. Your first officer, your helmsman, and your third shift crew have been removed to a facility where they will serve the war effort in another manner. I'm sorry."

No—Janeway had now determined that Lekket's constant appeals and apologies were nothing more than lies. He had a soft tone and a remorseful visage, but he was anything but sorry.

"You're making a mistake," Janeway said, knowing the risk to a ship that was half manned at red alert. She pumped her hands into fists at her sides. All her muscles coiled for action and she leaned forward across the table. "I want my crew. Every last member."

Commodore Lekket shook his head and took a napkin from a side table. "They are no longer your crew, Captain. They are soldiers in the Edesian fleet. They are, in fact, *my* crew, and I must deploy them as I think best."

He lowered himself back into his seat. "Please, do not waste this meal." He gestured for her to sit back down as well. "Everyone has to eat."

Refusing to sit, Janeway stalked away from the table.

"I suggest you get nourishment while you can, Captain," Lekket said evenly. "When *Voyager* is repaired, you and I will rejoin the battle. You must be prepared."

She turned and met his eyes. "I'll be ready," she said in a low whisper. "Very ready."

CHAPTER

8

MOIST WARM AIR BLANKETED CHAKOTAY'S CLAMMY SKIN. HIS eyes squinted open to lines of color and shadow. Harsh light softened into a bearable club that pounded at his head.

Where am I?

He was lying on something—he knew that much. But when he tried to rise, the motion made his head swim . . . he quickly lowered himself back down onto what felt like a sleeping-cot. Cradling his head with one hand, he wiped a film of sweat from his upper lip.

His lips were dry, his tongue chalky. He needed something to drink. . . .

He'd been standing next to Torres when it happened. He'd said something to her, noticed the sarcastic sparkle in her eyes, and then the darkness swallowed him whole, as if he'd been beamed instantly into the black of space.

"B'Lana?" Was she here too? Wherever here was.

He tried to rise again, and was slapped back by nausea. His head swam in tight circles. He hadn't been beamed anywhere. Starfleet training covered drug toxification simulations, and Chakotay remembered them all too well—he'd lasted as long as a few of his fellow cadets, then succumbed to the gas and found himself in Academy sickbay, vomiting.

He'd been drugged here, too. When the realization of that

struck, he gathered his anger and made himself rise against the nausea.

The room was dimly lit, but he saw enough to know he was on a cot in a row of like bunks. Other crewmembers . . . one in each bed. Some were beginning to stir—Holland, Seremak, Glavach. Storozuk. T'kengo, Chen, Dezago, and Briscoe. Gangle, Stone, Lessard, Townsel, Lothridge, Couls, Rossi . . . on and on . . . the gamma shift crew, present and accounted for. And Paris . . . Tom Paris . . . everyone was from Gamma shift but him.

Chakotay pulled his legs over the side of the cot. Awkwardly and barely he pushed himself to stand.

"Is everyone all right?" He looked from one end of the long hall to the other. How was he going to protect all these people? How was he going to engineer their safe return to the *Voyager?* Such questions choked off all other thoughts, and he needed to be clear-headed. The Edesians had obviously intended to separate the crew all along . . . it was the reason they had studied the personnel records so closely.

A few of the others had risen by now, and Chakotay shuffled into the middle of the room where they had gathered. "Everyone help someone else to their feet."

The standing crewmen nodded, and turned to rustle their comrades from their respective cots. Chakotay leaned toward Ensign Chen, who was sitting up and taking in long, deep breaths.

"You okay, Ensign?"

Chen nodded weakly. "Yes, sir. I just . . . I'm a little out of breath."

"You had that accident behind Holodeck Three."

The young man nodded again, his wiry frame sagging under the weight of injury and drug.

"Okay." Chakotay gripped Chen's bony shoulder. "Rest for a few. The doctor gave you a clean bill of health, right?"

"He told me to take it easy, that's all, Commander."

Chakotay managed a weak smile, and hoped that in the dim light it looked like a smile, not just pursed lips. "We won't tell him about the detour then."

Chen nodded again. He seemed to make the small gesture with great care, as if it pained him. Chakotay would have to watch him.

When they turned toward the center of the barracks, just about everyone was standing.

Lieutenant Paris staggered from the back and joined Chakotay in the middle of the gathering. "Heck of a hangover," he said.

Chakotay nodded. "I know everyone feels like they spent a bad night in a Klingon bar," he said, doing his best to lighten the dismal mood, "but we have to shake out of this and figure out what's going on. Assuming we're on the planet and *Voyager* is still in orbit, the captain will be trying to get us released. We're going to help her, or we're going to do it ourselves, right?"

Slow nods, and a few "Yes, sir" responses. Chakotay wondered how long the effects of the drug would last . . . would they all be sluggish for hours or days? They couldn't plot escape in that condition.

"Who feels well enough to walk around with me? One or two volunteers?"

Five of the thirty-five people stepped forward. "Good. Mr. Paris, you're with me. The rest of you, sit down. Try to wake up."

The crowd diminished quickly. Two or three crewmembers sat on each of the nearest cots.

Chakotay figured Paris must have been one of those people who'd lasted the longest in drug-tox simulator tests—he looked not quite fresh as a pressed suit, but better than Chakotay felt.

"Why do you look so good?"

"I've spent my share of nights in Klingon bars," Paris said.

"I want to know everything about this room," Chakotay told him as they walked toward what looked like a shut door. "Every vent, every door or window."

"Right."

Chakotay smoothed his palm against the cool metal wall.

"From there we press outward—every hallway we can see from the door, every guard. The captain will be trying to find a way to get to us, and I want to meet her halfway."

* * *

"In here." The Edesian guard—one of the two who had flanked Janeway since Lekket had bidden her goodnight— motioned toward a door. "You will be given four hours to sleep. Inside there is a change of clothes and a place to bathe."

"I'd rather be escorted back to my ship," Janeway said, not entering the quarters as the door slid back.

The guard shook his head. "Those aren't my orders."

No, of course not. Janeway nodded, entered, and the door closed behind her.

A spare cabin—a cot, a small table with a chair, a bureau with three drawers, and another doorway with a bath beyond.

"Don't you folks have something other than gray paint?" Janeway said aloud to the emptiness of the room.

She surveyed her new quarters, looking in the drawers of the dresser, under the bed, into the lavatory . . . and found no listening device. That didn't mean there wasn't one . . . it might just have been a sign that the Edesians were neither clumsy nor stupid.

Four hours. Too long, and yet not long enough.

Janeway closed her eyes and listened to the sound around her, thick with the hum of machinery. Processed air, artificial gravity, probably venting and cooling systems, and some form of defense for the space station. She heard it all, felt it too, then filed those sounds away so that if she heard something different, she'd know it wasn't background but a noise to which she must pay attention.

She tried to open the door. Locked.

She felt the walls, their smooth coolness. A bleak prison.

Gazing at the cot, Janeway thought how badly she wanted to sleep. Her hand smoothed the soft blanket, and she vowed she wouldn't sit. Sitting would give way to reclining, and reclining to sleeping, and then she would miss her only opportunity.

If she acted now she might yet save her ship. She was alone, for the first time since this began, and that in itself was an advantage. Yes, maybe there was a guard outside, and yes, there were guards between her and *Voyager*. She didn't have a phaser, or a communicator, or a tricorder. She didn't even have a club or anything that could be used as one.

A full inspection of her small cell reaped a pillow, a length of cloth that was probably a towel, an Edesian uniform meant for her use, and the thin gray blanket, which matched the walls, which matched the uniform, which matched the bulkheads, the ships, the food, and apparently the Edesian personalities.

Gray people on a blue planet.

She quickly peeled off her own uniform and pulled on the Edesian garb. If she was going to escape, it was better to look like one of them than one of her.

Her thoughts were rambling—she needed to focus.

Almost anything can be a weapon, and Janeway eyed the bed maniacally. She plucked off the blanket and tossed the scrawny mattress to the floor.

The cot's metal frame had hinges which allowed it to be folded for storage. She smiled. A military cot from any planet looked so uninviting and uncomfortable. . . .

Gripping the long support that ran the length of the cot from head to foot, Janeway tested its strength. She placed the heel of her boot at the uppermost joint and kicked hard—once, twice, then again, until the long strut clattered away from the rest of the cot frame.

Seizing the metal length with one hand to keep it from clanging against the floor, Janeway flinched at the raucous noise she was making. The last thing she wanted now was for the guard to come in.

Not yet, anyway.

As she worked on the other end of the cot, and finally tore away the long staff of metal, Janeway thought she heard a footfall in the corridor outside.

She froze.

Clank clank clank . . . boots on the deck outside. Walking past her cell. She waited until it was quiet again, then allowed herself to breathe.

Glancing down, she looked at her handiwork. It wasn't much—a long metal staff. But it was better than bare hands.

Now she had to wait.

Eyes heavy with fatigue, she wished the lights were not so

bright. She glared up at the blazing panels in the ceiling. If she could do something about those . . .

"Lights off."

Nothing happened. Not computer-controlled apparently, at least not to *her* voice, and no switch she could see.

Janeway set down her new weapon and stooped to pick up the thin blanket she'd tossed to the floor. She bit into the cloth about two inches in from one side, then tore down slowly, trying not to make a lot of noise.

Of course, if she was being monitored at all, the guards would have been all over her already. Maybe this was a makeshift cell, and security would be a little more lax.

Each slow tear sent a puff of cloth dust into the air. Toward the end of the rip, Janeway had to use her teeth again to separate the strip from the rest of the blanket. When she was done, and had bundled the long strip into one hand, she picked up her weapon again, and made sure her skin touched no part of the metal staff.

Stepping back from directly underneath the overhead illumination, Janeway thrust her long bar into the light panel. The covering cracked and sparks showered down on her as the light flashed brightly, then faded. She jumped away, small sizzles of spark finding her bare skin.

When her eyes adjusted, the spartan cube of a cell was dim. Only small accent lights near the bottom of the lavatory door lit the room.

She sank back against the wall near the main door and readied herself. Maybe she had four hours, or maybe she had mere minutes before a guard would be in to see why there was a disruption in the lighting.

How did they expect her to sleep with the lights on anyway?

Maybe they didn't. Maybe they didn't care. Maybe their race slept with the lights on. Or with their socks on. Did they wear socks?

Her mind was spinning in too many directions. *Focus, focus, focus!*

She began rubbing the end of the metal staff against the floor. She might need it to have a sharper edge. How was she going to do this all? Getting out of the cell might be easy compared with getting back to *Voyager*. Might be? Would be.

Minutes passed, and the only sound Janeway heard was her own breathing mixed with the rhythmic grinding she was making with the quarterstaff against the floor.

Quarterstaff . . . a funny thought. Visions of Robin Hood and his merry men. She was going to try an ancient weapon against a dozen guards with modern disruptors? Foolishness.

Her mind was wandering again, but at least she continued to listen—past the sharpening sound she was making with the staff and out into the hall, where a guard might be walking.

Seconds seemed to linger too long, minutes waited for them, and so an hour passed long after it should. Was time even passing?

Yes . . . she spun the end of her weapon toward her and felt one edge with her thumb. Sharper . . . good. She angled her next round of grinding so that the "blade" would be evenly sharpened.

Listening and waiting were not two of Janeway's favorite activities. In her mind's eye she tried to review her Academy hand-to-hand and simple weapon skills.

Eyelids heavy, she felt so much like sleeping. . . .

With her free hand she punched herself in the thigh. *Wake up, Captain! You're a captain! Remember your responsibility!*

Don't sleep . . . be alert . . . Her goal wasn't to do anything but get back to the *Voyager*. *Think only about* Voyager. She rearranged her grip on the length of metal and continued grinding it against the floor. It would make a good weapon, wouldn't it?

She couldn't do *anything* if she fell asleep. The guard would come in, see her snoozing with the weapon . . . then what?

Strangely, the longer she waited, the easier it became to stay awake. She'd found a healthy pattern—widen her eyes, jab at her own leg, sharpen her weapon. When the rhythm of the motion seemed to border on hypnotic, she reversed the sequence. Two jabs, eyes wide, and three grinds on the staff's edge. Then a few blinks, a grind on the floor, and a jab to her leg. She was probably giving herself a bruise. So what? She was awake.

After what seemed like six hours, but was surely less, she heard footsteps.

Janeway pulled her weapon into both hands and jolted herself erect next to the doorway. She held her breath, and listened. Adrenaline had her fully awake.

Footsteps—clomping, scraping, pounding . . .

She could feel sweat forming on her forehead, in the small of her back, on her tense shoulders. She tried to shake off the tightness she felt, tried to loosen the knots in her muscles. She let out her breath, but only in short, silent puffs.

Right now her ship and her entire crew depended on how many guards were placed between her and the spacedock. Could she get aboard *Voyager* safely? If so, this might all be over.

The footsteps stopped close to her door.

She steadied herself, calves taut, head cocked to listen to the silence.

The door slid open, too slowly.

The guard stepped in, hesitating in the dim light.

Janeway swung her staff behind him and pushed him into the room. He spun around as she leapt into the doorway. With the light behind her, she knew she was only a silhouette to him. But her eyes were used to the dimness and she saw him reach for a baton.

He swung; she countered and looped her staff around his forearm, trying to break his grip on his own weapon.

The guard used both hands and tried to pull her staff forward. She angled the long shaft away, swung around again and knocked his arm down.

As he recovered, she sliced across his chest. It was a glancing blow that cut through his uniform.

For a stupid moment, he looked down in surprise.

She thrust into his gut. The sharp edge of the staff pierced the guard's belly—an inch in and an inch up.

Staggering back, the guard sputtered, and fell over the wreckage of the cot.

Janeway stepped up, jammed her boot heel into his weapon hand, and he yelped in pain.

"Make a sound," she whispered to him harshly, "and you're dead." She flipped him over, grasped the torn lines of blanket she'd used earlier, and quickly tied his hands behind him, his ankles to his wrists. She stuffed a gag into his mouth. She finished by tightening another strip of blanket over the slash in his stomach. She wanted to escape, not to kill.

She searched his pockets, then his belt, but he wore no sidearm, no weapon but the baton. Very smart. If he'd had a sidearm, it would be hers now. As in almost every penal colony, guards were usually unarmed when inside a prisoner's cell and heavily armed on the other side of the locked doors.

She attached the baton to her tunic and slid out the door and into the hallway.

"Alert! Alert! All personnel, Main Alert!"

Janeway pressed herself against the wall as klaxons rang and voices squawked from up the corridor.

She looked left, right, and saw no escape.

CHAPTER
9

"ALERT! ALERT! ALL PERSONNEL TO DUTY STATIONS! TRANS-ports prepare for lift-off! Main alert! Main alert!"

"Where're we going?" Tom Paris tried to turn back toward the rest of the *Voyager* crew members, but was pushed forward down the corridor.

"What's going on?" Chakotay was also pushed forward by the Edesian guard.

"Just move."

Sirens, in the distance and in the foreground. Something big was happening. Chakotay looked back and was grateful that at least the crew shift was being kept all together. There were several guards, looking not hostile but urgent, waving them all up the corridor. And not just the crew, but Edesian personnel as well.

As they were being shuffled along, Chakotay strained to listen to the babble of their calls, hoping his universal translator could sort out what was going on.

"We have room in transports three and seven!"

"We're moving everyone to the west pad."

"Forget breaking anything down. Just get your people on!"

Everyone was moving out. Why?

If there were any time to escape, though, maybe now was the time.

"Paris." Chakotay tried to get the helmsman's attention.

Tom Paris turned his torso, but had to continue up the corridor. He was farther up than Chakotay, and though he tried to fall back, the Edesian guards wouldn't let him.

If they waited much longer, opportunity might pass . . . but how could they escape with all hands without any discussion or planning?

"This way! Hurry!" called one guard, motioning them quickly out onto a launch area. The air was cool, like an early spring day. Out past the concrete landing field was a meadow with wild flowers. There was a city in the distance, modern and sprawling. Sirens cut through the air, probably from as far away as the cityscape.

"Everyone on this side, board transport seven. Once in, continue toward the back!"

They were being transferred. Where? And why? Was it a drill? An emergency? A tactic to keep them confused or break them up? Nothing was very clear, and Chakotay wondered if, even after three hours, his mind wasn't still hampered by whatever drug had helped to bring them all here.

Suddenly Paris tripped, falling straight down, disappearing from Chakotay's view. He was helped up by two Edesian soldiers—not guards, but standard crew who happened to be alongside. The moving crowd slid around the three men as the Starfleeter was steadied. The two Edesians were gracious and patient as Paris so obviously pretended to be dazed. He patted himself to make sure he was intact, then slapped one guard on the back lightly, thanking him.

The Edesians treated Paris with kindness, brushing him off. Chakotay had the chance to catch up with them, and came up alongside Paris once the guards were on their way.

"You okay?" Chakotay asked.

Paris nodded and they all continued toward the transport pad.

A cool breeze swept over Chakotay's face. The smell of spring, pollen and flowers, brought a peaceful feeling—very illusory, almost dishonest, given their predicament. He turned away from the wind as he and Paris were pushed toward the personnel transport.

"If there's a chance," Chakotay said, barely above a whisper, "I'll take it. Follow my lead."

Before Paris had time to respond beyond a nod of his head, they were ushered into the transport. The ship was sparsely decorated. It was basically a giant box filled with seats from bulkhead to bulkhead, save for a T-shaped aisle leading from the main door to an emergency door, then perpendicular up the middle of the seats.

"Move along. March as far as you can, down and starboard, then sit." Edesian guards, two at the front, two at the back, guided people to seats once they were aboard.

"Seat-belts," Chakotay noticed and pointed out to Paris. "No inertial dampeners?"

"Well, weak ones probably. If there were none at all we'd turn to mush, even at low impulse speeds."

Chakotay nodded. "Of course." His *mind* still felt like mush, as he sat and buckled himself in next to Paris. If the drug were still affecting him, how would he know when his chance to act had come? Maybe he'd already missed it.

He thought he must wait—till all his people were aboard and until the ship was in the air, into space. Then maybe he could overpower four guards, find the controls to the transport, also overpower the pilots, and maneuver back to *Voyager.*

Right? Right. After that he would accept coronation as High Master Of All The Universe, and take his place among the physical and mental giants of all time.

As seat-belts throughout the transport clicked closed, Chakotay shared a glance with Paris and hoped they weren't all simply locking in their own fates.

If he'd waited too long to make his move, they might all soon be dead.

I'm dead, Janeway thought, klaxons blaring overhead. She twisted away from the doorway to her cell and looked up the corridor. No one in either direction. But where would they come from?

With her luck, both sides.

Her presence outside the cell must have triggered the alarm.

They didn't bug the room—they bugged me.

Janeway's heart sank. She'd blown it. How many guards would be on top of her in moments?

It didn't matter anymore. There would be no more pretense at cooperation. They might have her trapped, but they'd pay dearly to take her back into a cell.

She ran up the corridor, awkwardly trying to keep her long staff off the deck as she went. She paused, decided the guard's baton was an easier weapon to wield, and tossed her proudly made quarterstaff along the bulkhead.

A doorway, an alcove—that's what she needed. Some place to hide for a moment and get her bearings.

There were no hiding places. She pushed up the next long corridor. Gray walls curved forward, desolate of doors or crevices.

She was halfway to nowhere when she stopped and listened to a rumbling in the distance, trying to filter out the thousand sounds she wasn't used to.

Voices? Forward and to the left—around the far corner or in a room she couldn't see, she couldn't tell which. *My kingdom for a tricorder,* she thought, pressing herself against the left wall.

How far might she get? How many guards would she take down with her?

Count the voices . . . two—no, three. Getting closer.

Boot-stomps on the deckway. She could see them, three of them marching toward her—*running* at her.

She gripped the baton tightly in her right fist. Three against one. They were carrying disruptors, so she was nearly defenseless.

Three forms charged around the corner. They were almost on her, looking intently at her, their mission accomplished if she succumbed.

She wouldn't make it easy for them. She balled her left fist, felt her tense muscles loosen a little, warm with preparation.

Janeway pulled her baton hand back, ready to strike the first guard across the bridge of his nose.

"Get out of the way!" the Edesian yelled.

The trio of Edesian guards barreled right past her, pushing her out of the way. "Report to your station!" one of them bellowed. "We're on alert!"

They galloped quickly away.

She smiled a brief second, allowing herself a soft, nervous chuckle. Something else was up—the alert wasn't for her.

Janeway was renewed with hope. If everyone is distracted, maybe she still had a chance.

More footfalls erupted from up the curved corridor, dampening her shallow celebration.

The first door she tried spread open before her, and she slid in.

Frying pan to fire, two guards were rising from a table as she entered.

"Who are you?" the male guard demanded.

"Oh," Janeway began quickly, nonchalantly, "I'm here to help—" Before they could pull their weapons, she pounced forward, tossing the closest guard forward onto the table. He landed with a grunt and slid off to one side, onto a chair then to the floor.

Food and drink clattered to the deck as the female guard lunged toward Janeway.

The captain kicked the table over and on top of the male guard as she pulled out the baton. She pressed it into the other woman's neck, pushing her back.

Janeway spun the guard in front of her, pulling on the baton and cutting off the female guard's air supply.

"Stop squirming, or I'll take your head off!"

The woman writhed anyway, jamming her foot behind Janeway's right ankle.

Pulled off balance, Janeway dropped hard to her knees and took the female Edesian with her.

The guard sputtered under Janeway's tight grip and flailed chaotically as the captain tried to regain her balance and pull them both to their feet.

The woman guard had done her job, though. By the time she stopped fighting and Janeway had control again, the other guard was standing, weapon drawn.

"Disruptor down," Janeway snarled, "or I *will* kill her."

The male guard aimed at Janeway's head. "Kill her," he said, "and *you* will die."

Standoff.

Janeway pulled the baton deeper into the woman's neck. "I'm very serious about this."

The male guard flicked a switch on his weapon, making it hum louder. "I am serious as well," he hissed.

He *was* serious. She could see it in the angry slant of his brow. His jaw twitched, and he motioned her away from the other guard. "Let her go."

Janeway nodded once, released pressure on the female guard's neck, then spun the woman toward the disruptor in the other guard's hand.

A zapping sound—

Janeway felt the energy from the weapon as it cored into the female guard in front of her.

The Edesian woman tumbled to the deck, her body limp. Hers was not the slack of unconsciousness, for even a sleeping body holds a certain tension. Hers was the flaccid ballast of death, a body made of wet sand that was now slipping as low to the floor as possible—a mound of muscle at the male guard's feet.

"No!" the Edesian man yelled, and reached for the dead woman's head as it hung from her shoulders at an odd angle. "Yandal!"

He sprang up, aiming his weapon deliberately at Janeway. As she dove away, an explosion rumbled down from above and shook them both to the deck.

The lights dimmed a split second, then brightened, then dimmed again. Janeway rolled and whipped around onto a knee, trying to regain footing, but another blast shook the room and sent her twisting into the far bulkhead.

Explosion after explosion thundered around them. The station was under attack—this was no drill.

Voyager! What about her ship?

She leapt to her feet and by the time she was up, so was the guard. His weapon hand looped around. Before he could aim she lunged at him, taking hold of his weapon hand, bending back his wrist.

His disruptor clattered to the deck and bounced away. She took his fingers, jammed them back and spun him around. He growled in angry pain as she bent his elbow closer toward his neck and spread his legs apart.

Another internal explosion, this one feeling and sounding closer, sent sparks from the lighting above. Overhead ceiling plates twisted out of shape and fell on them. Both were forced to the deck.

Something burned the back of Janeway's neck as she pressed her captive down, then pulled him to his feet as she rose.

"Now," she rasped, "you're going to help me get out of here. Understand?" She pushed him away with one hand and scooped up his weapon with the other.

He stared at her, shaking, looking very young. Tears stood in his eyes, and for good reason—the young man didn't seem to know what was going on.

"The way I see it," Janeway said, "we've both gotten off easy."

He glared at her, then at the disruptor muzzle she placed at the level of his nose.

Explosions, now in the distance, sent dust and minute debris settling down on them.

Janeway coughed, but didn't take her eyes off the young Edesian. Were they all this wet behind the ears? He was frightened, and she could use that. "Show me a level that will stun without killing, and I won't have to test every setting on you."

"Step away from him."

Janeway spun, came up, her disruptor pointed toward the door.

Bolis edged a thin slice of himself around the doorway. Just enough so he could see to fire—

His left eyebrow was dripping blood over the half of his face that peeked forward. That's all she saw of him—an eyebrow, a weapon, and the tip of his boot.

"You'd never have escaped alone," he said.

Janeway was silent as his finger pulled the disruptor's trigger, and the weapon's whine filled the air.

CHAPTER 10

BOLIS'S DISRUPTOR WHINED WITH AN INTENSITY THAT HURT Janeway's ears.

She braced herself for the shot, but instead heard the Edesian guard behind her collapse.

"We are under attack," Bolis said, wrenching Janeway up, leaving his Edesian comrade where he lay stunned. "Come with me—I will take you to your ship."

He pulled her out of the room and down the corridor. Edesian soldiers, equipment in tow, were running repair detail and tending the wounded. They flew this way and that. Again, young people mostly . . . they all looked as though they were barely out of adolescence.

"This way." Bolis ordered Janeway in front of him. He pushed her toward a hatch that led to a ladder.

Looking down, Janeway could see down into the bowels of the station.

"Why?" she asked. "Why help me?"

"Move now," he said, and motioned her down.

Explosions continued, and the station rattled around them as she started down the ladder.

As smoke, dust, and debris settled across the decks of the station, Janeway was glad to be in the isolated—and cleaner—Jeffries-type tube.

"Is the *Marauder* out there?" Janeway asked.

"No. But there are three waves of Gimlon interceptors in attack formation. They came from three different sections of this quadrant—impossible to blockade with our low numbers. The first wave has all but been defeated. The other two are on their way." He was breathing heavily, and Janeway noticed how hot the air around her had become.

"We must hurry," he said, and a crack of some ship's disruptor fire punctuated the urgency in his voice as it crashed against the station.

"Why are you helping me?"

Janeway hesitated on the ladder as she asked her question, and Bolis's tone was pleading. "Move, Captain, and I promise to explain."

She did . . . and he'd better.

What about her crew? Was he serious about helping her?

How could she be sure this wasn't some elaborate ruse to make it look like she had escaped and he'd caught her?

"First safety, Captain," he said. "Then we will discuss the ramifications of your actions."

How cryptic.

What was he up to? And how could she use it? Now there was a real chance she could pull out with her ship and crew intact. The only worry for her was what Bolis wanted in return for his generosity. Janeway had been in space long enough to know that there were as many different political agendas as there were stars in the Milky Way. If Bolis didn't have some angle, he'd be unusual.

They both hesitated as another explosion raked the space station and the ladder vibrated in their hands. Janeway could tell the station was taking a pounding again—the second wave.

"What about my ship?"

Bolis didn't answer as another explosion gibbered the bulkheads around them.

"Your ship has been repaired, her shields restored," he said finally, "and your photon torpedo stores have been replenished."

Stunned at that last fact, Janeway staggered down the next rung and stopped. "How?"

"Move along," Bolis ordered. As she did, he finally

answered her. "We were able to reproduce the casings you use. They are not unlike our own plasma torpedo housings. Antimatter is abundant in our reserve; the actual circuits and guidance hardware were provided by your Engineer."

All right . . . *Voyager*'s safe, re-armed . . . for now.

One good thing in the last twenty-four hours. She was not exactly on a roll.

Janeway almost lost her balance, as her feet suddenly touched deck rather than ladder rung.

Wherever we are, here we are, she thought caustically.

She stepped out of the way and allowed Bolis to drop off the ladder.

He gestured to a doorway. "You must trust me now," he said, placing his disruptor in Janeway's hands. "Through that door will be two guards, then an airlock to your ship. I cannot go with you, I must stay here and search for the escaped prisoner."

Janeway held his warm disruptor in her right hand. She fingered the trigger but didn't fire. She aimed it at Bolis's chest, but not in a threatening manner. "You stunned your own comrade. He'll remember that."

"I will worry about the consequences of my own actions," Bolis said tightly, hurriedly. "You must go now."

They listened to the roar of a distant shot and the accompanying explosion . . .

"Voyager will be launched in minutes to deal with the Gimlon ships, Captain. Please—"

"Just tell me why," Janeway demanded.

Bolis thought a moment, looked at the doorway, then the hatch.

"Why should I trust you?" Janeway prodded. "Why your change of heart?"

"It is a philosophical matter," he said. "I am against this impressment policy. I cannot morally accept the most certain death of you and your crew in a war you neither started nor accept as your own."

"Wartime conversion to pacifism, Bolis? Sounds a little too convenient to me."

The Edesian pulled in a breath. "Captain, I could no sooner reveal my inner thoughts to you than to those who command me. There is an underground at work here, all over Edesia Prime. I risk much to do this, but I believe it important."

Should she trust him? No. Was he giving her a real chance to escape? Maybe, maybe not—but she wouldn't get closer to freedom if *Voyager* was just through the next two doorways.

"Prove you're of use to me. How many guards remain on my ship? And how do I deal with the warp-dampener?" she asked.

Bolis pushed her lightly toward the doorway. "I will help with that when I join you on board."

Janeway pressed his own disruptor into his breastbone. "Then come with me now."

He shook his head. "I cannot, Captain."

"I insist," she ground out, pressing harder into his chest with the business end of the weapon.

"Please trust me, Captain."

Janeway shook her head. "Lead the way, block my weapon as we approach the guards, then drop to let me stun them."

"This is not my plan. Captain, I am risking my life to do this for you. I am trying to help you." Bolis's expression was one of true worry, arched honesty . . . or was it? Maybe he just sold that look.

She didn't have time to weigh the truths he spoke against the reality she knew. "You don't seem to understand," Janeway said quietly. "We're changing your plan. And you're risking your life if you don't."

"Please! Stay in your seats!" the Edesian guard ordered. "This is but a minor skirmish! You must not panic!"

The sound of another explosion cracked the air.

"If this is a minor skirmish, I never want to see a major one," Paris said over the din of Edesian crewmen shouting orders to one another.

Chakotay's chair rattled under him as another volley of disruptor fire glazed off the transport's thin shields. He could see the shot on the small viewer at the bow of the hold. The ship could have avoided it if the transport had been equipped with even half-decent thrusters.

Most of the small vessel was filled with the entire transplanted *Voyager* crew shift, but many Edesian crewmembers were aboard as well, and Chakotay couldn't help but notice their general collective expression: frightened.

These are all trainees, Chakotay surmised. He'd mumbled as much to Paris and they'd both agreed that was the case. Young trainees too.

"The Edesians are losing their war," Chakotay told Paris, "and have to draw on younger and younger men and women to man their ships and fight their battles."

Paris nodded. They'd both seen the pattern before, and despite *Voyager's* situation, Chakotay felt sorry for the Edesians, for the waste of their lives and resources.

Slipping his hand beneath the clasp of his seat restraint, Chakotay leaned over to Paris, pretending to stretch his back. "Now's the time—while everyone is preoccupied."

Paris looked back at the relatively calm *Voyager* crew and contrasted them with the disorderly, agitated Edesians, who were caterwauling at one another in panicked voices.

"Frantic is more like it," Paris said, whispering. "You have a plan?"

"Sure." Chakotay frowned, straightened himself, and his seat belt slid away to either side. "We take over this vessel."

Nodding, Paris whispered. "I like it, but doesn't it lack a certain . . . specificity?"

His shoulders rolling a shrug, Chakotay pressed his lips into a flat line and couldn't help but agree. "What we need is to get one of their weapons."

"I can sell you one, but it'll cost," Paris said quietly.

Chakotay shook his head discouragingly. "I'm not in the mood, Paris."

Adjusting himself in his seat, Paris crammed his hand into the belly of his tunic via the V-neck opening. When his hand emerged, he had one of the slim Edesian disruptors in his palm.

"I think that's worth a week's replicator credits at least."

A chuckle bubbled up into Chakotay's throat. "Where did you get that?"

Paris shrugged modestly. "When the guards were picking me up from the little trip I took."

Taking the weapon from Paris, Chakotay hid it at his side

and motioned for Paris to unbelt himself. "Wish you could have gotten two."

"Hey," Paris protested quietly, "you weren't the one who had to pick the guy's pocket without him knowing it. If I'd tried for his compendant or something else, you'd be a pallbearer at my funeral by now."

"Come on," Chakotay said lightly. "Admit it. You were one of the Artful Dodger's boys in a previous life."

His head cocked to one side in mock dismay, Paris slowly removed his seat restraint. "What past life? I lived in France for a while, remember?"

Chakotay sniggered. Never in his life had he met anyone who somehow managed to annoy and amuse simultaneously—until he met Tom Paris.

Another explosion somewhere on the transport jostled them both, and Paris's seat-belt clasp rattled against the bulkhead.

Chakotay looked at Paris nervously, then around the cabin. That could have given them away.

The small viewscreen showed the starscape twisting wildly. The planet showed for a moment, then space, then the spacedock. These weren't evasive actions. They were evidence of a shaky helm. Or a shaky helmsman.

"I'm going to move. Back me up where you can," Chakotay said, and rose from his seat, the Edesian weapon held as inconspicuously as possible in his right hand.

He took only two steps forward before another salvo from the enemy raked the ship, sending sparks flying from above and Chakotay to the deck.

As Chakotay hit the floor the disruptor was knocked from his hand. It slid under a seat, out of reach. So close, and now so far. So much power in a such a small container . . . that weapon held salvation for the *Voyager* crew, *if* Chakotay could just get his paws on it again.

For just a quick moment he looked back to Paris, who'd been knocked from his chair. He then looked forward, saw the disruptor across the hold, and began to crawl toward it.

Damn!

The large vessel shook again under the brunt of further attack. The air sizzled. Chakotay could feel the structural damage through the length of his body. The transport's weak shields had been breached, and now the enemy would work on the ship's armor. No transport was meant to take such attack—not in the Federation—not anywhere.

Lights flickered again, and Chakotay struggled to maintain a bead on the weapon.

Explosions rolled over the ship's hull again. Chakotay was tossed one way, then another. The lights went out and didn't come back.

Something smashed onto Chakotay's back, sending waves of pain up his spine and down his legs into his knees. Hot metal cut through his uniform and into his skin, and he felt the flow of his own warm blood spread across his back.

He tried not to groan in pain . . . hoped for emergency lights that hadn't turned on . . . struggled to keep conscious as agony sliced into him.

Darkness persisted as explosions tossed the transport, and Chakotay with it.

CHAPTER

11

SMOKE SLITHERED THE DECK AND WRAPPED ITSELF AROUND Chakotay's neck as he scrambled to find the disruptor. His back stung, and he could feel his own warm blood under his uniform, but the pain was manageable.

The lights were still dim and intermittent. He elbowed himself forward and groped for the weapon awkwardly, knocking into the legs of his own crewmembers as they sat strapped to the transport's seats.

Why are the lights always the first to go? Chakotay grumbled to himself, wincing as he twisted wrong and aggravated his sizzling back.

His fingers found the butt of the disruptor and he quickly yanked it toward his chest, protecting it like a fragile egg. Hope was pent up in the packed energy of the Edesian ordnance. That's what a weapon could symbolize: death and tyranny, or protection and liberty—depending on whose hand fingered the trigger.

Chakotay's was the hand of protection for the crewmen under him, and he meant to see they all found their liberty. He hoped the disruptor was set for stun—and braced himself for his moment.

Again the small transport rattled around them. The sound of escaping oxygen hissed from the aft. Edesian trainees were being ordered to take care of the small breach, but they complained they didn't know how. *Complained.*

There was an opportunity here, beyond taking charge of the vessel with force. Chakotay could perhaps take charge with reason, and experience.

He stood upright between the rows of seats.

"You! Sit down!"

One of the guards who'd ushered the *Voyager* crew into the transport was trying to oversee the situation. Part of the problem was that the other three guards were trying to do the same. Orders were barked, countermanded, and given again.

"No, no! Use the other unit! The OTHER one! Seal that leak!"

"We need someone to work on the shield generator! Who has had shield training?"

"I did!"

"Get over here!"

"No, I need him for the navigation bypass!"

A cadet ship, trying to survive in a battle. The enemy knew the transport was defenseless, yet as Chakotay watched, the same Gimlon intercept kept tearing across the small viewscreen—it would attack, spin around, and attack again, with the single-minded goal of destroying the transport.

War was always dirty, but there was something especially unclean about trying to kill the defenseless—even when they were soldiers.

Chakotay stood there, looked back at Paris and across the faces of the *Voyager* crewmembers who were with them, then back to the Edesian guard who'd given the Starfleet officer an order to return to his seat.

Another explosion rocked the ship, harder this time. The hiss of escaping atmosphere grew louder.

"Call again for help!" The Edesian in command yelled. "Isn't there anyone to help us?"

"The pilot is injured, sir."

"How injured?"

"He's dead."

Very injured.

"Then so are we!"

Chakotay nodded to Paris, then stepped toward the guard, showing his weapon as he walked.

"Do as I say, and we all might live."

Maybe because Chakotay seemed like an authority figure, and maybe because the young guard just knew he was outmatched, he moved very slowly to unholster his weapon, and found he didn't have it. Paris had come around behind and taken it.

Tom smiled at him as the Edesian wheeled around to find two Starfleeters confronting every guard.

"I'm not trying to kill you," Chakotay said to the lead guard. "And you shouldn't be trying to kill us. We might be able to save everyone . . . and that's something I don't think your trainees can do alone."

There was a certain soft authority Chakotay let lace his voice. The tone one used when trying to persuade partly and control mostly.

The young guard, his brows knitted with frustration, nodded to his comrades to relent. He probably hadn't thought that his first command would mean his first surrender. "I could be put to death for treason."

Chakotay nodded. "Or commended for helping to save everyone's life."

Unhappily realizing his choices were few, the guard agreed.

Spinning about, ready to give orders to a new, combined crew, Chakotay let his weapon aim downward unobtrusively. "Paris, take any Edesian who was going to be a pilot and check out the helm. Get us on a course toward the *Voyager*."

Paris nodded. "Right." He turned, grabbed the nearest Edesian by the arm, and marched toward the bow of the ship. "You look like you've always wanted to be a pilot. You *can* read a control panel, can't you?"

The youngster nodded as he was dragged off.

"Chen, check into that hull breach!" Chakotay saw his own young ensign nod, and admired the man's strength, after the physical ordeal he'd been through. "Glavach, Spencer, Holland . . . and Lothridge. Work on the shields. I know they're weak even when they're up. Find a way to strengthen them."

"Aye, aye, sir."

Chakotay looked toward the small viewscreen. He was surprised to realize he had to squint past building smoke to see through to the view of space. He motioned about with his hand swiping the air. "Are there fans to clear this?"

He looked at the dazed guard still in front of him.

"Are there?" Chakotay asked again.

The guard shook his head slowly. "We are working only with auxiliary systems. This is a short-range transport, meant only for moving from the planet to other posts within this system—a ship or the space station."

Chakotay pulled in a breath and let it out slowly. *Wonderful.*

"Any weapons?"

"No, nothing."

"Tractor beams?"

"Yes, two, but what good—"

"Who knows?" Chakotay shrugged. Anything could be a weapon, for defense *or* offense. "Go on—what else?"

Chakotay noticed the Gimlon were scoring fewer hits since Paris had taken the helm. Good.

"I don't know," the guard said, his gaze cast down. "Five weeks ago yesterday I was a doctor."

A soft chuckle rose to Chakotay's lips. "You're a doctor, not a soldier," he said, more to himself than the Edesian. "Tell you what, why don't you see if anyone needs some medical attention, okay?"

The guard nodded. "How's your back?"

"Later. The rest of you . . ." Chakotay said, as yet another Gimlon salvo raked the ship. "Sit down . . . and hang on."

"Captain on the bridge."

Janeway stepped onto the Ops deck, having left Bolis's disruptor back on the station. That was the safer plan she'd chosen—to fool the guards and Lekket. But Janeway knew she was in command again, and that renewed her strength, mentally and physically. Her ship felt better to her as well— restored, repaired—but was about to take a pounding if she didn't get her out of dock.

"Lieutenant Bolis, I did not summon the captain," Lekket said, rising from the command chair.

"Commodore, I thought it prudent to have her aboard while the *Voyager* is under attack."

Lekket nodded slowly and seemed to accept that. Good.

Janeway marched toward Tuvok, who stood at tactical. Harry Kim was still at Ops, but Chakotay wasn't in his seat and Tom Paris wasn't at the helm. She winced and reminded herself to keep her priorities straight. First, get the *Voyager* out of the fish barrel into which the Gimlon were shooting. Second—get back her crew.

"Status report," Janeway ordered Tuvok.

"We are moored to the station. Station control cannot—or will not—release us. A third wave of Gimlon intercepts are on their way. We sustained minor damage from the first two sorties, but the Edesian defenses are almost exhausted."

Janeway nodded.

Some Edesian woman was sitting at the helm. Lekket looked over her shoulder, barking orders. "You must do something!"

"What?" The woman looked older than Lekket, and spoke to him in a frustrated, even arrogant tone. They didn't risk the *Voyager* to a kid. Interesting. "There is nothing to do!" the woman helmsman told Lekket. "A mooring is a mooring and these won't release us."

An argument . . . on her bridge, between two people who shouldn't even be there.

And at a time like this—another wave of Gimlon attackers on their way.

Janeway marched down to the command deck. "Red alert. All hands, battle stations."

The lighting changed, red lights tinting every surface in the crimson battle alert.

"Shields will not operate while we are moored to the station," Tuvok reported.

Lekket turned, looked at Bolis, then at Janeway, as he registered her presence and, perhaps, her new posture—more hardened than before.

"We can't break free of the moorings," the commodore

told her. "The controls are jammed, and station control won't respond."

Janeway nodded once. "Out," she snapped, motioning the Edesian woman away from the naviconsole. "Tuvok, take the helm. Transfer tactical down here."

Tuvok nodded once, jabbed at his board a fast moment, then dropped down from tactical to Paris's usual station.

The Edesian woman refused to release the helm. "I have studied your systems and know the proper protocols—"

Janeway leaned down, her voice a sharp sword. "Lady, if you followed protocols at all, you wouldn't even be on my ship. Now *move!*"

The Edesian woman didn't stand.

Tuvok stepped closer in behind her. He waited, hands behind his back.

The captain nodded at him.

He moved one hand fluidly to the Edesian woman and seemed just to touch her, a short squeeze where his fingertips met the top of her shoulder and side of her neck . . . She collapsed.

"Perhaps I should take the helm," Tuvok said dryly.

"She's not dead," Janeway told Lekket, then added, "Everyone gets a first mistake."

Tuvok pulled the woman softly away from the console and took his seat.

"Captain—" Lekket began in a protesting tone.

Janeway spun away from him. "Harry, get someone up here from Sickbay." She then turned back to Lekket and motioned to the Edesian woman who was sprawled on the deck at Tuvok's feet. "She disobeyed one of my orders. She'll be allowed to regain consciousness, and when she does, she'll find herself in the brig."

"I don't want—"

Janeway cut Lekket off. "What you want is to survive this battle," she told him over a tight jaw. "And so you'll take a seat and stay out of my way."

Somewhat to her surprise, Lekket responded with a nod. She wanted to glance up at Bolis as well, to get some sort of visual reading on his opinion of Lekket's submission, but she resisted.

"Show me tactical," Janeway ordered, turning back toward the main viewer.

Tuvok patted his console and a graphic of the starsystem appeared on the main viewscreen. The space station arm that enveloped the *Voyager* was at the center. Beyond it was the class "M" planet. Five small dots signified the Gimlon intercepts as they sped toward the station.

"ETA of the third wave?"

"If they maintain current speed," Tuvok answered, "one minute seventeen seconds."

Not a lot of time.

"Those other ships?" Janeway asked, motioning to some vessels leaving orbit.

Tuvok raised one eyebrow, the Vulcan shrug. "Various Edesian craft, transports, shuttles, and the like, and two Gimlon intercepts. The Gimlon craft have sustained damage and are no doubt waiting for the third wave as reinforcements."

"Maybe." Janeway was going to doubt everything until she had her ship and crew all intact and back on their original course.

"We have to get out of this dock," Janeway said aloud, stating the obvious. Her mind whirled with possible escape plans, then her rational side dashed those plans as too farfetched. "What about full impulse?"

"We'd tear away half our hull," Kim said. "We're too well connected."

Janeway nodded once. "Tuvok, what about—"

Three blasts roared into *Voyager's* hull.

The Gimlon hadn't maintained speed—they'd increased it.

"Two direct hits. More incoming!" Tuvok braced himself. "Plasma torpedoes!"

"Detonate—"

"Too close!"

The forward viewer blazed with white intensity before crumbling into static. Plasma detonations lit up the screen, and *Voyager's* hull darkened with burnt chemical residue.

Janeway gripped Tuvok's chair and wrestled against the quake that threatened to force her to the deck. The swollen knuckles she'd earned in her fight with the Edesian guards ached as she pressed her palms against the armrests. "Phasers?"

"Our range is limited by the arms of the station moorings," Tuvok said.

Kim called from the Ops deck: "Primary hull breach, Captain. S.I.F. failure at decks seven and eight."

"Damage control, Mr. Kim."

"Aye, aye!"

Chopped commands and clipped responses. The vessel rocked around them, creaking under the strain as *Voyager* was pounded by five Gimlon warships. Janeway choked on the thick air that suddenly filled the bridge—smoke, the odor of burnt connections, coolant steam. "Auxiliary fans," she coughed. "Return fire, Tuvok. Best possible targeting."

"They are taking cover from the station around us," Tuvok said. "I cannot get a weapons lock."

"We're sitting ducks," Janeway spat, her commands useless on a ship that couldn't move. She angled toward Lekket, who sat contritely in Chakotay's place. "There must be a way," she demanded. "Tell me what you know about those moorings. Where can they be manually detached?"

"I do not know," Lekket said. "I'm sorry."

Her muscles tight springs, as they had been for two days, Janeway wanted to strangle the Edesian commodore. "You're too young, Lekket. You're not a commodore. You're a kid. You haven't done this, and you're in way over your head."

Unwilling, or merely helpless to disagree, Lekket could only grind out another "I'm sorry."

Unable to maneuver, unable to raise shields and defend herself, "sorry" was not going to save the *Voyager* from destruction.

CHAPTER
12

FOR THE FIFTH TIME IN AS MANY SECONDS, PAIN SPASMED Chakotay's back and he struggled to raise himself at least to his knees. He groped for a handhold on the bulkhead and tried to pull himself up as the rickety transport shook around him.

Ensign Chen helped Chakotay to his feet. "We did what we could, sir, but we don't have many tools," he explained. "We rigged a magnetic bottle cap of sorts, but we're still losing atmosphere."

"Shields?"

"If we wanted to risk it, but we'd have to give up life support or inertial dampeners."

"Forget shields."

Chen looked better than he had just a few hours before. Perhaps struggling to save one's own life was good for motivation.

"How bad is the bulkhead leak?" Chakotay steadied himself, coughed on the smoke that was still spreading throughout the large hold, and wished it were only the soot in the air escaping into space.

"Pretty bad," Chen said. "Without a tricorder I can't get a specific reading, but that hissing sound tells us something."

"A few hours of air?"

Chen looked away a moment. "At the most." When he looked back, he had that there's-got-to-be-something-we-can-do look that ensigns wore as if they were General Issue. "What about hailing them—letting them know . . ."

"Comm systems are down. But I doubt it would work anyway," Chakotay said. "They're after defenseless transports. We stop moving and we're dead."

And moving was the only reason they were still alive. Paris had taken the helm and turned a flat transport into a bouncing ball that was dodging around more than a vessel of its design should. They were avoiding the Gimlon intercepts, and had shaken all but one, but the stress was tearing apart their Edesian transport in the process.

Chakotay's eyes flicked around the hold, from the *Voyager* crew, huddled in small groups, each working on a specific problem, to the Edesian crewmen, who had either joined the Starfleet-led bands or were sitting quietly with terrified looks on their young faces.

The Edesian guard who'd given command of the vessel over to Chakotay found himself without much to do. He possessed few nonmedical skills except menial ones, and no one had yet been injured except the pilot, who had apparently been quite old, and had died of a heart attack.

The very young led by the inexperienced and the infirm. These Edesians were desperate indeed.

Chakotay and Chen suddenly had to steady themselves, as the transport zigged in one direction too quickly.

"We're losing inertial dampeners," Chen said, eying the transport around them nervously as one might study the roof of an unstable cave that could tumble in at any moment.

"See what you can do to repair them."

"Sir, all we can do is look at the damaged system and reroute a few circuits. The Edesians aboard don't know much, and all we have is one tool kit."

A slender coil of smoke was being drawn into the small vortex created by the hull breach. It wasn't much of a breach . . . but it was enough to kill them all soon.

"What *do* we have to work with?" Chakotay asked.

"Six Edesian disruptors, eight Edesian communicators,

one of their tool kits, a portable field generator, a few crates of food rations . . . and that's it."

Chakotay nodded and tried to think as he and Chen hiked toward the cockpit. No easy task, thinking—as the vessel rattled, twitched, and jolted around them, a constant distraction.

"What about the transport itself?"

Chen bit his lower lip, then answered. "Thrusters? An impulse engine that's not very accessible from the hold, and not working anymore—"

"Not accessible from the hold? Why would they design a transport like that?"

The young ensign shrugged. "Maybe it wasn't originally a transport, sir. In my opinion, this was a small cargo ship. We're in the main hold."

"Interesting." Chakotay crammed himself through the small door to the cockpit and Chen followed. "What else, Ensign?"

Checking a panel to his left, Chen continued. "Tractor beams . . . I don't know how strong."

Chakotay nodded and plucked a weapon from Chen's hand. "Find a place to cut through the bulkhead and get access to the impulse drive. I want it up and running."

"Aye, sir."

"I'll work on these tractor beams." He slid into a seat next to Paris.

"Oh," Paris huffed, "I was beginning to think I was the only one aboard." The helmsman's tense fingers fought with a console with which he was obviously unfamiliar. He jabbed at the controls, paused a moment, then jabbed some more. On the viewer before them, the starscape dodged about. For a moment, Chakotay caught a glimpse of *Voyager* still in space dock—and being attacked.

Attacked in dock. Defenseless.

"Can we help them?"

"We can't even help ourselves." Paris pounded at the helm. "We're losing power. I've stayed away from all direct hits for three minutes, and we're still losing power."

"The impulse engine will help if Chen can get it on-line," Chakotay said, then turned to call back into the main hold. "Lothridge, Rossi—get in here."

Two young Starfleet crewmen bounded through the cockpit doorway.

"See Ensign Chen. I want you to rig those Edesian comms into something that can signal *Voyager*," Chakotay ordered.

They accepted with a nod and squeezed themselves back into the cargo bay.

"You know how to use the tractor beams on this thing?" Chakotay asked Paris.

"Nope."

"Can't be harder than the helm."

Paris looked up a moment, his hands frozen on the console. "Who said I knew what I was doing with the helm?"

Chakotay pursed his lips into a frown. There was and wasn't a time and a place for clowning, and Paris never seemed to know which was which. "Stow the attitude, Paris. I'm not in the mood."

On the viewer, they watched the Gimlon intercept come about again, firing disruptor shots.

"Evasive!"

"What do you think I've been doing?" Paris twisted his body to port as if that would help them steer. "We've only got thrusters here! They're gonna catch us—"

The transport pitched aft. Chakotay and Paris tried to keep their seats. A rumble came from the hold—maybe another hull breach.

"We've got to get them off us," Chakotay said.

"Right," Paris agreed. "Wish I'd thought of that."

"I'll find out how to work the tractor beams," Chakotay said, studying the console next to Paris. "You just shut up and drive."

"Janeway to Engineering." The captain thumbed a button on the arm of her command chair.

"Torres here."

"Prepare for a jump to warp one. I want all available power transferred to the structural integrity fields. Batten down and engage warp on my mark."

"Captain," Torres protested, *"we'll tear the ship apart. We can't warp out of a spacedock we're moored to. I have crews working on cutting us free. Just give me some time."*

Janeway flexed her fingers, hoping that might help the swelling knuckles she'd bruised. It didn't. "How much time?"

"Ten minutes."

Another explosion sent vibrations trembling through the bridge. Her ship had been healed, and now it would be killed in its hospital bed. "We don't have ten minutes," Janeway said. "Carry out my orders. Janeway out."

"Hull breach under control, Captain," Harry Kim said. "Deck seven, section 15 through 18 are sealed."

"Seal off all sections near the moorings."

"Aye, Captain."

Janeway nodded and turned to Bolis at the useless tactical station. Tuvok had transferred control of tactical to the helm, and all Bolis could do was check readouts and sensors.

"Turn off your warp-dampener," Janeway ordered, swiveling back toward the main viewer. "We're getting out of here."

If Lekket disagreed with her plan, he didn't let Janeway know it when she glanced at him. He sat remorsefully, quietly, allowing *Voyager*'s captain to run the show.

And she did.

"Set a course, Tuvok," she said. "Out of orbit, then back in at two hundred thousand kilometers perigee."

"Course set and on the board."

"Stand by all phaser banks. Focused cutting beams."

"Standing by."

"Engage at full impulse!"

Voyager tensed, gathered itself, but couldn't move as the entire ship strained against the space station's mooring locks. The engines whined and grunted, and Janeway could hear the creaking of the vessel's inner structure as it began to buckle.

"Visual on moorings! Phasers, fire!"

A port mooring-lock crackled onto the viewscreen. *Voyager*'s thin phaser beam sliced into the space-station structure a few meters from the outer hull of the Federation Starship.

Orange chemical flame snapped from the mooring clamp to *Voyager*'s skin.

A tremor pressed the ship forward, only slightly, as one mooring was sliced away from the space station but still clung to *Voyager*'s hull.

"Aft phasers, fire!"

The engines complained in harsh high-pitched tones as another phaser shot carved off a starboard mooring—hot energy cutting through space-cold alien alloy, sending globs of molten metal rolling into orbit and onto the surrounding station.

Another bounce forward, and this time Janeway heard the strain on the two remaining moorings that creaked and moaned as tremendous stress pulled them apart.

"Hull intact, minor damage only," Kim said, his voice notched with excitement.

"Fire number three, Tuvok!"

The Vulcan poked at his console and another lean phaser shot separated the space station from its mooring.

"Three mooring lines cut, Captain," Kim said as *Voyager* lurched forward this time, pulling the last lock away from the station as the starship hurtled into open space.

Behind them, the space-station dock was now empty, four blossoms of electrical flame where the moorings had been.

Tuvok punched up a graphic of the sector on a corner of the view screen. "Reading five Gimlon intercepts on tactical." A Gimlon squadron swooped in from the other side of the planet.

"Ahead warp factor one! Raise shields and prepare to come about. I want three-twelve, mark six." Janeway grabbed Lekket's arm. "Where's the rest of my crew?"

The Vulcan tactical officer shook his head. "We are at warp one, but shields are unstable due to plasma discharge from the remaining mooring lock attached at starboard aft."

"Blow it off," Janeway ordered, her hand still clamped onto Lekket's forearm. "I want those shields up! Now!"

"Damn, I wish we had shields!" Tom Paris had taken the transport on a zigzag course, randomly looping one way then another, but the Gimlon intercept was playing with them, looping the same way when it could, and taking potshots to frustrate any hope of escape. "He's the cat and we're the mouse."

Chakotay huffed an angry breath as he struggled with the second cockpit console. "I thought I told you to shut up."

Paris turned and met the other man's eyes. "I thought you were kidding."

"Nope."

"Well!" Paris said in mock anger. "This is the last time I allow an alien race to draft me into their army with *you* around!"

Paris pointed to a distant spot on the forward viewscreen. "Chakotay, look!"

His eyes searching for whatever Paris pointed out, Chakotay finally focused on *Voyager* and the space station.

"Magnify that."

Paris shrugged. "How?"

Forced to see it from afar, they watched their ship break free of the space station, sending debris into orbit like ejecta from a volcano as they plowed away from the planet. *Voyager* disappeared into warp, then popped back into view.

"We have to get to them," Paris said.

"Agreed. I think I can get the tractor beam going."

"Great," Paris said. "Does that mean we can tow ourselves the hell out of here?"

Ignoring his annoying comrade, Chakotay twisted out of his seat and went to the hatch. "Chen, get in here!"

Ensign Chen appeared in a few seconds. "Sir!"

Chakotay almost smiled at the young man's exuberance. Almost.

"Any luck getting to the impulse drive?"

"Not yet, sir."

"Put someone else on it. See if you can help Lothridge and Rossi get some communications going for us. We either get those to work, or we'll be raising signal flags on the ensign halyard."

"Who's that, sir?"

Chakotay sighed. What happened to the days when Starfleet cadets had to get sea legs before they got space legs? "Forget it. How big is our hull breach if we take off the magnetic patch?"

The young man looked aghast, his Asian features wide open with surprise. "Sir?"

"Answer me, Ensign! How big? Big enough to put my fist through?"

His brows knitted in confusion, Chen nodded slowly. "Aye, sir."

"Good. Stand by to push something through that hole." Chakotay turned back into the cockpit and sat back down next to Paris.

"We're losing thruster power," Paris said. "You have a plan for the hull breach, or are you going to make us row?"

"I'm planning to get *Voyager* to notice us. If we make that happen, maybe we can tractor onto them."

Paris nodded. "You don't even know if the tractor beams work."

"You're right," Chakotay agreed. "That's why we're going to test them." He jabbed at his console. "Best speed to *Voyager*."

"On our way . . ."

Chakotay pulled up his weapon, studied the controls of the Edesian disruptor for the fifth time, then called Chen back into the cockpit. What he was thinking was risky, but sometimes life-and-death decisions were easier when one knew death was the only alternative to inaction.

"Sir?" The ensign appeared in the hatchway.

"Here, and here." Chakotay pointed to two buttons on the weapon, then handed it to Chen. "Arm it to overload, then push it out the hull breach."

"Sir, the breach will open—"

"The magnetic field should mold around it. It'll be fine."

"But, sir—what if it detonates near our hull?"

"Have some faith, Mr. Chen." Chakotay smiled reassuringly. "You have your orders. But don't start it on overload until you're ready to push it out."

Chen nodded and ran toward the aft of the transport.

"Dangerous," Paris commented, grunting with effort, as if he himself were physically pushing their vessel through the evasive maneuvers. "Do we know how long it takes one of those things to build to an overload?"

"I'm guessing," Chakotay replied.

"Ah."

"You could have a little faith too," Chakotay said.

"Hey, I'm faithful as a puppy," Paris answered. "I just don't know how that's gonna help anything."

Chakotay shook his head, glanced down at his scanner. "I have a lock on the weapon. Prepare for a starboard turn."

"The Gimlon ship is coming by for another swipe. I'm reading no shields and damage to their armor."

"Probably why they're chasing a defenseless transport," Chakotay said. "Too damaged to join a real fight."

"Ready when you are," Paris said confidently, as if he'd been piloting the Edesian transport for years. "But our Gimlon friend is coming in fast."

"Good," Chakotay murmured, bowing into his console. "Now! Turn!"

The display to their right showed a blip that was the target of the tractor beam—the Edesian weapon. A thin tendril of energy seized the disruptor and Chakotay dabbed at his controls, swinging the beam around.

"This could actually work," Paris said.

"Shhhh!"

Feeling like David against Goliath, Chakotay used the tractor beam to slingshot the weapon at the passing Gimlon vessel.

"Damn!" Chakotay watched as the disruptor missed the enemy vessel. But it detonated, a bubble of exploding energy that sent a shockwave into the Gimlon ship and knocked it off course.

"Not a hit, but a good miss," Paris said, smiling.

A moment later the shockwave hit the transport, and Chakotay and Paris had to struggle to keep their positions.

"No, no. We need a direct hit to do anything against their armor," Chakotay chastised himself. "We need to be closer, then get away."

Paris tapped him in the arm with the back of his hand. "You'll get your chance—here he comes."

On the screen, the recovered Gimlon vessel turned back toward them.

"Mooring debris is blown clear. Shields are up—full power."

"Continue evasive." The captain wanted to avoid the

Gimlon for now . . . and she could, now that *Voyager* was free of the space station. "Tell me something, Harry."

Ensign Kim stooped over his monitor. "Scanning . . . a different design of Gimlon intercept . . . five of them . . . smaller than *Voyager,* maybe a crew of fifty or sixty. Technology similar to state-of-the-art Federation science circa 2240."

Janeway blew on her sore knuckles, trying to cool them. Circa 2240. Before the first Constitution-class *Enterprise.* Early phasers, simple photon-burst torpedoes, no transporter technology, warp factor four maximum . . . like a war of large shuttle craft.

"You can easily defeat them, yes?" Lekket asked.

"War isn't supposed to be easy," Janeway said. "It's hard, and the harder the better. Maybe there would be less war if it were just a little harder."

Lekket snickered, that bitter laugh that struck Janeway as if it were coming from a cynical child who'd been hurt young and now trusted nothing in life. "Would there be less need for food if our fields were bare, Captain? No, hard war means hard war, not less war."

He was a pathetic figure, Janeway decided, but she wasn't sure if Lekket sickened her or was merely to be pitied.

A small blast against the *Voyager's* shields shook the bridge.

Again Janeway chastised herself for letting the situation go too far. She was separated from part of her crew, and the umbrella of her protection was stretched beyond stability. She had to gather them up, retreat, and release herself from the Edesian grip.

She stood, leaning into the rail that ran against the back of her bridge.

"Where are the rest of my crew?" Janeway demanded of Lekket.

"My crew now, Captain," he said. "You have other duties with which to concern yourself."

Janeway spun toward Tuvok. "Can you scan for human readings on the planet?"

"Negative."

"Can we—"

A smash of energy against the shields, and Janeway recognized the sound immediately.

Space electrified, broke into light, and the forward viewer flashed bright for a moment before going dark.

Janeway dove for the command chair, but the deck pitched her forward.

The universe lost itself for a second time, and Janeway again felt death crushing in on her.

CHAPTER

13

"I HAVE AN ENERGY WAVE—ZERO-ONE-ZERO MARK SEVEN!"

The bridge spun. Janeway grappled with a new physics as space became savage. She hung onto her command chair and felt its grip on the deck weaken.

"Impulse engines are off-line!"

"Port thrust."

"Thrusters sluggish—"

Storm-tossed and creaking with strain, *Voyager* wailed. The lights flashed, dimmed—and power left the ship. Weak, Janeway felt a spasm of pain and struggled to crack out orders.

"Emergency power!"

Hot embers of wire spat from above. Janeway felt them on her neck, her hands, and as she turned, also on her cheek and jaw.

"Switching." Tuvok's voice.

Pale lights replaced flickering orange alert beacons.

"Don't lose the shields!"

"Shields are up. Energy wave is leaving them undisturbed."

The captain was forced to the deck again, her shoulder jammed into the hard bulkhead. She didn't hear a crack—

but she felt it, as pain burned its way down her arm to her fingers and back up into her neck.

Then, as suddenly as it had begun, it was over. Janeway was able to pull herself to her feet. She felt depleted and nauseated, and her shoulder was either broken or dislocated.

She smothered the agony through gritted teeth. "Sensors?"

The Vulcan nodded once. "Short-range only."

Janeway pulled herself up with her good arm, then unconsciously tried to use her other to swipe at a length of hair that had come down across her face. She winced in pain and jammed her lips together to stifle the bulk of a groan.

"The *Marauder?*" she grunted.

"Affirmative. Bearing zero-one-zero, mark seven. We are on thrusters, twelve thousand KPS, holding steady on a parallel course."

"Maintain."

"Helm still sluggish, Captain."

"Do your best."

The captain didn't help Lekket to his feet. She didn't even look at him. She brought herself over to Tuvok, glanced at Bolis for just a second, then looked at a tactical readout.

"Their entrances pack less of a wallop than their exits," she said, squinting through her pain. "I think this was easier than last time."

Tuvok agreed. "We were also at closer proximity when they disappeared."

Janeway pushed out a tired breath. "Thank you for small miracles."

"I assure you, Captain," Tuvok said, "I had nothing to do with it."

She nodded and whispered to him. "Doctor to the bridge."

Tuvok flicked an eyebrow, showing his acknowledgement.

The captain tried to cram her pain into the back of her mind as she pivoted toward Harry Kim. "Try to raise the *Marauder* on the comm. Tell them we won't fire on them if they return the gesture."

"No, wait!" Lekket yelled as best he could with his weakened voice. "You must destroy them!"

"Where are my people?" Janeway demanded with a painful huff. "That's the only thing we have to discuss."

Lekket was gaunt, spiritless, his eyes sunken with exhaustion both physical and mental. What had *he* broken or dislocated?

He balled his fists at his side and struggled with the words he squeezed through gritted teeth. "I *will* follow through on my threat, Captain."

Janeway nodded to Ensign Kim. "Carry out my order."

Kim's hands dabbed at his console, and Lekket spun toward the young man and ordered—*pleaded*—that the ensign be wiser than his captain. "Do as *I* say, or you and your shipmates all die."

Harry Kim glared at Lekket a moment, then looked to his captain. "Message sent, Captain."

No matter what the threat, no matter what war *Voyager* had been forced to fight, she was a Federation vessel with a Federation crew. Lekket held the crew only as long as he held their captain . . . and he no longer held Janeway.

She stepped toward the Edesian commodore, down into the command deck. "You don't have power here any more," she said in a low, angry voice.

On the forward viewer, the *Marauder* lumbered toward the planet. It left *Voyager* alone. Whether that was because they'd received Janeway's hail or because *Voyager* simply wasn't in the plan yet, there was no way to know.

"Where are my people? Return them to me," Janeway demanded, "and I might let *you* live."

Lekket's left eyebrow twitched and he clasped one of his pendants in his hand.

"I will destroy you, and myself with you," he choked over his own anger and fear.

Janeway took one more step toward him.

"I'm ready," she whispered. "Are you?"

Lekket tore his pendant from around his neck and thrust it between them. He pressed an indentation in its middle. "You have thirty seconds to do as I say. You will place me in command of this vessel, or we will all die in a matter of moments."

"Paris, get us out of here."

"We're losing thrusters—I can't get power!"

"It's the *Marauder*'s disruption! Ride the wave, try to move with it."

The Edesian transport spun end-over-end in the torrent of energy that was the *Marauder*'s return.

When it dissipated, there was calm.

Chakotay raised his head from a crouching position. The transport hadn't caved in on him—just the lighting panel from above.

Dust caked against his sweaty neck—the temperature was rising. Somewhere a coolant system was off-line. Or *the* coolant system.

He tossed the panel off his shoulders and brushed off some of the debris that had fallen with it.

"Status?"

"Uh . . ." Paris coughed, squinting through a thick smoke at the Edesian transport's helm console. "We're dead."

"Don't editorialize." Chakotay wiped his forehead and leaned toward the control board. "What about scanners?"

"I'm serious, Chakotay. We're dead in space. No power. At all."

Chakotay waved away some debris on the console before him. There were no lighted buttons. No working panels. No display screens. Above him, small emergency light sconces were the only illumination.

A creaking sound from above rattled the ship. Metal against metal.

"Uh oh."

"That's an understatement," Chakotay said, looking for one of the Edesian weapons that were left. "We're being boarded." He tossed a disruptor to Paris and then scooped one up for himself.

Paris set the weapon and held it ready. "Yeah, but why? They destroyed the other transports."

Shaking his head, Chakotay shrugged. "If we had a tricorder, we could tell where they'd attached themselves."

"If we had ham, we could have ham and eggs, if we had eggs."

Chakotay frowned, if only because he was suddenly hungry. A strange sensation to notice when one was about to die.

"How long before they cut through the hull?"

"Of this thing?" Paris said, rising as he pulled a long metal strut away from the doorway to the transport's main hold. "Not long at all." He stabbed at a button on the wall next to the door, but the panel didn't open.

"Jammed?"

"No internal power."

Frustrated, Chakotay shook his head. "They have power going to emergency lights but not to the door."

"Well, you have to be able to see that you're trapped."

Chakotay pressed his lips into a line and tried to think of *something* that might be of use. No power, except the emergency lights, a locked door, two weapons . . .

"Can we route power from the lights to the door?"

Paris shrugged. "Without tools, without a computer? I don't know the systems, or where to look, and I'm afraid I left my magic wand back on *Voyager*. We'd be better off vaporizing it with a disruptor."

They stood silent a moment, listening to the scraping of metal against metal—armor against their small vessel's hull.

"Does that weapon have a setting like that, and do we know it could limit the blast to the door?"

Biting his lower lip a moment, Tom Paris examined the settings dial of the Edesian weapon. "Those buttons overload it, we learned that from experience. If the bottom setting on the dial is stun, then the middle might be kill, and the third . . ."

Chakotay looked over his own weapon. *"Might* be vaporize. But does it have self-setting limits so we vaporize a door and not the wall with it? No one said it was that much like our phasers."

"Stand back," Chakotay ordered.

Paris looked around the small cabin. "Where?"

"Just . . . cower over there."

Crouching behind the helm chair, Paris held his weapon at the ready. "Not a problem."

Chakotay stood as far as he could to the left of the door, reached his hand around, and hesitantly fired the Edesian weapon point-blank.

An elliptical, head-sized portion of the door dissolved into molten metal, then disintegrated into the thick air. The smell of burnt paint and liquified ore filled the small room.

Paris stood. "I'd say that's limited."

Twisting around so he could see out the hole he'd made, Chakotay watched as part of the ceiling above the main cabin crashed toward the deck. The Gimlon had cut a small opening—not big enough for an average-size biped humanoid.

What *did* they look like?

A softball-size object bounced down onto the deck from the ceiling above.

Chakotay had only a moment to see it through the crowd of people suddenly rushing away from the metal sphere. He yelled "Take cover!" but far too late—even if there had been cover to take.

An all-enveloping green wave of luminous energy washed out from the small device and leveled those gathered like so many grass stalks plowed over by a flooding river.

Chakotay felt as if he'd been slapped in the face—hard—and he was flung back into Paris, who also collapsed with a thud.

Chakotay's weapon fell from his grasp and clattered to the debris-strewn, soot-covered deck.

The dim lights played with him now, consciousness passing over him. When he tried to look up, he saw shadows, and struggled to determine whether they were moving or not. Paris groaned beneath him, and Chakotay dragged himself to one side so his comrade could move. He didn't. Neither of them moved much.

Voices—in the main hold? Disembodied orders, and the sounds of people groaning with strain.

After what seemed like a frustrating hour of struggling to make out words or at least tones in the voices, Chakotay felt himself being dragged up to a standing position. He strug-

115

gled, perhaps only in his mind rather than in reality, but either was futile. He was pulled up and out of the transport, and the cold Gimlon vessel's lighting still was too dim to help him much with his surroundings.

He moved his head to glance around, and it bounced lethargically on his neck. He'd been stunned by a phaser before, and this was what the lowest setting felt like.

All the *Voyager* people were here, he could see that much, or so he thought—but where were the Edesians?

A hatch near him clanged shut, and Chakotay felt the vibration of the slam as it moved through the deck beneath him.

"Is it readied for self-destruct?" One voice broke through the haze.

"Edesian garbage," another said. "Hard to *keep* it from falling apart."

The muffled explosion, just a shockwave against their shields, drilled its way into Chakotay's mind.

How many young Edesian people had just died on that ship?

And why had the *Voyager* crewmembers been saved?

"What about them?" Another Gimlon voice? Certainly not one of Chakotay's drowsy comrades.

"We use them," was the gruff reply. "Then we kill them, too."

Chakotay felt as if he'd dropped in the lake again, and he was being drawn into unconsciousness also coupled with a thud.

Chakotay's reason fell from his grip and deposited in the debris strewn, soot-covered deck.

The dim lights played with him now, consciousness passing over him. When he tried to look up, he saw shadows, and struggled in dark color whether they were moving or not. Pain welled beneath him, and Chakotay dragged himself to one side so the dimness could move. He didn't want one of them moved nearby.

Voices. In the faint, solid Throbbing of feet, and the sounds of people groaning with strain.

After what seemed like a lifetime, hours of struggling to make some words or at least tones in his voice, Chakotay felt himself being dragged up to a solid up-straight standing

CHAPTER
14

JANEWAY'S BRIDGE. THAT'S HOW IT FELT TO HER AGAIN, AS Lekket's fist grasped at the control that should have killed them all—but didn't.

The commodore's eyes widened with panic, and droplets of perspiration dripped down his forehead. Nothing had happened—no computer alert signaled increased radiation. No sound. No klaxons. Just his own tense breathing . . . and Janeway's raspy whisper: "It's over."

"Bolis! Initiate the radiation manually!" Lekket ordered.

Bolis, his brow still dark with his own caked blood, took a step back from Tuvok's usual console and let his hands slip to his sides.

"Lieutenant Bolis! That is a direct order!"

Grabbing Lekket's tunic at the collar with her one good arm, Janeway pulled him toward her. Pain shot from her dislocated shoulder down to her fingers and up into her neck, but she ground the agony between her teeth and hissed into Lekket's face. "This is my bridge. I give the orders here."

"Mutiny!" Lekket yelled and grabbed at another of his control pendants. "Security—mutiny on the bridge!"

The two young Edesian guards who were near the turbolift finally stepped forward, weapons in hand.

Captain Janeway took a step back, pulled in a deep breath, then spoke quickly. "Computer, initiate program Janeway five-one-seven!"

"Acknowledged."

"Tuvok," Janeway said, twisting toward the helm. "Everyone but Lekket and Bolis!"

The Vulcan nodded and hit a keypad on his console.

Of the two guards, one stopped in his tracks, held his head in his hands, and began to yell. The other dropped to the deck screaming. Both were covered in a flowing stream of light and sparkle—then vanished to nothingness.

"Where are my men? What have you done!" Lekket stomped toward Janeway, his ashen face angled with anger and frustration.

The captain took another step back—away from Lekket—as the turbolift doors spread open. The doctor slid onto the bridge, and when Tuvok motioned him toward the captain, he slid down to the command deck and began scanning Janeway with a medical tricorder.

"Captain, your shoulder—"

"Kill the pain and clear the bridge," Janeway ordered.

"Where are my men?" Lekket demanded again. *"Tell me what you have done!"*

"Mr. Tuvok . . ."

At Janeway's order, Tuvok brought the transporter alive again.

The captain held out her hand, which appeared to cradle a ball of light—until a phaser materialized in her palm.

"Now *that* is magic," she said.

Lekket was astonished, which showed clearly in his widened eyes.

Janeway leveled the phaser at him. "Your men aren't dead, but they would've been if I'd ordered it. Now I ask you the same question," Janeway spat at Lekket as the doctor took a hypospray and touched it to the captain's neck.

A final wave of pain washed over Janeway, then thinned into a dull ache.

The doctor nodded as if he'd been about to say something but had thought better of it, then backed up to the turbolift and left.

"Where are my people?" Janeway sparked, the refreshing lack of pain bolstering her strength as well as her anger. "I want exact coordinates. Now."

"Captain," Tuvok's urgent call pulled Janeway's attention. "We're reading an energy buildup on the Gimlon Marauder."

Janeway, her shoulder giving her a slight twinge when she moved, twisted awkwardly to look at Ensign Kim. "Harry?"

"Confirmed," Kim nodded. "Gravimetric subspace energy signature."

"Gravimetric?" Janeway's brow furrowed in perplexity as she pivoted back toward Tuvok and the helm, cradling her bad arm with her good. "What's their heading?"

"They are closing on the planet," Tuvok said. "A possible attack vector."

"You must defend the planet!" Lekket pleaded. "There are three billion people—"

"First my crew—"

"Captain!"

Janeway slipped forward, her good hand slipping away from her sore shoulder as the bright flash from the *Marauder*'s maw filled the main viewer.

Not so much a beam of light as a wave of luminous space distortion, the *Marauder* spat forth an energy path that snapped into a corner of the planet—and made it vanish.

Before orders could be given or scanners read, the massive planet was torn apart by space itself. It collapsed inward in a desperate attempt to reestablish its spherical shape. Another bright flash, and the missing block reappeared, a large continent of crust and magma—a good fifth of the planet—that swiftly crashed into the body from which it had come.

White-hot molten rock splintered up from a now fiery orange mass as the two sections of undulating spheroid collided. Slabs of rock, entire mountain ranges, and somewhere millions upon millions of people were blasted apart or into space. Oceans vaporized and tectonic plates crumbled as the planet's crust crumpled in and then out, in a massive torrent of raw destruction.

Janeway's jaw dropped an inch. She caught herself and moved a step back, wanting to pull her ship back with her.

Her body tensed, sending a twinge of pain down her shoulder again.

"Warp evasive! Get us out—"

As if Janeway's order was for the *Marauder,* the massive Gimlon ship turned and warped away from the ejecta sphere that was pushing forward into the starsystem.

Voyager followed, pitching away from the planet and the explosion that rushed out in all directions.

Rolling white debris cooled red in space, leaving chunks of planet careening off into the starsystem at hyperspeed.

A subspace shockwave followed, catching up with *Voyager* as she muscled out deeper and deeper into space. The ship shook, riding the wave as she fled a now lifeless solar system.

The little blue planet . . . gone. Now it was just a field of asteroids that peppered empty space around a yellow star.

"Three billion people!" Lekket wailed, his body crumpling to the deck, his bony back curving under his tunic as he shook with horror. "Three billion—"

"Oh, my God—" Janeway rasped, pulling the Edesian up with her good arm. "How?"

Lekket pulled himself away and spoke in a bitter tone. "I told you, Captain—they are evil with power and magic! And now your people are with mine. *All dead!"*

"It is unfortunate, as all harsh duties are, but history *will* record these pitiable deaths as necessary to the dawn of a new Gimlon Empire. That I promise you."

The Gimlon commander stood on a small pedestal in what was the Gimlon ship's small cargo bay. His voice was high and squeaked with pomposity, and it stabbed into Chakotay like a giant bee sting.

For reasons yet unknown, the Gimlon had gathered the *Voyager* crewmembers here, dragged out a small platform on which the ship's commander could stand and be seen, then began this . . . *explanation,* for lack of a better term, of the Gimlon Empire's motives.

"Whether you number yourselves as one of the dead," the Gimlon commander continued, "or one of those who walks on the side of fate, is your only question now."

"Who are *you?* And what specifically do you want from

us?" Chakotay demanded for his crew. He shot one more glance at the five guards and their heavy disruptor rifles. Right now they outnumbered the Gimlon, and they weren't restricted in movement or space. If he could delay, get an advantage. . . .

He had to wait, though, at least a little while longer. Until his mind was less cloudy, and his strength greater. He felt awful, but probably better than most of the other *Voyager* crewmembers. He'd been farther from the stunning device, and somewhat protected by the door he'd been standing behind. He wasn't sure just how much time had passed since then, but he knew it hadn't been too long. He felt the blood that had dried and caked under his uniform, and wondered if the crew could see the slices in his back. He itched, but refrained from scratching at the wounds.

"I am Stith-ta." The Gimlon commander smiled. "And I want many things. A good harem. Strong children. A house near the capital city's square. Eventually an elegant and yet ostentatious tomb . . . and of course, the death of every Edesian man, woman, and child and the submission of the known galaxy to the Gimlon Empire."

"In that order?" Paris asked, groggily.

Cocking his head toward the *Voyager* helmsman, the Gimlon commander smiled a bit wider and answered. "No."

Paris leaned toward Chakotay and whispered, "Is it me or did this guy just step out of a bad Cardassian War holo-novel?"

He couldn't muster a chuckle, because Stith-ta was so obviously not joking, but Chakotay did nod his agreement.

Stith-ta was arrogance personified, with the power to back it up. An annoying combination.

"I believe you want all that," Chakotay said finally, trying to give his voice as much strength and resonance as he could. "But you wouldn't waste your time telling us all that . . . if we didn't figure in your plan in some way. Correct?"

The Gimlon commander, his features also very Ocampan, much like Lekket's, again smiled the evil grin he had shown them just moments before. "Does that mark on your face signify your standing as leader of these people?"

"No." Chakotay shifted his weight from one foot to the other. Why was this man playing with them so?

"*Are* you their leader?"

Stiffening his shoulders and straightening his legs, Chakotay answered. "Yes. I am Commander Chakotay. First officer aboard the Federation Starship *Voyager*. Do you have any plans to state your intentions?"

With a nod, the Gimlon commander summoned one of the five guards forward. Then, at a gesture of Stith-ta's hand, the guard seized Chakotay and pulled him from the rest of the *Voyager* crew.

Paris stepped forward, but the guard backhanded him with his rifle-butt and continued muscling Chakotay, as Paris fell to the deck.

"Stand down, Paris," Chakotay said as he was whisked out the door.

The Gimlon commander watched the door close as Tom Paris picked himself up from the cargo bay's floor.

"Commander Chakotay, great leader that he is, will be executed with military honors."

Paris and the other *Voyager* crewmembers shared fleeting glances.

Smiling viciously, the Gimlon commander looked over the gathered Starfleet refugees. "Now . . . who else among you wishes to be a leader?"

CHAPTER
15

THREE BILLION RIVULETS OF SWEAT DRAINED FROM JANEWAY'S face, down her tunic. Three billion needles of pain jabbed at her shoulder. And three billion waves of nausea raked her belly.

Three billion people were dead . . . and she could have stopped it. Chakotay, Paris . . . a third of her crew were among those numbers—and it was her fault.

And *his:* Lekket's.

She glared at his shrinking figure, his face still darkened in horror, his shoulder blades arching up like gargoyle wings as he stood crouched in mental agony.

Janeway grabbed his arm and pulled him up. He grunted as he was yanked straight. She felt her eyes tear, and saw his were doing the same. But she squeezed her tears away.

"We didn't have to be here. *You* brought about this turn of events. You!" She wrenched his arm around and he groaned in pain.

Lekket stood even straighter and tugged himself from her grip.

"The deaths of those souls are on *your* head, Captain. Not mine!"

The accusation clubbed into her and she felt it was true. But anger spiked from that guilt—anger at Lekket and his forceful hand that had shaped these events. Yes, she should have acted more quickly, and perhaps more rashly, to excise herself and her crew from this fight, but it was *Lekket's* fight. He was the cause of those deaths. *He* was.

Janeway seized Lekket again and grappled him closer to her. "You take us by force, steal my crew, and then dare to put the death of a planet on my shoulders!" She threw him back down to the deck with all the might her one good arm could muster, then as he tried to rise, she curled his tunic in her fist and brought him back up herself. "You're the murderer here, Lekket! That planet is dead because of your filthy war and your petty impressment!" She said it—spat it at him—but only half believed it. She could have saved the planet. Maybe. But she hadn't tried. She didn't think it was her affair. And maybe it wasn't—but *three billion people* . . .

She pinioned him against the bridge rail. She wanted to jam her elbow into his stomach, his chest, his head. She wanted to pound him with a heavy, angry fist.

All she wanted right now was to lose control. To pull back her knuckles and release her rage into Lekket's soft body with a good pummeling. He'd bullied the *Voyager*. Bullied her. She'd let him. *Bastard!*

Control . . . it kept her fist from breaking Lekket in two.

Control was hers—it was what made her captain, and she willed herself not to lose that control—ever again.

"I'm in command of this vessel," Janeway said. "Do you understand that? *I* am in command."

And she was. For the first time in two days. She could not change the past, but she could choose the future. She *was* in control again.

Lekket looked into her angry eyes, and he seemed afraid.

She nodded, glanced around her bridge, at a suddenly liberated bridge crew, then looked toward Tuvok. "Get him to Sickbay."

Chakotay turned to face the guard, then dropped to his knees. Raising up his head, he placed his hands into a pleading steeple and begged the Gimlon stormtrooper to spare his life. "I'll do anything! Anything, just please don't kill me!"

The guard's narrow eyes almost disappeared into a perplexed squint. "Get up! What is wrong with you?" He took a step closer, reaching to pull Chakotay to his feet.

As the Gimlon leaned down, Chakotay's clenched hands rammed into the man's stomach, then swooped around to the back of his head as the guard doubled over in pain.

Two fast jabs to the back of his neck and one swift kick in the jaw knocked the guard out fast, as Chakotay leapt to his feet.

He rolled the Gimlon over and looked for anything that might help him to free the others. "Thanks," he said, taking the guard's ugly-looking rifle. "Hope it's fully charged."

The Gimlon moaned. He'd been knocked out, but only briefly.

Chakotay searched the guard's pockets, then inside his tunic, and found what might be a code-sequencer to open some kind of lock. He pocketed that, slung the disruptor rifle over his shoulder, and pulled the guard by his shoulders into an alcove off the corridor.

He pulled the rifle back into his hand and aimed it point-blank at the Gimlon's head. "Where can we go that's more private?"

The guard made another groaning sound.

Chakotay pressed the business end of the rifle against the man's skull. "I will kill you if you don't tell me what I want to know."

The Gimlon guard tried to raise his head but Chakotay did not release the pressure of the rifle barrel. "I do not care if I die," he said in indignant pain.

"You know what? Neither do I." Chakotay studied the rifle's controls on either side of the weapon just above the grip. "I bet one of these would vaporize you, but I bet another setting would just leave you to die a slow, agonizing death. Am I right?"

He forced the rifle harder against the Gimlon's head and the guard let out a grunt.

"Am I?"

"Yes," the guard said grudgingly.

Chakotay smiled. "See how we can get along when we just cooperate? First contact isn't that hard, is it?" He pulled the rifle back a bit, then put his free arm under the guard's shoulder and dragged him up to a standing position. "Let's go to some place no one is likely to happen by."

"You are as vile as the Edesians to help their cause," the Gimlon said.

Shaking his head, Chakotay pushed the guard forward out the alcove. "How many crew on this ship?"

The guard was silent, but did shuffle forward reluctantly.

"My friend," Chakotay said, letting the rifle barrel lie against the guard's back, "you're less of a risk dead than alive. It's up to you."

Fear was a galactic constant, and the Gimlon said, "Fourteen crew."

"Good. Is there a control room or communication room that would be unguarded and empty?"

Again the guard was hesitant as they walked up the cold corridor. Cold in looks, cold in temperature. Chakotay hadn't noticed before because he hadn't been focusing on anything but getting the upper hand over his new "friend." Now that he had that, he took in some details of the ship and of the guard himself. The guard looked young, but his uniform was garnished with medals and regalia—unlike the corridor, which was austere and strictly utilitarian. The uniform was a diametric contrast. It was built up to convey glory, whereas the ship was merely a means to an end.

"Well?" Chakotay prodded, more with his weapon than his voice. "Communications hub. Where?"

"It's all guarded."

Chakotay shook his head. "You have only fourteen crew-members, and every place where someone can communicate out is guarded?"

"It is the truth," the Gimlon said, half whispering, as if he didn't want anyone to know he was being a traitor. "There are only two places for communications on this vessel."

"Where?"

"The bridge is one, the commander's quarters the other."

Noticing a door to his left, Chakotay grabbed the guard's elbow and stopped him from continuing down the hall. "What's in here?"

The guard glanced at the door only a moment. "Access to a coolant system."

"Should anyone be in there?"

The guard's answer came quickly. "No."

Chakotay pulled the code-sequencer from his pocket and placed it on the door. "Open it."

The guard did as he was told, and as the door slid open Chakotay pushed him roughly through the doorway.

Stumbling into the room, the Gimlon toppled over two of his crewmates. Another Gimlon came up from behind and all three stormed forward, weapons raised.

Chakotay snapped his rifle toward the doorway and fired. Once.

And once was all it took.

Disruptor waves shot forward, dropping all four men instantly. The guards collapsed. Blood drained from their mouths and ears.

Peering down incredulously at the weapon in his hand, Chakotay assured himself that the lowest setting had been chosen. At least he'd thought it was the lowest.

He checked, and checked again. There was no other explanation—the barbaric truth was that the Gimlon rifle had no stun setting.

"Damage report." Captain Janeway made a vain attempt to smooth her tunic with her good right arm as two guards escorted—almost carried—Lekket from the bridge.

The odor of smoke still lingered, and sweat, and tension—if tension could have an odor. She felt its presence nonetheless.

Tuvok returned to the helm and glanced down at a screen. "Minor hull damage, decks three through seven. Damage control teams are active."

"Shields?"

"Ninety-three percent."

Her shoulder again a dull thud of pain along her upper left side, Janeway lowered herself gingerly into the command chair. "Where's the *Marauder*?"

"Gone."

"Long-range scans, Mr. Kim?" Janeway spoke, but didn't bother painfully turning toward the aft deck.

"Reading the subspace residue of their weapon, Captain. That's it."

Janeway began a nod, but was stopped by the pain. "Hit and run."

"Captain . . ." Bolis stepped down from the upper deck. "Now is the time to escape."

"To where?" The captain swiveled to meet the Edesian's gaze. "We have forty of your comrades in our brig—"

"Sickbay, actually, Captain," Tuvok interrupted.

"Sickbay?" Janeway blinked in astonishment. "Why?"

"The brig is too close to the warp-dampening device. Excess radiation made transporting ineffectual. I chose Sickbay as the next best possibility, considering its containment fields."

Keeping herself from nodding, Janeway drew up her brows in agreement. "The doctor must be thrilled."

Tuvok pursed his lips. "He *has* requested a word with you at your earliest convenience."

"Hmmm." Janeway was sure that the doctor's tone wasn't quite as controlled as Tuvok's. She looked back up to Bolis and continued. "Mr. Bolis, do you have any idea what the range of that *Marauder* is? How fast can it go? How long before it can use its cloak again?"

Bolis furrowed his brow. "Why?"

"Captain," Tuvok interrupted again, "I do not believe we are dealing with a cloak of any type."

She might have smiled, but the thoughts of the dead still kept her lips from curling upward. Magic was only magic so long as one was ignorant to the method behind the feat. Maybe she had a hunger for vengeance, or perhaps it was just disgust at the number of lives the *Marauder* had so easily snuffed out. Either way, she wanted to satisfy the feeling. "What do you have, Mr. Tuvok?"

"Strange readings—on the gravimetic level, on a subspace band not usually seen," Tuvok said. "And only from their *Marauder*. Not from the other Gimlon ships."

Janeway rose, warily, and patted Bolis on the arm with her right hand. "We might not leave just yet," she said to him. "Maybe we can save the Edesians and Gimlon from fighting further and involving the rest of the galaxy in their war."

"But what about your escape, Captain," Bolis asked. "It is immoral to have you involved. I cannot ask you to stay after all you've lost."

Her jaw tight, the pain in her shoulder resuming its strong pounding, Janeway cleared her throat and rasped: "This time, Mr. Bolis, no one has to ask."

CHAPTER

16

PARIS KNEW WHAT THE NOISE MEANT, THE SOUND THAT CRUSHED against his ears and sent a chill from his neck down his spine.

"That shriek you hear—it is the disruptor blast that disintegrated your Commander Chakotay. Were there time, I would allow you to pray to your gods for him."

Chakotay—dead? Hard to believe, hard to swallow— and hard to just stand and wait for someone else to be next.

Paris wouldn't wait. He reached into his pocket and felt for something that might be of use. The two isolinear data chips in one pocket would hardly be helpful. Seething, he searched his other pocket; he felt a small power coupler he'd used on the Edesian transport, and a small length of stiff wire that he'd been planning to use to bypass a circuit whose access plate he never did find.

Not much to help him overtake four guards and the Gimlon commander.

He needed a distraction—and decided he would supply it himself.

"We won't help you," Paris told Stith-ta. "Not one of us." The muscles in his back tensed and he gripped the stiff wire in his hand so tightly that it hurt.

Stith-ta looked down from his small pedestal with bemused curiosity. "Really? I sincerely doubt that." He gestured to a guard. "Kill any five of them."

One of the guards stepped forward, his rifle raised and ready.

"No!" Paris almost stumbled forward. "Wait!"

Still half-smiling, Stith-ta raised one hand and stopped the guard. "But why? You aren't going to help me, are you?"

Paris hesitated. "What do you want?"

The Gimlon smiled. "How many vessels are there like yours? Where is this 'Federation of Planets'?"

"That information won't help you," Paris said.

Looking down at Paris, as if to admonish a scornful child, Stith-ta lost his smile. "You have courage. That might not serve you well within my ranks."

Paris was silent. He studied the bridge of Stith-ta's nose, his brows, dark and arching. He'd found a way to hate this man—*hate* him—in just slightly more than a few minutes.

"How many vessels like yours," Stith-ta repeated, "are within a month of this sector?"

With great difficulty, Paris tried to keep his expression blank and even. "Forty-three."

Stith-ta nodded to the guard. "A lie. Kill him where he stands."

The guard stormed forward, his rifle pointing upward. Paris leapt to meet him, taking the stiff wire in his hand and pushing it up into the Gimlon's neck—and straight into his throat.

With the briefest of surprised looks and a chopped gurgle, the guard fell into Paris's arms, dead. The wire had found a main artery.

Then, protecting himself with his Gimlon shield, Paris swung the guard around, exposing the man's macabre death-mask to Stith-ta as the other guards yanked up their weapons. Paris's fingers wrapped around the dead guard's rifle hand and sent a pulse of disruptor blast forward, into one guard, who abruptly vaporized. Then the beam turned as if in some swift, morbid dance, shifting to each of the three remaining guards in turn.

Within fractions of seconds the guards were all gone, and only three hot bronze mists remained.

Foolishly, Stith-ta either had no weapon or was paralyzed with surprise, or—Paris hoped—fear.

Wrenching the rifle from the dead Gimlon's fingers, Paris let the guard drop to the deck without his weapon.

He aimed the disruptor at the small platform on which Stith-ta stood motionless. Paris strode forward, hate and anger burning his eyes. *Move and give me some excuse,* Paris thought, then said it aloud.

When they were inches apart, Stith-ta's left eye twitched and Paris swung the butt of his new rifle into the Gimlon commander's neck.

Stith-ta collapsed to his knees, clutching his throat in both hands.

"You moved," Paris said. "And I'm not even going to kill you for it."

"Harry, you have the conn. Best speed to the coordinates Mr. Bolis has provided."

"Aye, Captain." Harry Kim nodded and allowed a more junior officer to take over his station as he slid down to the command chair.

"Tuvok, Mr. Bolis, with me," she ordered as she staggered into the turbolift.

Lieutenant Tuvok and the Edesian turncoat followed her.

"Sickbay," she told the lift, then turned to Bolis as the doors closed. "How sure are you that these coordinates will lead us to the *Marauder?*"

Bolis didn't look at Janeway, but rather at her feet. Perhaps he was feeling the loss of the Edesian colony left destroyed by the Gimlon, or perhaps he felt bad for betraying Lekket and his comrades. Janeway didn't know which, and couldn't have consoled him on either point anyway.

She couldn't console herself on the deaths of those three billion people, either. She could stop it from happening again, though, and she wanted to.

"We have had some intelligence reports that they have a

repair facility in that sector," Bolis said. "That is all I know."

"Long-range scans this far out would be inconclusive," Tuvok offered. "And we have no data on those coordinates." There was some skepticism in his voice, perhaps about the honesty of Bolis's information, perhaps about Janeway's wish to pursue the *Marauder*.

She nodded only slightly—and even that slight movement caused her great pain. Whatever the doctor had given her had completely worn off.

The lift doors parted, and Tuvok and Bolis followed her out.

"Tuvok, tell me something new about the *Marauder*."

The Vulcan hesitated. "I would rather we discussed this in private, Captain."

Janeway looked at him a moment, then continued up the corridor. "Okay," she said softly. "We'll talk later."

Sickbay seemed too far, just at the end of the corridor. When Janeway entered, the doctor came right to her. "Captain, how good of you to visit. Finally." He led her quickly to a bio-bed and helped her up onto it.

The captain took a moment to glance at the medical treatment areas, all filled with numbers of Edesian personnel behind containment fields. Lekket was in the one to the left. She could see him talking among his people. He hadn't yet noticed her.

"Captain," the doctor began, as he ran some humming multilight flashing thingamabob over her left shoulder, "I really must protest the conversion of my sickbay into Botany Bay. I'm not a prison guard."

"Right now," Janeway said, grunting as the doctor took her shoulder with both hands and ran it through an exercise, "you are. This is the only safe place to hold them. Unless you think we should put them in the brig and then bring them back up here for radiation treatment an hour later."

The doctor pursed his lips and looked up a moment, as if considering it. "Well, many of them *would* be unconscious then . . . I often prefer my patients unconscious."

"No doubt," Tuvok said dryly, "they might prefer it as well."

He stood at Janeway's side and watched Bolis try to shield himself from the other Edesians' view by standing behind the bio-bed.

The doctor wedged himself around Tuvok, making it clear that the Vulcan was in his way. "Is there some special reason you're here, Mr. Tuvok? I assure you I can't cure arrogance."

Tuvok moved his gaze to the doctor a moment, then back at Bolis. "That much is evident, Doctor."

Janeway shook her head in displeasure—and for the first time in some hours it didn't even hurt to do so. "Gentlemen, this isn't the time."

"Of course," the doctor said. "Your shoulder is going to be fine. Try not to lift heavy objects for the next six days, and there will be a special exercise regimen to follow. I'll have it sent to the computer in your quarters."

Janeway slid off the table. "Thank you."

The doctor curled his fingers around her upper arm. "I'm not finished with you, Captain."

She turned toward him and nailed down a harsh glare. "Excuse me?"

"It's evident to me that you haven't slept in days. You're slightly anemic, and obviously exhausted."

"I'm not in the mood for a lecture, Doctor."

"No one ever is." The doctor pulled a hypospray from the tray next to the bio-bed. "So I've prepared a mild stimulant, knowing you can't take my advice until this ordeal is over."

Janeway softened her expression. "Am I that predictable?"

The doctor frowned. "Unfortunately."

The captain accepted the hypospray and felt the rush of new strength it gave her, mere moments after its application to her neck. "I haven't seen a casualty report." She looked around sickbay and noted that she was the only patient.

"Only minor broken bones, some abrasions and contusions, and one concussion I sent to quarters rather than house here, considering our guests."

"Well," Janeway sighed, "that's the best news I've heard in a while."

"Captain—"

It was Lekket's voice, but less weak than before—the doctor must have treated him for fatigue as well.

Janeway felt the muscles in her neck tighten, as she moved toward the containment field that held Lekket and the other Edesians wedged into a corner of sickbay. She readied herself for the pain in her shoulder to return but, of course, it did not—the doctor was very thorough.

"I'd like a word, Captain," Lekket said, making his way to the front of the force field.

"I have very little I want to say to you." Janeway squared her shoulders, and with her renewed strength came renewed anger. She felt her face flush, and knew it wasn't merely her proximity to the energy field that locked Lekket away from her. "But I would like to know why, Lekket. Why did you play some childish game with me? Why not tell us the *Marauder* had this much power? And would use it so destructively?"

"I didn't know, Captain. I knew of their ability to cloak, and of the beam they struck you with on your first encounter, but not of this, I swear. You understand that we were without hope, that I feared you would not fight for us if you knew the true odds—and that if you did fight we'd need your fresh perspective . . ."

Janeway wasn't sure if she should believe him. He'd been spouting lies and half-truths since their first meeting. Why should he stop now, especially when at a tactical disadvantage?

The captain decided to test her new captive. "Tell me, Lekket, where do you think the *Marauder* is headed?"

His look tacking toward surprised, Lekket stammered out his answer. "I . . . to Edesia Prime—I'm sure, Captain—you see what they are capable of—you see—"

She cut him off. "I see that you disagree, again, with Mr. Bolis. He suggests they are heading for a repair facility."

Commodore Lekket's visage bent to disgust as he spied past Janeway to glare at Bolis, then softened into sadness as he took back the captain's gaze. "He is a traitor. Who can trust the lies of a traitor?"

"I trust him," Janeway said. "At least more than I trust

you." She looked to Tuvok. "Find Mr. Bolis some quarters. He's our guest."

With that she turned on her heel and marched toward the door.

Tuvok followed, and Bolis was probably behind her as well, but as she stepped into the corridor she only looked forward, trying to push from her mind Lekket's last call to her as it faded. "Trusting him is a mistake, Captain! I swear on my life—a mistake!"

CHAPTER

17

"WHAT'S THE STUN SETTING ON THIS?" PARIS LIFTED THE weapon, gesturing with it. Stith-ta gazed at it almost longingly. He'd gone from the man in charge, with four guards securing more than four dozen *Voyager* refugees—to the man held captive, his four guards dead.

Paris fingered the setting dial, spinning it to one end. "Is this the lowest?"

The Gimlon commander was silent, his eyes twitching again, a grayish bruise forming on his chin and spreading to his cheek. He was scared. And Paris liked that.

"You will be dead soon," Stith-ta said, still coveting the rifle, his threat sounding hollow.

Paris almost hoped the Gimlon coward would make a grab for the rifle so he could get clubbed again.

"Maybe I just don't need the stun setting for you," Paris said. He wanted to poke the barrel of the disruptor into the Gimlon's chest and knock him over. Stith-ta had ordered Chakotay's death—now he deserved to die as well.

"Chen," Paris called. "Get up here." He had to get away from the gutless murderer and he backed away as far as he could without falling from the small pedestal.

Chen quickly bounded up to join them, looking refreshed and recovered. Youth . . . Paris had that once, and not too

137

long ago. Lately he was feeling very old. Chakotay . . . all the Edesians on the transport . . . all dead. That would age anyone.

It had become obvious who the real villains were in this conflict. The Gimlon were ruthless. The Edesians had treated the Starfleeters with relative kindness, considering the circumstances. Maybe that was only part of the story, but certainly it was enough to make Paris no longer care if Stith-ta lived or died.

"Search him," Paris ordered Chen, gesturing to the Gimlon commander. *"Carefully."*

Nodding, Chen approached the Gimlon slowly, his expression apprehensive. As the young ensign patted down his subject, Paris wished he knew for sure if there was a stun setting on the rifle. He'd have liked to stun Stith-ta and *then* search him for weapons or communications devices.

"You're lucky," Paris said, his voice so hard it somewhat surprised even him. "If I didn't think I might need you, you'd probably be dead now."

Stith-ta said nothing as Chen finished frisking him. The young ensign had come up empty, and shrugged his shoulders.

"Nothing, sir."

Paris nodded, but decided the search had been too cursory and superficial, and he wasn't satisfied. Chen was from Engineering, not Security.

Neither was Paris, but he'd been searched enough times to know how it should be done.

"We want communications equipment," he told Stith-ta.

The Gimlon commander smirked his nervous smirk. "I will spit on your corpse—if anything is left after you've been killed."

"Trying to convince me or yourself?" Paris stroked the rifle's trigger with his index finger, ready to fire.

Then again—they *were* on Stith-ta's ship, and the Gimlon seemed to combine the worst attributes of the Romulans and the Cardassians, and with more than a little Colonel Greene thrown in.

"Everyone spread out!" Paris spun toward the door through which they'd taken Chakotay.

If they were being watched—if Stith-ta's men had seen all

that had happened . . . Gimlon Security would be on its way—that's why the Gimlon commander could afford to spit threats.

Reinforcements would come without being called. Paris had given that some thought, but figured he'd have more time than a few scant minutes.

Now he had to tense for an underdog fight. And without knowing just where the stun setting was on his new Gimlon Issue rifle . . . well, it wouldn't be nice.

Paris looked up toward the ceiling, wondering where the sensor device was, then back down to the doorway.

"Get in front of the door." He motioned from Stith-ta to the hatchway with the disruptor rifle.

"That won't save you," the Gimlon said, his tone bitter and unfortunate. "I am considered expendable."

"Great," Paris said. "That makes it unanimous. Now move."

Too slowly, Stith-ta moved down from the platform and toward the door.

Paris gritted his teeth and growled, "Move!"

When the Gimlon was in place, Paris shifted his head back to the rest of the *Voyager* crewmen. "Chen, you and Holland tip up the platform and try to make some cover out of it. See if those cargo containers can be moved too. And make sure something explosive isn't in 'em."

"You're all dead," Stith-ta said, turning his face from the door and toward Paris. "But especially you." The Gimlon was turning his fear into hate. It seemed an easy trip for him.

"Oh? I'm going to be deader than most? How does that work?"

The Gimlon commander's smirk returned. "If we both live, I will see you tortured."

Paris didn't feel like smiling, but he didn't want his full feelings to show, lest Stith-ta think he was getting under the Starfleeter's skin. Which he was.

"Interesting hobby. When I was a kid, I collected computer programs."

"If you have children," the Gimlon said coldly, "they will collect tears because their father has died a fool and a coward."

Paris tried to broaden his false smile, as counterfeit as the Gimlon's. "Tell me, how does your engineer compensate for the gravity well caused by the mass of your ego?"

Before Stith-ta could retort—and Paris was sure he would have—the door began to pull into the wall, opening almost in slow motion.

Chen and Lothridge had raised the platform into a barrier, but only part of the crew would be protected, and the cargo containers had not yet been moved.

Paris readied himself. One man, one rifle . . . against how many, he didn't know.

He edged to the left a little and prepared to fire past Stith-ta and through the opening door.

Finally, the door was open . . . and no one lay beyond.

Paris looked past the Gimlon commander and up a very empty, silent corridor.

"Tuvok, tell them what you told me." Janeway couldn't sit. She had to keep moving, couldn't rest. Her mind wouldn't let her, and now that her body wasn't in such pain she didn't have to relax.

Three billion dead . . . and she'd failed her crew.

She marched back and forth along the briefing-room table, her officers—what was left of them—watching as she paced. Soon she would have to force herself to sit—her neck and back muscles were beginning to knot again.

Par for the course. Torres and Seven-of-Nine, seated opposite each other, probably felt the same.

Well . . . Torres probably did.

Harry Kim, the other officer present, needed to see Janeway in a relaxed state, the captain thought. So she tried to look calm, yet attentive.

Unsteepling his entwined fingers, Tuvok straightened from his reclining, less anxious position. "Preliminary data indicate that the Gimlon do not, in fact, employ a cloak of any kind. At least not as we define it."

"Are we defining it wrong?" Torres asked.

"No." Tuvok pressed a data padd on the table, and the viewer to his left flashed alive with a graphic of some sensor data. "The Marauder creates around itself a subspace field at such a frequency that we did not read it *as* a subspace field. They are using a very complex warping of space-time, with what I believe are a series of gravimetric fields of unknown genesis—and immense power."

"So they're using this as a method of transportation? Moving so fast we can't track them?" Torres asked.

Tuvok shook his head. "I think not. They are not moving. Rather, they seem to cease existing in one place, then exist again someplace else."

"But where?" Janeway tossed the question over her shoulder as she twisted away from Tuvok, continuing on her in-place hike.

"At this point we cannot know exactly where they go."

"Is this anything like Borg technology?" Torres asked Seven-of-Nine.

The young lady, her smooth Nordic features only slightly marred by the remnants of Borg technology that had not yet been totally purged by her human body, glanced at the data on the screen. "This is not Borg. But very interesting. And highly developed."

"Is it like anything the Borg have encountered, to your knowledge?" Tuvok asked.

"As I said, it is not Borg."

"I did not ask," Tuvok said calmly, "if it was Borg. I asked if the Borg had encountered it. There *is* a difference."

"The difference is irrelevant. If the Borg had encountered this, it would have become Borg technology."

Tuvok raised an interested brow.

"How have the Edesians stood against this technology for as long as they have?" Janeway asked no one in particular. "Are the Gimlon playing some cat-and-mouse game?"

Torres shrugged, and the others were silent.

"Perhaps they have but the single vessel with such capabilities," Tuvok said.

"Rushing into war with their prototype for some political reason would explain it too," Torres said.

"Why," Tuvok asked, "if planning a war of aggression, would they not build all their infrastructure with their new technology?"

"Because they're not as logical as you," Torres said.

"Or they lacked the resources," Seven said.

Harry Kim looked down at the padd in front of him and seemed to have nothing to offer.

Janeway stopped her gait and leaned toward him slightly. "Something bothering you, Mr. Kim?"

"No, Captain."

The captain shared a glance with Tuvok, who gave the slightest of shrugs.

She looked back to the ensign. "Try again, Harry," she said softly.

His eyes shone up at her for a moment, and then he apparently decided to gather his determination and speak. And when he did, it was with raw emotion. "It's just that—I know three billion people died, and I feel awful about it. But I feel worse knowing that Tom and Chakotay and . . . and—well, and everyone . . . We've lost a lot of our shipmates—I . . ."

Everyone was looking at him, especially Seven-of-Nine. He suddenly stopped, self-conscious.

"I'm sorry," he said finally.

"No," Janeway said. "Don't be. I'm sure we've all had the same thoughts."

"I have not," Seven-of-Nine said.

"Well, isn't that nice!" Kim snapped.

Captain Janeway glared at Ensign Kim, and he lowered his gaze again.

"Sorry, Captain."

She nodded. "This is hard on everyone, but we'll need to get through the entire event before we mourn. We need to stop the *Marauder,* and stop further bloodshed, and then . . ." She felt her eyes lose their focus. She saw Chakotay's face again . . . Tom's . . . Chen's . . . Lothridge's . . . the entire complement of missing crew.

Finally she spoke again, her voice thick and heavy. "Then we can bury our dead."

She blinked her eyes clear, and considered the sad or flat expressions of her various officers.

More than a third of her crew was gone . . . how would she get the rest of them home?

Perhaps she never would. She'd always held out the hope that they'd find a wormhole somewhere or stumble upon someone with technology similar to the type that had flung the *Voyager* so far from the Federation. She'd held on to that hope—kept it and slept with it every night. She kept it in her left hand on the bridge, as she saw the *Voyager* across the quadrant. And she carted it out for others, wearing it like a badge of faith, showing her crew that even though home seemed so far away, it need not be.

Hope. Hope didn't touch reality, and it was reality that was stabbing Janeway in the back right now. Sometimes she wondered if she wouldn't have been better off deciding to cannibalize *Voyager* and make a colony on some nice little out-of-the-way green planet.

Home and hope . . . two words just one letter different, and both now seemed so remote.

There was a very good chance they'd all perish in this fight between these two parties—a fight in which they had no real stake.

"Dismissed," Janeway ordered finally, but as they all rose and Tuvok reached the door, she asked him to stay.

When they were alone, he sat back down in his seat across from where his captain stood.

She was quiet, just looking at him. His expression of serenity, self-possession . . . was it mask or was it real?

Janeway shook her head to herself. She'd known Tuvok for too many years to ask such a question. She knew it was real—she just wished it wasn't sometimes.

She chewed her lower lip a few moments, when he finally prompted her.

"Captain?"

"Yes, there *is* a reason you're here, Mr. Tuvok."

"Indeed. I did not think otherwise."

She nodded, drew herself together to begin pacing again, then decided against it and forced herself into one of the chairs. But she couldn't lean back and recline. Instead, she leaned forward and rested her elbows on the table top. "I don't know if we'll survive this," she said finally.

"We may not."

She nodded again, this time at Tuvok's matter-of-fact demeanor. "I'm glad I didn't ask you for a pep talk."

"Captain, I cannot relate to you anything save what I understand to be the facts of reality."

"No," she said softly. "And I wouldn't have it any other way." She swiveled away from him and toward the window, which showed the stars spooling by quickly, colorfully. From here the universe looked crisp and clean. "I'm risking this ship, and the remainder of my crew, on a mission which might very well fail. We're understaffed, damaged, tired . . ."

"Yes."

"Am I . . ." She turned toward him. "Am I right about this? Am I being logical, Tuvok?"

The Vulcan pulled in a long breath and let out a slight sigh. "I fear," he began, "that a simple 'yes' would not suffice. Are you familiar with the works of T'Ayn Ral?"

Janeway turned her gaze back out the window. "No."

"A matron of Vulcan philosophy. A contemporary of Surak's, usually noted for her rejection of those who proposed the concept of Kholinar—the ceremony and study of purging all emotions."

"Blasphemy?"

"Hardly. Those who wish to attain Kholinar are a minority. Those who actually attain it, a much smaller minority."

Janeway nodded warily. "Tuvok, if there's a point—"

"There is, Captain. T'Ayn Ral once stated: 'Morality is a path to guide one's choices. A reasoned path leads one to a moral choice. An unreasoned path leads to the unknown, and eventually to self-destruction."

She stood and walked over to the window. "Very profound."

"Captain, you are a being of reason. You make logical choices, and your values are moral ones, in my opinion."

"Thank you."

"But," Tuvok said, rising and stepping up behind her, catching her gaze in the reflection off the window, "I ask you to remember that while the path chosen must be rational, the *reason* for your walking that path must also be based in logic—in noncontradictory concept formation. It is the only method I know to ensure that you are *not* in conflict with reality."

She turned and met his eyes, face to face. "Logic will fit any argument, but not every premise on which the argument is based."

"Correct," Tuvok said, pleased with the definition.

"The logical argument here is that the *Marauder* must be stopped because innocent life should be protected."

"Yes."

"And the premise on which that's based is an individual's right to his own life: the Federation's founding principle."

"Indeed."

Janeway frowned. "My crew have a right to their own lives."

Tuvok shook his head. "Less so—if only because they have pledged their lives to the Starfleet and to the protection of the Federation."

Janeway pursed her lips. Not quite a smile. She took one of Tuvok's forearms in her fingers. "It all comes back to morality not changing based on your location. If we have a duty to protect the innocent in the Alpha quadrant, we have a duty here. And the Gimlon would eventually seek out other peoples besides the Edesians."

"Your logic, Captain," Tuvok said, "is based on a solid premise."

She nodded. "Stalin. Hitler. Kahn Singh. Li Quan. Maltuvous."

"And the Gimlon."

"Thank you, Mr. Tuvok."

"I did nothing," he said, "except confirm that which you knew."

Janeway gripped his arm tighter, and was warmed by his friendship, even if he was not. Then again she knew he was, in his way.

"Tuvok—my Patron of Vulcan philosophy," she quipped.

He shook his dark head. "Logic is not a Vulcan philosophy. It is merely a philosophy embraced by most Vulcans. Any sentient being, who chooses to think, can be logical. Real thought—where contradictions are not allowed, and morals codes are based on reasonable values . . . it is the universal philosophy of reason. And it's a Vulcan philosophy only as much as it is Human and Andorian and Orion . . . and Gimlon, if they were to choose it."

Janeway nodded in agreement. "But for now they won't, and so they have to be stopped. I want to know more about this technology they use. I want to know what they're doing and how."

"I will employ Mr. Kim, and we will endeavor to supply you with that information as soon as possible."

She nodded. "And we'll need a series of battle drills, Commander."

"Aye, Captain."

Turning toward the door to her bridge, she marched forward with conviction, a new hope in her left hand. "This time," she said, "we won't back down."

CHAPTER

18

"*SHHHH*—NO ONE MOVE." TOM PARIS CLENCHED HIS FINgers around the butt of the alien disruptor rifle and readied himself to pull the trigger. He'd moved the power selector to the lowest setting—still too high for his liking, but certainly more useful than bare hands.

If only he hadn't had to vaporize the other Gimlon guards *with* their weapons. Then the odds would have been at least slightly less than impossible.

The corridor beyond Stith-ta was as silent as the eye of a massive storm. The Gimlon were obviously taking cover, waiting, and Paris felt exposed. Stith-ta made a rather inadequate shield.

"We have your commander," Paris called out. "Lay down your weapons!" He extended the rifle toward the Gimlon commander. "Order them!"

"I order you," Stith-ta barked, "do as he says!"

"But I like my new weapon." Chakotay's voice—from beyond the door. A trap? Did they *not* kill him, but instead were using him as a pawn? Or did he escape? Or did they have a voice synthesizer? Almost anything was possible.

Paris tensed, aimed his weapon past Stith-ta's head, and waited to fire.

"It's me, Tom," Chakotay said. He let his voice linger a moment, then stepped out from behind the doorway.

Stith-ta slumped—perhaps even came close to collapsing—as Chakotay marched into the room, a disruptor rifle in hand.

Paris couldn't contain his smile. "We thought you were dead!"

Chakotay nodded. "Came close."

"How did you manage without *me?*" Paris asked, incredulous.

"Starfleet Martial Arts Course One."

"Excuse me?" Paris knitted his brows in skepticism.

"I surprised him with my fast moves." Chakotay smiled and gestured for the other *Voyager* crewmembers to come from behind their makeshift barricades.

"You gloat now," Stith-ta said, "but you only postpone your own inevitable deaths."

Paris and Chakotay exchanged a glance.

Pressing his disruptor rifle into Stith-ta's shoulder, Paris pushed the man forward a step. "Giggles over here is annoying, but he might be right. Maybe we've secured our prison cell here and nothing else."

A slight smile still traced Chakotay's mouth. "Mr. Stith-ta isn't being quite honest. If I read their internal sensors correctly, we outnumber what's left of his crew by about seven to one." He turned to the Gimlon commander, but didn't raise his weapon, probably because Paris already had the man well covered. And covered he would stay. "Two on the bridge, three in Engineering, and that's about it, right?"

"That's it?" Paris was taken aback. "Six guys, including the high-and-powerful-commander-of-all-that's-arrogant here?"

Chakotay nodded, gestured from Stith-ta to Paris with his free hand. "With a title like that I'll be confusing the two of you." He motioned one of the *Voyager* crewmembers toward the door. "Someone close that for now."

Lothridge acknowledged the order and tread to the door's controls. After the blank corridor was again hidden from view, Chakotay continued.

"This ship is highly automated. And I'm pretty sure it is supposed to be. Which makes manning it easy but repairing it a little more difficult."

"You found all this out from some internal sensors?"

The *Voyager* commander stepped back a bit, and glanced around the cargo hold that had been their makeshift brig cell and was now their base of operations. "The guard I captured thought I'd walk into their automation room and let myself be killed. He said it was an empty communications room."

Following Chakotay's gaze around the room, Paris wondered what the man was looking for. "And I assume it wasn't a comm hub *or* empty."

"No. And because these thugs don't believe in stun settings—"

"Yeah, I found that out—"

Moving toward the other end of the bay, Chakotay looked at the cargo containers that the *Voyager* crewmen had tried to take cover behind. "Well, the three people manning the automation room aren't there anymore."

"Vaporized?"

"I wish it were that clean."

Stith-ta turned his head, but kept his feet planted on the deck. His jaw slackened a bit, and Paris saw him move it from side to side as if someone had punched the Gimlon in the face.

Was he upset because he'd lost men or because his ship had lost crew? Or because he'd found that the *Voyager* crew was now firmly in charge?

"What's in these?" Chakotay pointed to the cargo containers with his rifle.

Paris pressed his weapon into the Gimlon's back again. "Well, Stick-ta. Answer him."

Stith-ta was stiff with conviction, though, not choked up with remorse for his crew—Paris could sense that now.

"I will not help you," the Gimlon said.

"I could kill you now." Paris grabbed the man with his free hand and spun him around so they stood face-to-face.

"Then do so," Stith-ta said. "But I will not help you any more." The Gimlon spat his words, and under the hum of his universal translator Paris could hear the Gimlon's real words—guttural and harsh. "No more calling into corridors and ordering my men to stand down," Stith-ta continued. "My situation was different when I believed I had control of this ship. Now I know that if I help you it is merely a matter of time before you are on my bridge."

"You won't help us, even to save your own life?" Chakotay asked, walking back toward the Gimlon commander.

"I am dead," Stith-ta said. "Even if I am given to the Edesians they will return me to my people as a prisoner of war. As someone foolish enough to be captured, I will be killed."

Seeming to consider that, Chakotay exchanged another look with Paris.

"What if we make sure you can escape, and won't become a prisoner of war?" Chakotay offered.

"If I am missing and presumed a deserter, my family will be sent to a Harmony Camp, where they will be taught to live without me."

"I take it that's not as pleasant as it sounds," Paris said.

"It is an effective means of keeping myself, and others, loyal."

Paris shook his head. A victim of his own government, Stith-ta still agreed with a policy that would kill him and maybe even his family.

The Gimlon commander looked toward the doorway a split second, then down to his boots. "I would be loyal without the threat."

"He's stalling," Chakotay said finally. "We're headed back to Gimlon space, and he's stalling for time."

"Okay," Paris said. "So we stop that from happening. What do we do with him in the meantime?"

"Take him with us. Where we can keep an eye on him."

He didn't like it, but Paris nodded because there really was no other answer. They could knock Stith-ta over the head, *maybe* knock him out—but for how long? They could kill him, but that just wasn't the way Starfleet liked to work.

Chakotay slid toward the controls to the door. "We split into two teams—since we have two weapons. Team one heads for Engineering, team two for the bridge." He pressed a pad on a control panel and the door to the corridor began to open again. "Paris, you take team one. Secure Engineering and contact me on internal communications by sending a burst of static to the bridge. If you hear back from me, I'm there. We'll do the same if we get to the bridge first."

Paris nodded. "Aye, sir." He liked the plan—simple and to the point. Get the ship and head back toward *Voyager*. And hope an Edesian wouldn't attack them on the way. He felt the muscles in his legs tighten. He wanted to get started. Now.

"Move out," Chakotay said, crooking a thumb over his shoulder. "Stith-ta, let's look at your bridge."

Stith-ta stepped forward, then ran—out the door and up the corridor.

"Computer! Self—" He was running, yelling, "—Destruct program one!"

Paris and Chakotay leaped forward. Chakotay was through the door first, his rifle raised. "Stop!"

Stith-ta stumbled, yelped as he fell forward, then regained himself and ran on. "Begin—"

"Stop!" Chakotay gained a few feet on him, but the Gimlon commander was too far ahead now to be within physical reach. Paris watched as Chakotay's weapon extended before him and fired a pulse of sonic disruption that screeched through the air.

The blast caught Stith-ta and forced him forward faster than his limbs could carry. The Gimlon commander fell—his legs sheered apart beneath him. He rolled out of control as he careened up the corridor.

Paris and Chakotay stopped a few feet from the Gimlon commander, who gasped and sputtered and moaned all in one breath.

"What did you do?" Paris demanded of the Gimlon commander, but his question was moot. It was obvious.

His universal translator interpreted the Gimlon ship's computer flawlessly.

"Self-destruct in forty seconds . . . thirty-nine . . . thirty-eight . . ."

Orangish-red blood was pooling on the deck at their feet. Stith-ta reached out a hand to clench the floor before him. He dragged what was left of his body an inch or so forward.

"How do we stop it?" Chakotay demanded, as if Stith-ta would answer now.

"You . . . can't."

"Of course not," Paris said grimly. "It's just not a real self-destruct command if you can stop it on a whim."

Stith-ta cried out in pain.

He'd be out of his misery soon, Paris thought.

"Thirty-five . . . thirty-four . . . thirty-three . . ."

In thirty-three seconds.

They'd all be out of their misery . . .

"Thirty-two . . . thirty-one . . . thirty . . ."

Stith-ta was still writhing, and Paris wondered which was greater—the Gimlon's pain from his vaporized legs, or the glee he must be feeling, knowing he'd won.

"What now?" Paris asked.

"Twenty-eight . . . twenty-seven . . . twenty-six . . ."

Chakotay looked down at Stith-ta, then up to Paris. "I'm open to suggestions."

"You . . . you'll die," Stith-ta sputtered, spittle from his mouth flying off and combining with the pond of blood that now surrounded him.

"Twenty-four . . . twenty-three . . . twenty-two . . ."

"Yeah," Paris said. "Same to you, fella."

What could they do? How did they threaten a man who had decided to kill himself and everyone else with him?

"Twenty-one . . . twenty . . . nineteen . . ."

There was nothing to do.

It would end here . . .

Paris looked at Chakotay—wanting to say something.

All they heard was the Gimlon computer, flat and mechanical—not even taunting.

"Seventeen . . . sixteen . . . fifteen . . ."

CHAPTER
19

"MAY WE SPEAK, CAPTAIN?"

"Yes." Janeway motioned to a seat and Bolis slid fluidly into the chair before her office desk.

He sat, hands clasped on his lap, thin lips semi-pursed. His close-cropped hair showed some gray strands among the dark black, and Janeway realized this was really the first time she'd actually allowed herself to look at him.

He was quiet for some time after sitting, as if not knowing where to begin their conversation. Janeway didn't like the quiet. Quiet meant her mind was forced to swirl around thoughts of the billions of lives so recently lost. Chakotay, Paris, Chen . . . so many among those numbers. Her own people. She felt she shouldn't think about it in those terms—shouldn't count her own people above those she didn't know . . .

But she *did* know her people, and not the others. She saw their faces in her mind's eye when she thought about the dead on that planet. And she missed seeing those faces on her bridge.

Her bridge.

Bolis had helped her regain her bridge . . . and now he sat before her, seeming to hold back troubling words.

"Is there a problem?" She prodded.

He shook his head. "No, Captain. I . . . I would like to see Commodore Lekket."

Janeway was surprised, and was sure that showed in her expression. "Why?"

"I wish to explain to him my . . ."

"Betrayal?"

Bolis pursed his lips, looked away. Surely he didn't like the word, but it *was* what Lekket had called it, and in fact it was accurate.

"That's what it is," Janeway said. "But that doesn't make it wrong. Betrayal of an immoral value—is moral, Mr. Bolis."

Nodding slowly, Bolis seemed to take little comfort in the captain's words. "If so," he said, "I need to explain that."

"I see."

He turned his gaze back to her, and his eyes looked very strange. Not cold or distant, but somewhat detached from what he was saying. "I've disobeyed my commander. I've made decisions which affect my homeworld, my family, and hundreds of thousands of families—"

"I understand."

"I may speak with him? Privately?"

Janeway nodded. "Of course. What will you tell him?"

After pulling in a long breath and holding it a moment, Bolis sighed. "That I resign my position, stand by my decision, and will give myself up to the Edesian authorities, should there be any left when this war is over."

"There will be if I have anything to do with it."

Bolis smiled slightly, strangely—as if it was an effort. "You possess a persistent confidence, Captain."

"Yes," Janeway said. "I do."

The gall! The unmitigated, unabashed, arrogant gall! Lekket's rage was stoked higher every minute he was left to sit and wait in the small conference room. Even if Bolis— the worst traitor ever to be born of Edesia—were to be tortured and killed . . . well, that would be too good for him.

A flood of failure and torrential anger battled for sway over Lekket's attentions. Was it thanks to Bolis that the commodore had lost command of the situation? Or was it his own weakness which had led Edesia down such a disastrous path?

Did it even matter? Bolis obviously held Captain Janeway's ear, and on that treason, Edesia would perish.

Finally, the door to the room slid open and a Starfleet guard allowed Bolis to enter. It was all Lekket could do to keep himself from plunging forward and placing his fingers around the neck of his once-close friend.

That would have felt good for a moment—his fingers pressing the life out of Bolis's body—but that was not Lekket's way. He probably couldn't have even finished such an attack.

Instead, all he did was glare at the man who had betrayed him, and ask, in a near whisper, "Why?"

Bolis stood silently before his former commander, looking all too normal. Lekket didn't want him to look normal. Such a man should have fangs, or horns, or a scar across his cheek—something that would indicate he was not to be trusted, that he was evil.

But evil didn't often wear signs or have scars. Sometimes evil looked like your neighbor, or your brother . . . or your friend.

In Bolis's face, Lekket could not help but see his former friend, and now a new enemy. And that Lekket had chosen Bolis to be his lieutenant made Lekket feel as if he himself was perhaps his own worst enemy.

Before the war Lekket had been just a businessman. Yes, he'd had military training as a younger man . . . but that seemed so long ago. He hadn't wanted this responsibility—hadn't asked for it. But he'd felt an obligation when asked, and he intended to live up to that duty.

Bolis was now keeping him from fulfilling his charge.

Why? Why? Why? Bolis had been a friend for so long. Now, that was no longer the case—for reasons Lekket wanted to hear.

"Why?" Lekket repeated. "Why have you done this?"

His jaw quivering, Bolis was apparently taut with emotion. Slowly, his mouth moved to speak . . .

"I have done little," Bolis said finally, almost bitterly. "Captain Janeway is determined to stop the *Marauder* at all costs."

"But you have her going to the Sortika Nebula! You *know* the *Marauder* will be headed for Edesia now! You *know* it! Why have you done this as well?"

"I do not know it," Bolis snapped. "I believe the *Marauder* has never been this damaged and will head to its repair facility in the nebula."

"I do not understand you at all anymore, Bolis!"

"Why? Because I did not want to see these good people die in *our* war. I could not—"

Pushing back his chair, Lekket bounded from the seat and almost leaped over to Bolis. Instead, he held his ground about a meter away, clenching his fists at his sides. "Spare me the sermons and contrived elevated discourse, Bolis! Never have you questioned this policy, even when I myself have voiced concerns. How do you explain that?"

Silent another moment, Bolis seemed to study Lekket's face. "I cannot."

"You cannot?" Lekket mocked. "Of course not! Not once did you ever indicate to me you had doubts about this policy. Or any Edesian policy, for that matter. You've been the perfect soldier. The perfect everything!"

Bolis looked away.

"How many ships have we impressed together?" Lekket snarled. "Eighty? Ninety? How many had my predecessor, before he was killed? Never have you spoken of moral grounds against this policy. *Never.*"

Lekket pounded his fist against the table next to them and Bolis looked back up.

"I did not because I could not before. I did not mean for it to happen this way."

"Why now?" Lekket demanded. "Why when we were so close to destroying the *Marauder?*" Jutting forward in two quick steps, he grabbed Bolis's tunic front in both fists and shook the man before him. "Three billion people! Had you no one on that planet to call your own, you putrid, *evil* man? Can you sleep knowing that three billion souls should be haunting your every moment until your dying day?"

Lekket stared at Bolis, hoping for some sign of regret, some sign of anything but coldness. The man was full of emotion—but what emotion?

Slowly, Bolis pulled Lekket off him and pushed him away.

One hand kept Lekket at a distance, while the other removed the pendants from around Bolis's neck.

Bolis held out the pendants to his former commodore. "I resign my position, and give myself up for court martial—if I am alive to present myself to an Edesian authority."

Turning quickly on his heel, Bolis left Lekket in solitude.

As the door slid closed, Lekket looked from the rank pendant to the scanner pendant, and finally to the communications pendant.

Lekket shook his head in disbelief. Bolis clearly wasn't in his right mind. Only a madman would overlook the opportunity he had just given his own enemy. Either that, or in his final act as an Edesian soldier, Bolis had made a grave error.

Lekket quickly placed all three pendants around his neck as the guard came in to escort his prisoner back to sickbay.

The Edesian commodore made sure not to even touch the communications pendant on his chest—but he could barely resist. He could very well hold Edesia's survival in his hands.

Maybe Janeway was going to go running in the wrong direction. Lekket was sure of that now—but with a method to communicate to his own people, he could do something in these final moments that might actually help Edesia—or at the very least avenge her.

Bolis had lost his mind, and Lekket had lost every life on Edesia's largest colony . . . but now the Gimlon would suffer a loss as well—and Lekket would make sure it was the largest loss of all.

CHAPTER
20

"SEVENTEEN . . . SIXTEEN . . . FIFTEEN . . ."

The countdown to self-destruct continued, the Gimlon computer ominous, imperative, and yet serene in its presentation.

"Fourteen . . ."

Panic swelled in Chakotay's chest but he bulldozed it aside as he pushed past Paris. He ran down the corridor as fast as he could. His spine tingled—the pain in his back was barely noticeable. He was about to die. What did pain matter?

"Thirteen . . ."

He tried to turn, but lost his balance and skidded past the doorway for which he'd aimed. He laid down his free hand to slow his momentum, and grit from the floor ground into his flesh.

"Twelve . . ."

With his other hand he clutched the Gimlon disruptor rifle close to his side. He vaulted up, catapulting himself through the door and onto the bloody bodies of the Gimlon he'd accidentally killed just minutes before.

"Eleven . . ."

Struggling in a tangle of slack alien limbs, he fought to get a footing between the spent corpses of the Gimlon soldiers.

158

"Ten . . ."

The automation room: everything on the Gimlon ship—every control, every command—came through the automation hubs in this room. Not the heart of the vessel—its brain.

"Nine . . ."

Which panel should Chakotay choose? Which console could stop the self-destruct command? He had only seconds to find the computer that controlled the countdown—

"Eight . . ."

Chakotay looked from wall to wall: computer monitors, input displays, terminal screens—buttons and switches and a lever or two—

"Seven . . ."

Which one?

"Six . . ."

Paris pushed himself quickly through the doorway. "What—"

"Five . . ."

Which panel controlled the computer? The propulsion? The shields? Life support?

"Four . . ."

He aimed his weapon at the console before him, pulled the trigger, and moved his arm so that every control, every computer panel, and every terminal was covered by the wave of sonic disruption his weapon spat forth.

"Three . . ."

From the corner of his eye, Chakotay could see Paris ducking behind the doorway as a spray of spark and electrical flame burst out in all directions.

After another moment, Chakotay released the trigger, jumped and rolled out the door, knocking into Paris as he went down onto the deck. Explosions seemed to rumble all around him—splinters of spark now pouring out the door of the automation room, skidding onto the floor and against his knees.

If the computer counted "two," Chakotay didn't hear it. He couldn't have over the din of exploding computer equipment.

The lights above them dimmed and in a final flash, went dark.

Finally, all explosions stopped, and the only sound Chakotay heard was the sizzle and hiss of what had been the automation computers.

In the complete darkness, he pulled himself up. He knew Paris was somewhere near him, and he instinctively reached out for his shipmate, helping to hoist himself to his feet.

"I think that stopped the computer," Chakotay said, choking a little on the smoke that was surging from the equipment he'd wrecked.

"I think it stopped everything," Paris said. "Not a bad idea—knock out automation, knock out everything—including the self-destruct. Even if it has a certain flavor of overkill."

Chakotay looked around, but the darkness persisted, and although his eyes strained to adjust there just wasn't enough light to focus. An occasional spark could be seen through the doorway, but all that did was light up the puffs of smoke as they gushed toward the ceiling.

"At least we're not going to die," Chakotay said, mostly to himself, but loud enough so that the *Voyager* crewmembers could hear him.

"Or if we do," Paris added, "at least we won't see it happen."

"Shut up, Tom," someone called out.

"Who said that?"

"Whoever it was," Chakotay said, closing his eyes since they were useless anyway, "is right."

"So . . . this is a bad time to tell you I'm afraid of the dark?"

Someone chuckled.

Then someone else.

And another—until finally Chakotay allowed himself a short laugh.

On the brink of death, in a ship without power, in alien space, with Lord only knows how many Gimlon enemies still alive and after them, they all laughed.

As the laughter died down and the silence grew awkward again, Chakotay cleared his throat and spoke.

"Okay, people, this is where we stand: there are other hostiles on this ship, but they're in the same situation we are, and we outnumber them. Anyone not like those odds?"

"No, sir!" came a number of replies.

"Good." He turned in the direction he'd heard Paris's voice from. "Tom, I need light."

"You'd think after leaping into the fire from the frying pan, light wouldn't be a problem."

"I swear to you, Paris, *no one* thinks you're funny."

"I do."

"Who said that?" Chakotay asked the darkness.

"Whoever it was," Paris said, and Chakotay could *hear* his smile, "is right."

"Serious-time now. Options, Lieutenant?"

Before he answered, Paris must have thought a moment, as there was a pause.

"I don't hear even an engine, so I'd say we're completely dead in space. I don't hear fans, or anything electronic, which is why the lights are out. Does anyone have a flashlight?"

"Of course not," Chakotay said dryly. "But there must be some battery system for the lights?"

"Hey, somethin's working. We're not all floatin' around," Crewman Josh Lothridge said.

"Yes," Chakotay said. "Somewhere something's powering that."

"How do we find it and manually transfer that power to everything else?"

"I don't know," Chakotay admitted, and in the darkness, that sentence seemed like the wrong thing to say. With as bright a tone as he could summon, he added: "But let's find out."

Moving his hand along the Gimlon rifle he still held, Chakotay felt for the rod that ran along its top and acted as a sight. When he grasped it well at one end, he pried it loose and then handed the remainder of the weapon to Paris.

"Hey—"

"Oh, sorry." He must have hit Paris with it. "You okay?"

"Yeah."

Chakotay felt for the seam of his tunic where his shoulder met his neck. He tore down, ripping the cloth at first smoothly, and then raggedly with a few rough yanks.

"What are you doing?" Paris asked.

Taking the length of cloth, Chakotay found the end of the

metal rod he'd split off the rifle, and tightly wrapped the torn sleeve around its end. "I'm making a torch."

"And you're going to light it with what?" Paris asked. "We're going to rub two ensigns together?"

Chakotay motioned his completed though unlit torch toward the ceiling, despite no one's being able to see the gesture. "Where there's smoke . . ."

He stepped toward the brief flashes of spark and pushed himself back into the automation room. Immediately, the smoke and soot choked him, burned his eyes, and made them water.

Wishing he could close out the irritants, he forced himself to keep those stinging eyes open. He needed to see the arcs of electricity or scraps of fire that might kindle his make-shift torch.

Hard to be sure through the thick smoke, but Chakotay thought he saw a flicker of light that could have been a piece of insulation on fire. He coughed roughly, and extended his arm until the tip of the cloth-covered rod touched the fire.

Ignition took a moment, but even the best Starfleet-issue fire-retardant weave would inflame if exposed for a long period. It might not last long, and Chakotay wished he had some kind of accelerant, but all he needed was a little light—until some flashlights could be found.

As soon as the torch seemed bright enough, Chakotay turned quickly and pushed back out the doorway. He was gasping for a clean breath, and even though the corridor's air wasn't clear as nature, it was better than the drafts of smoke he'd been choking through.

Panting, sucking in the comparatively cooler air outside the automation room, Chakotay peered past his torch down the now dimly firelit hallway.

Paris stood just a few steps away. Beyond him, about half their people.

"Where are the others?" Chakotay asked.

Paris motioned toward him. "Behind you."

Chakotay turned, held the torch high. He counted heads and gauged faces. Everyone was present and looked intact.

"How many weapons do we have?"

Holding up the rifle he held, Paris shrugged. "Four, maybe?"

Commander Chakotay nodded. He felt a rivulet of perspiration drop from his left sideburn down toward his neck. "We make four torches, split into four teams, each with a torch and disruptor. We'll reconnoiter the vessel—deck by deck."

Everyone nodded. A few said "Aye, sir."

"And when we find a Gimlon crewmember?" Paris asked, already prying the metal baton off his other rifle.

Chakotay looked up the corridor, toward where Stith-ta was lying dead. He couldn't see him there—the torchlight only radiated out a meter or two—but the Gimlon commander *was* there, dead, his legs vaporized out from under him.

"As we've found, there is no stun setting on these," Chakotay began slowly, holding up his weapon. "When you find someone, make an effort to get them to surrender. If they have a weapon, though . . . you do what you have to. If we can find some of their stun grenades, like the one used on the transport, I'd like that. But no unnecessary risks."

Again, more nods. They were a cohesive unit again—a real crew, even separated from *Voyager*. They were not just Federation refugees—which was how Chakotay had felt about them just an hour before.

"Paris, you and I will try to get some internal lights working, then head for the bridge. Give your torch to Chen. The rest of you, split up evenly into teams. Chen's team toward Engineering, where we'll meet you when we've secured the bridge. The rest of you, take one deck at a time until you reach top or bottom. Find weapons, communicators, whatever you think can be useful."

Paris traded Chakotay's torch for a rifle, and led the way up the corridor. Chakotay looked back a few times, and the remaining *Voyager* crew melted into the blurry glare of their own torchlight.

The ship held an eerie silence—no engines, no fans, no hum at all.

"We must be almost completely stopped in space," Chakotay said, more to himself than Paris.

"I noticed," Paris said. "Good for us. In fact, after we get some lights, assuming we can keep a hold on the Gimlon crew left, we'll need their help to get deflectors and structural integrity fields going. Otherwise a stray atom could knock a hole in us at any useful speed."

"I know," Chakotay said, and chewed his lower lip a moment. "But we can't count on getting Gimlon help. So far, they don't seem cooperative."

Paris grunted his agreement, and gestured to an access panel on the bulkhead to their left. "Let's see what this does." They made their way to the wall, and Paris handed back Chakotay the torch.

Despite the light shed on the panel, Paris felt for depressions that might snap the cover from its housing. He found them, one on either side, and pressed both until the panel came off in his hands, revealing a circuit bank.

"Am I good, or what?"

"Until you get the lights on, you're an 'or what.'"

"Fickle." Paris laid the panel against the bulkhead at his feet, then reached for the torch and brought it close. "This is interesting."

"What?" Chakotay leaned forward as near as he could, but tried to also keep an eye on the corridor both ways. It was possible that any remaining Gimlon would soon be looking to restore these same systems.

"I could be sure if we had a tricorder—"

"We don't."

"I know. So we'll fall back and punt."

"Huh?" Chakotay turned from the circuit panel to look at Paris.

"Forget it," Paris said. "You probably didn't play games as a kid, if you ever were one."

Chakotay often wondered just how much Paris believed his own jokes. Did he really see Chakotay as that stiff? "I played soccer, pereci squares, and tennis."

"Impressive. Now look here." Paris pointed to where two circuits met. "These are basically duotronic conduits. Fairly old technology by our standards, but not ancient. If there's a schematic somewhere here, I could find out—"

Chakotay shook his head. "Schematics—you always want it easy." He picked up the panel Paris had placed on the floor and tried to tilt it into the dim torchlight. "There's some kind of diagram etched into the back of this plate."

"Fantastic." Huffing out a breath, Paris studied the

controls before them, then the schematic. "You read Gimlon?"

"How hard can it be?"

Paris shrugged. "I don't know if this is lights or not, but I think this and this here will bypass the computer and just apply power. I could be completely wrong." He fingered one of the circuits, then another.

"Why so tentative?"

Shrugging again, Paris fingered a few more. "Want me to try it? It could blow us to atoms."

What was there to lose? "Do it."

"We could wait for the Gimlon to get the lights on themselves," Paris suggested.

Yes, they could. Chakotay thought about that a moment, as the muddy light lapped against the circuits and Paris's face. "If they get the lights on, they'll find us. If we do, maybe we have a chance of catching them still recovering from all the damage we did."

Paris nodded. "Okay . . . here we go." His fingers moving slowly, he pulled a plasticlike housing away from one circuit line, then a second, and finally a third.

Trying to get a better look, Chakotay horseshoed around Paris to peek over his other shoulder.

With some hesitation, Paris rerouted alien circuits he was barely able to see. When the final changes were made and all the cables he'd pulled had been clicked into new places, there was still silence.

"Well?" Chakotay prodded.

Paris frowned . . . then shook his head. "This could take some time."

His chest tight, Chakotay nodded cheerlessly. "I know. I just wish I knew if we have it to spare."

CHAPTER

21

"WHAT ELSE DO YOU KNOW ABOUT THIS SECTOR?" CAUTIOUSLY, Janeway eyed the forward viewscreen, and the darkly colored nebula *Voyager* approached.

Bolis stood to Janeway's left, right hand on his chest, his fingers nervously stroking up and down. "Just that the *Marauder* has been known to retreat to these coordinates after battle."

"Mr. Kim?" Janeway twisted toward the Ops station.

"Sensors still inconclusive at this range, Captain. We'll need to be a lot closer, if not inside the nebula itself."

Closer was dangerous. The Gimlon vessels were heavily armored to compensate for their limited shield technology—and *Voyager* was the opposite. Entering the nebula would limit shield strength, if not make shields useless altogether and the ship would be like a turtle without its shell.

The *Marauder* had to be lured into the open.

"Composition of the nebula, Mr. Kim? Is it something we can ignite?" That had worked once, maybe it would again.

"Negative, Captain. Mostly inert gasses. Relatively low amounts of ignitable material."

Janeway looked at the expansive nebula as it filled the screen. On a cosmic scale it was probably collapsing inward to form a star, or was perhaps expanding outward as the

166

residue of an exploding sun. She hadn't bothered to check the astrometrics report that would tell the tale of this system, mainly because she didn't care. Life or death on the cosmic scale wasn't her concern. Life or death of her crew, and of billions of Edesians, held a firmer grip on her attention. "Let's get ready to go in—just in case Gimlon reinforcements show up," she said finally of the nebula, then tapped at her combadge. "Bridge to Engineering."

"Engineering. Seven-of-Nine reporting, Captain."

"Where's Lieutenant Torres?"

"Lieutenant Torres and Lieutenant Carey are sealing a plasma leak in conduit thirty-three delta."

"I need power rerouted from all nonessential systems to sensors and shields. Be ready to transfer away from shields and to the SIF generators if the nebula disrupts our deflectors beyond use."

"Yes, Captain. How much power should I reroute?"

The captain sighed. "As much as possible. Janeway out."

Two of her top engineers working on a plasma leak as *Voyager* went into battle, because Janeway had been unable to keep her crew together. One third of her crew gone at normal cruising could be dealt with . . . but at battle stations? Damage-control teams were composed of personnel not at duty stations during battle. With so many of her crew missing . . . she was fighting with one hand tied to her foot.

Even if they made it through this battle—through this war—how would they manage on their long journey home? How would her crew react once the loss of the others sank in? How would she react herself?

Janeway poked at the console screen next to her command chair. A tactical map of the nebula appeared, three-dimensional and spinning to show her all angles. "Harry, what about a probe?"

"I doubt we'd be able to receive telemetry from within the nebula, Captain."

The captain nodded and pushed herself up from her seat and toward the helm. "We can send a probe in here," she said, pointing at a coordinate on the navigational console, "have it store all data, then pick up the signal here when it comes out the other side."

Ensign Kim nodded, already plotting the course a probe

would need to go in at that point, read the interior of the nebula, and come back again. "Yes," he said. "That could work."

Janeway looked over to Harry's station. "Surprised?"

"No—not at all, Captain." If he wasn't, he looked it anyway.

Almost a light moment, but it didn't help the tension, and Janeway nodded instead of smiling.

"Launch probe."

Harry Kim pecked at his console. "Probe alpha away."

Janeway angled toward the main viewscreen. She needn't watch the probe as it streaked swiftly toward the extensive nebula, but seeing it gave her comfort. She was taking action, and that filled a little of the void she felt without Chakotay and Paris on her bridge. A little, as measured in nanolitres.

"Tuvok . . ." Janeway didn't return to her command chair, but instead hovered next to her security officer and temporary helmsman. "You said the frequency of subspace the Marauder used was unusual. Not usually scanned for. Will the probe pick up that wavelength?"

The Vulcan nodded once. "Yes, Captain, I have modified all sensor procedures to scan for that frequency. However, there is no certainty that such a low wave signature will be readable within the nebula, even by our probe. Obviously they chose this nebula as a place for regroup and repair specifically because of its sensor-dampening qualities."

Obviously. That was a standard tactic for many spacefaring military operations. Starfleet had no less than twenty bases or relay stations in different nebulae scattered across the Alpha quadrant. Perhaps more Janeway didn't know about. And despite its unstable nature, Chakotay and other Maquis used to hide in the Badlands along the Cardassian border.

Chakotay . . . the Badlands . . . Janeway barely ever thought about all that ancient history. The Maquis had become members of her crew, and Chakotay, their captain, had become the best first officer she'd had.

Anger, at Lekket and at herself, gnarled around her stomach like a starving dog. Chakotay was gone . . .

"Set up a random shield modulation," she ordered. "See if we can't get *some* protection."

Tuvok nodded. "Aye, Captain."

Pressing her lips into a thin line, Janeway took the feeling in her stomach and tried to push it away. "Take us to the intercept point with the probe. Ahead full at zero-seven-zero mark twelve, then z minus one A.U. at one-eighth power."

"Course set," Tuvok said, his nimble fingers dabbing at the helm console.

"Engage."

Only the hum of the engines and the forward viewscreen showed Janeway any movement. The nebula swirled around until it was below *Voyager,* and only the topmost swoop of dust and gas showed at the bottom of the screen.

Harry Kim bent over his scanners. "Probe should be here in seven . . . six . . . five . . . four . . . three . . . two . . . one."

Janeway tensed with anticipation, but the probe didn't emerge from the cloud. Not a speck of nebula moved to reveal the spent probe. Not when Harry said "Zero," nor when he counted "minus one . . . minus two . . ." until Janeway motioned for him to stop.

"Maybe it hit a thick chunk of gas and bounced off course," Janeway said ironically, more to herself than anyone else.

"Unlikely," Tuvok said.

"Sensors at maximum plus twelve percent," Harry reported. "Still unable to punch through interference."

"Someone destroyed it," Janeway said finally, then turned to Bolis, who rolled his neck in a sort-of shrugging motion.

"The *Marauder* is undoubtedly in there," he said.

"Undoubtedly," Janeway said, but she wasn't quite certain. "How many Edesian ships have been lost in this nebula?"

Bolis hesitated. "I cannot be sure of the exact number. More than we could spare."

"This is a trap. Come about. Reverse course," Janeway ordered, returning to the center seat. "One-half impulse power."

Stepping down to her side, Bolis leaned toward her. "Captain? Are you going to remove yourself from this conflict?"

"On the contrary. Grab a seat, Mr. Bolis," she said, gesturing to where Chakotay usually sat. "We may be in for a few bumps."

Bolis slowly lowered himself into the seat next to the captain.

"Tuvok, short out the shields."

"Captain?"

"Make it look like we're losing our shields. Either the *Marauder* isn't in there, or she's not alone. We're going to find out which. Harry, open a channel to the Edesian fleet."

"The entire fleet, Captain?"

"That was the order, Ensign. The entire fleet."

Harry patted at his controls. "You're on, Captain."

"Edesian fleet. This is Captain Kathryn Janeway of the Federation Starship *Voyager*. Proximity to the nebula at the coordinates provided have damaged our shields beyond swift repair. We are returning to rendezvous sixteen hours earlier than planned."

Janeway mouthed "close" to Kim, then turned to Tuvok. "Full shields on my command."

"Aye, Captain." Tuvok's hand hovered on his controls.

Cocking his head at Janeway, Bolis looked at her with narrowed eyes. "Why do you think this a trap?"

"I know it's a trap," Janeway said, taking in a short breath. "The *Marauder* is big. Nebulae like this hamper shields *and* impulse engines. She might even be more helpless in a nebula than we are—unable to maneuver as we could. We'd be all over her. Had there been some ships to defend her on the way here, maybe I'd have thought she was alone. But the chances of her destroying that probe, with her low maneuverability—without sensors and at the speed a probe travels . . . I don't believe it."

"If the Marauder is more vulnerable, then why not attack?" Bolis asked.

"Because if that massive vessel is in there, either it's not alone, and has a fleet of defenders, or *just* the fleet is in there, waiting to attack us. I don't think the Gimlon would leave their most powerful weapon unable to defend itself."

"You are very wise, Captain," Bolis said, the slightest smile twisting his lips.

Janeway simply nodded.

"Captain, I'm reading a disruption in the nebula," Harry said. "Shifting patterns within the normal flow."

"Stand by on shields."

Tuvok still had his thin fingers hovering just over the shield controls. "Standing by."

"Captain—" Harry's voice sounded anxious. "I'm reading three—no *five* vessels. Gimlon configuration."

"Let them chase us," Janeway ordered. "Course one seven nine, mark forty. Warp two."

"Aye, Captain."

"Raise shields."

"Full power available."

Voyager took off like a playful stallion, and the dogs she had taunted sped to follow.

Maybe the *Marauder* was hiding, repairing the damage Janeway and her crew had inflicted. Maybe—but *Voyager* would have to deal with five ships to find out.

The Gimlon ship closest fired first—plasma torpedoes that spread out into space and missed *Voyager's* maneuvers.

"Evasive substarboard," Janeway ordered. "Phasers, fire at will."

Voyager lanced out energy and caught one Gimlon vessel in its underbelly. Another Gimlon ship took two shots as it passed quickly, turning away and firing disruptor lines across the aft shields. A glancing blow, but not enough to slow Janeway down.

In unison, the three other enemy ships plunged toward *Voyager*, disruptors glowing. Powerful lightning sparked against the shields and buffeted the Starfleet vessel from side to side as it plowed through the attack.

"They are targeting our plasma conduits, Captain," Tuvok said, struggling with his dual duties of navigation and tactical control. "As well as our still-weakened dorsal shield generators."

"Target their impulse engines and deflector screens," Janeway ordered, grabbing onto the command chair as a flutter of sparks and smoke spread from the console next to her. "Why is this circuit overloading? Shut down this panel!"

"Targeting their impulse and deflector centers. Aye."

"Fire and maintain."

Again *Voyager* spun around and hurled forth massive bars of phaser power. Every shot hit, riveting each Gimlon vessel back against velvet space as if Janeway were pinning dead butterflies to a display board.

"Keep it up! Maintain!"

Unlike a normal phaser spread, once *Voyager* connected with each ship, the beams kept pounding in against the enemy's armor. Fiery spits connected *Voyager's* hot phaser ports with the Gimlon ships. The enemy tried to maneuver away, and had they been smart enough to move in opposite directions, that would have worked. But instead each captain was attempting to retreat back into the nebula. *Voyager* moved with them, raw energy punching almost directly from her warp core into the armor surrounding the enemy's engines.

"Captain—our phaser arrays are overheating!" Harry Kim's voice sounded the warning, but phaser arrays could take a pounding, and Janeway wasn't about to give up. Not yet.

"Maintain fire. Transfer coolant procedures."

"We don't have the coolant to spare, Captain."

In the pit of her stomach she knew she was taking more risk then necessary. But she also knew she could not give up—that it would only take a few seconds more before—

"Automatic phaser shutdown in five seconds, Captain!"

"Override!"

"Captain—we cannot risk you losing your offensive capabilities!" Bolis—on the edge of his chair—yelling at her.

Janeway heard him and ignored it. These people had killed a planet and her friends with it. They would succumb—they must—

One explosion, then another racked *Voyager* as debris scraped against her shields.

"Two hostiles destroyed, Captain."

"Discontinue phasers!" Janeway ordered as her ship

regained a level course and she took in a settling breath. "Slow to one half."

Voyager pulled back her powerful talons and the three remaining Gimlon vessels sped away at odd angles toward the nebula. They were flying out of control, through the debris left by their two destroyed comrades.

Janeway raked a strand of hair from her sticky forehead. "Status report."

Harry Kim's voice was much calmer now. "Semi-fusing of one phaser bank. Damage looks repairable. Coolant leaks on decks three, seven, nine, and in Engineering."

"And them?" She looked at the three ships, sparkle and electrical flame dotting the wake of their paths. They were leaking plasma and coolant both.

"Two ships completely destroyed. The other three have sustained major damage. Their engines are disabled. Deflectors too. Two of the three have life-support off-line. The other one's in trouble."

"Good shooting, Mr. Tuvok."

The Vulcan clicked at his console and turned just slightly to meet his Captain's eyes. "It is difficult to miss a nail with a sledge hammer, Captain."

"Hail them. Tell them we're willing to take them aboard. Unconditional surrender."

Harry nodded, sent the transmission, then looked up as the Captain met his gaze. "No response, Captain."

"Are their communications out?"

"Negative."

"Captain," Tuvok began, "with their deflectors disabled, they cannot enter the nebula."

"I know, Tuvok. It would tear them apart, even at half-impulse drift."

"They are getting very close, Captain."

Janeway rose. "They must know it. Why no response?" She looked to Bolis, but he was silent, watching the three ships on the forward viewer as they spiraled out of control.

"Ready tractor beams."

"Tractor beam control is off-line. Coolant leaks in the tractor generator."

"Stand by, transporter rooms."

His voice now a mirror of Janeway's own feelings, Harry Kim sounded very frustrated. "I can't get a lock. They're too close to the nebula."

No escape pods spat off their ships. They twirled toward the nebula, mere dots on the spacescape now . . .

Finally the gas cloud enveloped them, and Janeway could only watch as one explosion, then another, and finally a third made the giant gas cloud bubble and spurt in a momentary fit in its otherwise placid existence.

Sensors wouldn't tell her they were dead . . . but they were.

Janeway stared at the viewer and the nebula beyond, as it calmed after the unnatural disturbance. Five ships had attacked, and five had been beaten back.

Perhaps the *Marauder* was still hiding in that gaseous cloak. *Voyager* had beaten the guards, and now would have to find out if anything was even being guarded.

"Plot a course into the nebula, Mr. Tuvok."

The bridge was very silent, except for Bolis, who fidgeted awkwardly in his seat. Janeway glanced at him a moment, wondered what he was thinking, then looked back to the main viewer.

"Course plotted."

Janeway gathered herself. "Take us in."

CHAPTER

22

"DO YOU WANT ME TO TRY FOR A WHILE?" CHAKOTAY OFFERED Tom Paris the torch and the Gimlon rifle.

"I'm fine," Paris grumbled, not accepting relief from his work. "Just fine."

Chakotay nodded, but if Paris didn't get at least the lights on within five minutes he'd have to step aside. Time was running out. There could be a Gimlon soldier around the next corridor. "Interesting plan—just moving things around randomly."

"Ouch! Damn!" Paris pulled his hand away from the console as a cascade of sparks exploded forward. "What kind of stupid engineer puts the artificial gravity on its own system, but not life-support or the lights?"

"You okay?"

"Nope." Paris waved his hand back and forth, fanning his fingers. "I have now ten matching burns on each finger."

The rifle under his arm, Chakotay warmed one hand over his torch. "At least your hands are warm. This ship is losing heat. If it weren't so dark, I could see my breath."

"So, I'm the lucky one, burning my fingers off, is that it?"

"More or less."

"Hmmm."

For a while they were silent, but the awkwardness of that was nearly unbearable. Quiet made the situation seem more surreal, spooky. Here they were, standing in the middle of a dark ship, set adrift in strange space, air and heat leaking away. Chakotay wondered if they'd suffocate or freeze first. The numbness in his nose and ears told him that the cold would get them first.

"It's possible any remaining Gimlon soldiers used escape pods, otherwise they'd have had their systems back up by now."

"I'm working on it, Commander."

"I wasn't chastising you, Paris. I was making small talk."

Paris shifted his weight and glanced at Chakotay a moment, then looked back toward his work. "I'm sorry. This is very frustrating."

"We don't have to talk at all . . ." Chakotay was sure to make his tone soft. "But ten minutes ago you told me to keep talking because you were exhausted."

"I know . . . just talk about something else, okay?" Paris zapped his hand again, pulled back in pain, then dove back into the access port console to go at it again. "By the way, I've confirmed these *are* live circuits."

A soft chuckle from Chakotay broke the tension some, and he tried to talk about something lighter than their predicament. Almost anything would do.

"What's the first thing you'll do when we get back to the Alpha quadrant?" he asked.

"What?"

"You heard me."

Paris paused without looking up. "I don't like to think about it."

Surprised, Chakotay felt his brows crinkle and he noticed his face was getting colder and felt very stiff. He moved his head closer to the torch flame. "What do you mean?"

"Just what I said."

"Come on, Paris. You don't want to go home?"

"I don't want to think about going home right now," Paris said, reaching deep into the access panel. "Do you?"

"Of course. Why not?"

Paris chuckled mockingly. "I know we're closer to home, but do you feel it right now?"

"I guess not."

"You know what else? I've been working with the doctor a lot recently. What happens to him when we get home? What happens to Seven? To B'Elanna? I'm very close to these people. I'll feel like I've lost my family."

"We don't have to break up. Who knows?"

"This crew is a ticket for the Delta quadrant, Chakotay. It's not being played back home."

Chakotay took a step closer to Paris and the access panel. "I'm sure that considering all that's happened, all we've been through—"

Again, Paris gave a short, pained laugh. "They'll give us all Starfleet commissions? Even the Doctor? And Seven? And B'Elanna? Where would we all go?"

"I don't know."

"Neither do I. And I don't always feel this way. I don't always think about it. Hardly ever. But . . . with the hope that we get home soon . . . is the feeling that I don't want to be anywhere but *on the way* home. You know?"

"Yeah. I guess I do." Chakotay hadn't considered it, but Paris had some valid points.

"We're a good crew together." Switching hands, Paris maneuvered himself around for a better reach, then realized it was too awkward and switched back. "Even Seven is shaping up."

Chakotay shook his head. "Is that a pun?"

Tom Paris pulled his charred hand from the Gimlon access console and straightened himself. "Nope. B'Elanna would kill me."

"And I would tell her," Chakotay said.

They both laughed, but once they were silent an eerie stillness settled and connected them for a long moment before Paris returned to his work.

Chakotay looked from Paris to the torch, then back to Paris. How many other people would be slightly more content with their lives now than before? How many others now on the *Voyager* crew, especially from the Maquis part of the crew, felt the same as Paris?

"I don't know what to say," Chakotay admitted finally.

"I'm pretty sure that's a first," Paris said, his head half in the access panel.

Another electrical snap resonated through the corridor, and a flash of spark spat past Paris. With that, the lights came on.

Dim emergency lights, but lights nevertheless.

Paris laughed as he looked up at the illuminated ceiling and sucked on his blistering index finger. "Let there be light."

"I'm impressed."

"Don't be," Paris said, still smiling. "I have no idea how I did it."

Chakotay dropped his makeshift torch on the deck and snuffed it with his boot. "Are you sure you *did* do it?"

"Are you doubting my ability to stumble into a good thing?"

"It could have been Chen or one of the others . . . or it could have been the Gimlon."

"What about your escape-pod theory?"

"Just a theory."

Paris nodded slowly, and suddenly the light didn't seem as bright to Chakotay.

"This is about all I can do from this access console, according to the schematic," Paris said.

"Assuming you're reading it right."

"Assuming that, yes. Engineering or the bridge should be the next stop. It looks like I could reroute more circuits from one of those two hubs."

"Okay. We have to get to the bridge," Chakotay said.

"There could be Gimlon on the bridge."

"You want to hold the rifle?"

Paris shook his head and held up his red, burned fingers. "Only if it's made of butter."

"This isn't the best way to surprise them," Paris whispered as Chakotay attempted to pry open the hatch to the bridge.

"There *is* no way to surprise them," Chakotay grunted.

"They'd have to be dead not to hear me forcing the door open."

"That was my point."

Paris was teetering on being annoying again. He might have pain in his fingers, but Chakotay couldn't feel *his* fingers, toes, nose, or ears at all anymore. But his back still stung from the injury he had sustained hours ago.

"Just be ready to fire," he told Paris.

"Then you be ready to duck," Paris said, his voice hushed.

Chakotay would be, if he could get the door open at all. He had wedged his fingertips through the small crack between the hatch slabs, but no power was going to that door, and there didn't appear to be a manual override.

The door gave a little, perhaps a quarter of an inch each way, but wouldn't budge past that. Chakotay pulled his hands away, and when he looked down at his fingers he saw deep white indentations where he'd been pushing against the door. "We need a lever," he said finally, giving up whispering altogether.

Paris handed him the rifle. "Here," he said, and Chakotay saw the frost of the man's breath. "Blast it already."

Chakotay hadn't wanted to do that. He didn't want to cause more damage to an already crippled ship. But he took the rifle anyway, apparently pulling it too quickly from Paris's grip. Paris waved his hand in pain and blew on his fingers.

"Sorry," Chakotay said, then motioned for Paris to step back.

"It's on the highest setting," Paris said.

"You going to assure me we're not knocking out more circuits?"

"Not according to the schematic we found."

"If you're reading it right."

"Details, details . . ."

With a sigh that felt too cold because it was pulled through his mouth and not his nose, Chakotay aimed at the door and fired.

The sonic whine crushed forward, collapsing the hatchway at first, then vaporizing it in a cloud of gaseous metal.

Chakotay felt the warmth of the blast, even as it quickly dissipated, and he stepped forward partly to continue to feel the heat on his face. But he held his rifle up as well, and called into the bridge "Don't move!"

No one did.

As he and Paris stepped through the doorway, making sure not to touch the still smoldering bulkhead, five Gimlon soldiers lay at their feet, centered in the middle of the bridge, around what was probably the command seat.

Cold air had preserved their bodies, and the bridge didn't smell at all. In fact, there was a layer of frost all about.

"Suicide?" Paris wondered, still whispering.

"Because the ship was going to self-destruct," Chakotay supposed. "Or maybe to keep us from using their knowledge." He shook his head gravely.

Then he realized that shaking his head actually hurt. He felt a bit dizzy, and had to lean against the nearest console for support.

"We need life-support back fast," he said. "The air is getting thin."

Paris nodded and reached out to hold Chakotay's arm. "I'm surprised it's this thin and this cold so fast. There might be a hull breach somewhere."

"Maybe not," Chakotay said, regaining his footing, trying to take his breath in with short but filling heaves. "If all engines are shut down, there's no super-hot plasma to keep the ship warm."

"Sit here," Paris said, guiding Chakotay to a seat next to a console. "Watch this console, and I'll see if I can get it running. I'll look for access to the circuit hub."

Chakotay sat, the rifle still in his arms, and looked at the dead Gimlon soldiers, frost-covered and peaceful. Paris looked for an access panel along the bulkheads, and found one about two meters from the station where Chakotay was.

"According to the other schematic, this should be it," Paris grunted as he pried off the access plate.

Feeling more refreshed, Chakotay pushed himself up so he could see better into the port Paris had opened. As he did, he rested his hand on the console and felt a powdery substance stick to his fingers. He rubbed it between thumb and forefinger, then smelled it but didn't taste it.

"Fire suppression," he said quietly. "There was no air in here before we cracked the door. It was probably sucked out—and this fire retardant released."

Paris was now lying on the deck, his head at the access port, the schematic on the reverse of the panel propped up against the wall. "Maybe it was their preferred method of suicide."

"Maybe," Chakotay said and readied his rifle. "Or maybe there was just a fire and they were caught. An offline computer can't read life forms."

"Without the computer, maybe the fire suppression wouldn't have been triggered," Paris said, almost absent-mindedly as he continued to study the new circuits.

"I'm not going to assume they've all committed suicide," Chakotay said, taking a few steps toward Paris, but also keeping an eye on the hole they'd blown in the hatchway. "Finding anything?"

"Yeah. This is beginning to make sense," Paris said, eyeing the hub circuits with new intent. "Gravity seems to have a fail-safe power supply so that other areas can be worked on."

"They thought of this for gravity but not lights and life-support?"

"Well, according to this—again, if I'm understanding these symbols—lights and life-support and structural-integrity field generators are all on an even more powerful fail-safe system, which you blew out with the automation." After a moment, Paris looked up, smiling. "But you also saved our lives, so I guess it evens out."

"So we've got lights, why don't we have life-support and SIF?"

"Look here." Paris propped himself up on one elbow and took hold of the plate with the schematic. He held it so Chakotay could see the etchings. "Lights, life-support, SIF, all on this line here."

"Got it."

"We blew that line when we torched automation."

Chakotay shrugged. Alien technology could seem so familiar, and yet be so confusing. "Why?"

"Because they were using that protected circuit net as the basis of the automation power. Probably smart if you didn't have anyone to quickly reroute power when a normal line was frizzed."

"I see," Chakotay said. "That line is safer, more protected, so they used it for automation. Which I knocked out. How do you know all this?"

"Ever go picnicking with B'Elanna?"

Yes, he had. But it was no secret that Paris and Torres were an item, and so Chakotay decided he needn't relate his picknicking experience. "Can't say I've had the pleasure."

"Me neither," Paris said, re-propping the schematic panel against the bulkhead and leaning back into the access port. "Last two times we tried, we ended up in a Jeffries tube rerouting power to something."

"And you picked all this up like that?"

"And I can hand someone a laser-spanner like a pro."

"Can you reroute power here?"

"Eventually, I think. But I don't know what everything is."

Chakotay had been getting more excited at their prospects, but now he was a bit disappointed. "You can't prioritize—find life-support and get that on-line first?"

"Nope. We have lights. Next I might get life-support back on, or for all I know, the showers. If the Gimlon bathe."

"I don't need the showers on—"

"Well . . . I wasn't going to say anything, but in fact—"

"Very funny, Paris, but that's not what I mean. We need life-support back—fast." To emphasize his point, Chakotay blew warm air into the hollow of his cold clasped hands. A stream of breath frost filtered through his fingers.

Paris glanced up, a sincere look painted on his face sideways, as always. "Look, there's just no way to know what line is what."

"How did you get the lights on first?" Chakotay asked, pacing back toward the chair he'd sat on when they first entered the bridge.

"I didn't. I just stopped when I got to the lights. For all the connections I made and pulled apart, I could have had life-support on a dozen times by now."

"Wonderful." What if he couldn't find the right connection in time? All aboard would either suffocate or freeze. And there was no way to know how long Paris had to keep looking for the right circuit.

"Start hooking things up," Chakotay ordered. "And hurry."

23

CHAPTER

23

"ALL STOP," JANEWAY ORDERED, AND *VOYAGER* SLID TO A hover just before where the nebula's gas would begin to hamper sensors.

"You're not going in, Captain?" Bolis asked.

The captain turned slowly and met the Edesian's eyes. "I was going to," she said. "But then I decided to waste another torpedo casing and send in another probe." She turned to Harry Kim. "Ready, Ensign?"

"Ready, Captain."

"Ready, Mr. Bolis?"

Bolis looked at Janeway, then at Kim, and then at his own boots. "Of course, Captain."

Janeway nodded. "Now, Mr. Kim."

The probe marked a line of space into the nebula, bisecting the main viewer with a plasma trail that quickly dissipated into nothingness.

Moving into the nebula after one trap had been uncovered would be too hasty, she'd decided. Crashing about without shields, possibly against ships with more armor than *Voyager* had, would be a dunsel move—more gut than gray matter. She was letting her passion run too hot, and her mind needed to be in control if she was to stop the Gimlon from destroying more billions of lives.

"Intercept the probe, Mr. Tuvok."

"Aye, Captain."

And moments later—long moments—the probe slid out the other side of the gas cloud, with *Voyager* there to meet it.

"Receiving telemetry now, Captain," Harry Kim called from the upper deck of the bridge.

Janeway waited silently, her eyes lingering first on the nebula, then on Harry's face as he read the incoming data.

"No disturbances of sufficient mass to suggest the *Marauder* is within the nebula, Captain," he said finally.

"Readings that suggest any other vessels?"

The young ensign shook his dark head. "No. All readings are nominal."

"Empty," Janeway whispered to herself as she rose from the command chair and slowly turned to Bolis. "Except for the five ships that attacked us."

"I don't know what happened, Captain," Bolis offered, shaking his head with regret.

Janeway felt her lips press into a line. "Of course." Her voice was calm, still almost a whisper. "No one could have predicted this." She motioned to one of the guards who flanked the turbolift. "Collect your thoughts in your quarters," Janeway said evenly. "I'll want to talk to you at our briefing in thirty minutes. We'll want your help in planning our next move."

Before rising, Bolis seemed to pause, as if considering her words one by one. Finally he rose, and with the guard, departed the bridge.

As soon as the lift doors closed, Janeway pounced up toward the tactical station. "Mr. Kim, transfer all subspace frequency logs for the last six hours up here."

A ghost of perplexity rippled across his face. "Aye, Captain."

Already hovering over Tuvok's usual console, Janeway saw the data as it was transferred. She saw what she expected to see, what she hoped she wouldn't see, and called to her Vulcan security chief. "Commander, have Commodore Lekket brought to the bridge. Bring Bolis back here too. Then come look at this."

With a short nod, Tuvok followed the command and gave the order to his subordinates. He then released the helm to a junior officer and joined his captain at the computer console, which held her glare.

When he saw the data, and its unmistakable spike of subspace communication activity, he nodded gravely.

Bolis was ushered back onto the bridge by his Starfleet guard, and a look of confusion was very obviously etched into his alien visage.

Moments later, when Commodore Lekket was escorted onto the bridge, Janeway noted that he did not look surprised or confused. He looked somber, as always, but also a little indignant. He had gotten his second wind, perhaps, and was ready to spit in Janeway's face for trusting Bolis, the man who'd betrayed him and let her escape.

Neither Edesian, however, asked why they had been brought before Janeway, who with a gesture had them taken to the lower deck of the bridge.

As they stood there, each man with a guard at his side, Janeway first passed one and then the other on her way to the command chair.

She didn't sit. Instead, she went up to Lekket and placed her fingers around the pendants that hung from his neck. "Here," she said, "was my mistake." A quick, sharp pull, and the chain snapped at his neck and the pendant was in her hand completely. "You've been contacting your government." She wasn't asking a question. "And that's my fault. I let Mr. Bolis give you his rank pendants without thinking that it was also your method of communication." She gripped the offending piece of utilitarian jewelry and studied its simplicity. Slightly warm to the touch, it must have enough compressed energy stored to reach quite far. Not like her own combadge, which needed to be relatively close to *Voyager* to work over any distance. "I was foolish," she said finally. "But I won't underestimate either of you again."

"Captain—" Bolis began a protest, but Janeway hammered him with a glare.

"I know. You didn't expect this," she said, pivoting toward him. "You didn't think he'd use your ceremonial gesture in such a manner, right?"

Janeway didn't wait for an answer. Moving his communicator between her hands, she turned back toward Lekket. "You contacted your government."

"Yes," Lekket said, but he did not say it sheepishly. He sounded proud of his action. Why not? She would have been, if she'd been in his position. Which she had been several hours earlier.

"And you told them what happened, and that we were going after the *Marauder,* and that in your opinion we were headed to the wrong place." She let her voice fill the bridge. Let everyone hear anger in her voice.

"Yes."

"Did you send any other message?" she asked.

"No," he said hesitantly.

She knew what he was wondering: Why did she know everything, but ask that?

"This is a unique piece of equipment," Janeway said, admiring the communicator, holding it up to her eye. She tossed it to Tuvok, who caught it with ease. "It seems to have the ability to focus its broadcast to a specific coordinate."

Lekket's expression grew more befuddled. "Yes, that's right."

Janeway glanced around the bridge and noticed that the only expressions that were not confused were Tuvok's . . . and certainly her own.

She was doing this in a roundabout way, but she wanted to know for certain that her grim hunch was correct.

"We nearly fell into a deadly trap," Janeway said, "because you sent a message to your government."

Shaking his head before she even finished her charge, Lekket protested adamantly. "No, Captain. I swear to you. I made sure my transmission would only be received by the Edesian homeworld. To intercept it, a vessel or listening post would have to be directly in the path of communication, and then I wouldn't have been able to communicate with those I wished to contact."

"You gave him the ability to send a message in the first place," Janeway accused Bolis.

"Unwittingly, I assure you, Captain," Bolis said, his voice much calmer than Lekket's. "If his transmission gave away your position—"

She cut him off. "It didn't."

At this, finally Bolis did look somewhat surprised. His eyes gave him away. They flicked toward Lekket, then to each security guard, to Tuvok, and avoided Janeway directly. She could tell he was looking at a point just beyond her . . . and not into her eyes.

"There was another transmission interlaced with your transmission, Lekket," Janeway announced to the commodore, but kept her glare firmly locked on Bolis. "This vessel keeps data records of every subspace spike and transmission. Detailed records. Records that can be analyzed for location of origin, duration, and about thirty other things you probably can't imagine."

Bolis said nothing. He probably knew there was nothing to say.

"Betrayal seems to be a habit with you, Mr. Bolis," Janeway said, her teeth gritted in anger. She wasn't sure why Bolis had rigged the communicator to send a message toward Gimlon space, but she would know eventually—by the time she was done with him.

"I don't know what you're talking about, Captain. I—"

She silenced him with a raised hand. "Please," Janeway said. "I think many things of Commodore Lekket. Treason against his people, in the form of communicating knowingly with his enemy, isn't one of them."

The captain took a step forward, and her muscles seemed on fire. "You rigged your communicator so that it would transmit a covert message to the Gimlon when Lekket sent his message to the Edesians. If we noticed this, you expected us to blame Lekket for his transmission, but not for yours. You didn't think we'd see that, did you?"

Again, Bolis said absolutely nothing. Something in his look changed, however. His eyes glazed over a bit, and his jaw seemed to tense.

"Why?" Lekket asked the question of his former confidant, and the commodore's voice was heavy with real emotion—regret, confusion, anger, and probably some fear. "You come from a good family . . ."

Bolis didn't answer. He looked only at Janeway, who had motioned for Lekket's guard to move toward Bolis.

"Were you recruited by the Gimlon, or are you a plant? Don't you even care about the billions of lives lost on that planet?" Janeway asked.

"Does it matter, Captain?" Bolis said roughly, almost a hissing.

The captain shook her head. "Not to me." She motioned to the guards. "Get this trash off my bridge."

"You'll die a painful death, Captain," Bolis said as the guards wrenched him through the lift doors.

Janeway turned back to Lekket. "I should have listened to you," she told him.

Seemingly drained again, Lekket's soft voice broke Janeway's tension. "We should have listened to each other. Now it is too late."

The captain disagreed. "Not yet it's not—"

"Yes, Captain. It is," Lekket said. "The *Marauder* is headed toward the heart of Edesia. And because we do not have enough vessels to stop her, my government is sending every last ship to the Gimlon homeworld."

"No," Janeway said, and lowered herself absently into the command chair. "Mutually assured destruction? What does that solve?"

"Perhaps the *Marauder* will be diverted back home," Lekket offered. "Long enough to evacuate some people from my planet. Some of us might survive. And if we destroy their homeworld in the process, they won't have time to come after those that do survive."

Janeway couldn't believe what she was hearing . . . from three billion dead to thirty, or sixty—who knew how many?

"They must have planetary defenses . . . you must have—"

"Our last ships are on a suicide mission, Captain. Filled with antimatter. So long as we make it into orbit, their world is dead. And without their world, the Gimlon have nothing. It will take them centuries to recover—those who are left."

"And your world? How does that save Edesia?"

Lekket lowered his head sadly. "It does not. But at least we will be the last to die."

Small consolation, in a universe of corpses.

"There must be another way—" Janeway protested.

"Captain—we're reading an energy buildup. Radiation is flooding the ship!"

She turned to Kim. Tuvok was already at the ensign's station as she twisted around.

"It's the warp-dampener," Tuvok reported. "It's on a buildup to overload."

Janeway leaned over, pressing against the handrail that separated the lower and upper decks of the bridge. "How long?"

"Three minutes before the radiation becomes fatal."

Her mind searched for an order she could give. A way to stop this from happening . . .

"Bolis must still have control of the device, Captain," Lekket said. "We won't see the end of this war."

Somewhere there was an answer to it all . . . but Janeway had precious little time to find it.

Perhaps no one would see an end to this war, she thought bitterly. *Because no one will be left.*

CHAPTER
24

CHAKOTAY'S FINGERS WERE WARMING UP. HE COULD FEEL HIS ears. He could feel his toes. He could feel the pain in his back again.

Paris had gotten the life-support systems on, and the computers as well. Progress seemed so slow, however, that Chakotay couldn't help but wonder how many things had happened to *Voyager* since they'd been split from their ship. Did Janeway think them dead? Missing? They were missing, and perhaps close to being dead.

The other thought that Chakotay didn't like to contemplate was that Janeway and *Voyager* might be dead by now.

No, he didn't believe that. He couldn't.

He had to remain positive. Things were looking up. Chen and his team had found Engineering, and with it more dead Gimlon soldiers. Mass suicide, apparently a rule when the ship was in self-destruct. Probably to ensure that no one would get cold feet before the ship was destroyed and try to cancel implementation.

Cold feet. That's what they all had now.

A shudder went down Chakotay's spine. Partly because of the chilled air, and partly because he feared he was beginning to think like Paris. Puns were not his usual style.

As Chakotay tried to get the computers not just on-line

but translating into a language he could understand, Paris got communications running. Soon Chen was able to make his report from Engineering, using the internal Gimlon intercoms.

"Commander, everything seems intact down here, but the engines are completely off," Chen said, his voice more excited than scared.

"Understood, Ensign. Have you got power to the computers down there?"

"Aye, sir."

Paris looked up from his cubbyhole on the deck. "Told you I knew what I was doing."

"As I remember it, you said you didn't have a clue what you were doing," Chakotay said.

"I was trying to lower expectations."

"It worked." Chakotay returned to the comm. "Chen, I'm working on using previous *Voyager* communications this ship intercepted as a template to create a translation program. I'll let you know when you can try the computers again. In the meantime, see if you can get battery power warming up the engines."

"Yes, sir. The other teams are here. We should have enough to get this bucket going soon."

"Keep up the good work. Chakotay out."

"You know," Paris began, his voice muffled by the duct around his head, "it will take at least an hour to warm the plasma enough to get the engines going. And the batteries might be too drained to do it that quickly. Chen is dreaming."

"Let's worry about crossing one burned-out bridge at a time, huh, Paris?"

"Right."

The Gimlon language as displayed on Chakotay's computer screen was as confusing as any he'd seen before. There were perhaps three dozen different letters, or characters, and so far he was unable to even determine what was a number and what wasn't. It was possible that letters doubled as numbers and one could tell what was what only by the context.

That wouldn't be helpful, since he didn't even know in what order the alphabet went.

"I wish I had a tricorder," Chakotay said.

Paris could be heard "harumph"-ing from the deck below. "You wish? I wish I had a toolbox the size of a shuttle craft."

A flash drew Chakotay's attention, but the flicker didn't come from anywhere near Paris. It came from the small viewscreen that must have been the Gimlon bridge's forward viewer.

"Was that you?"

"If something happened," Paris said, "then yes, it was me. What happened? I just connected a circuit."

"Stand by." Chakotay stepped toward another console, one that had just come alive with lights and colors. "I think you got the viewscreen working. Which wouldn't be on its own circuit. Maybe that's the sensors?"

"Could be." Paris pulled his head from the access port and sat up to watch Chakotay.

Rows of switches and blinking panels with symbols Chakotay didn't understand seemed to flash randomly. He looked for a pattern, but didn't see one. "I guess I'll just see if any particular switch does something."

"Hey, that's my plan," Paris called.

First he pressed one panel, then another. The console bleeped at him pleasingly, but seemed to do nothing.

After thirty seconds of this, on his twelfth button, the viewscreen opposite them came alive.

Space . . . the stars were unmoving, but were there . . . Suddenly Chakotay felt like they were part of the universe again. They were on a ship, not adrift in a tin can. Well, they were still adrift in a tin can, but now they had a window.

Looking down at a screen that had changed from a bland Gimlon insignia to grid-map space, Chakotay studied the new console. "Short-range sensors," he said. "You're really catching on to these systems, I guess."

Paris held up his hands. "And I only had to lose half my fingers."

"Uh-oh." Chakotay saw a large blip, and wished he'd had some way to run a sensor diagnostic—or at least refresh the display. "We might have company."

"Company? I don't like the sound of that," Paris said.

"I don't like the look of it." Chakotay pointed to the viewscreen. "I'm going to try to get a visual."

After a few meanderings around the console panel, he did, and as both Starfleet officers looked up, the *Marauder* filled their viewer.

"The *Marauder*, with about seven escorts," Chakotay said, his throat suddenly dry.

"It looks like they're headed right for us," Paris said incredulously.

Chakotay checked the sensor console. "I think they are. I don't suppose you could get warp power and navigation up in the next five minutes?"

Paris didn't turn. He kept staring at the screen—at the *Marauder*, as it lumbered toward them—a giant hulk whose ugly form meant death itself. "Before or after I write my will?"

"Either."

"Not a chance."

CHAPTER

25

"WARNING, LEVEL ONE RADIATION CONTAMINATION. DANGER-ous levels of radiation detected. Warning . . ."

"Shut that off."

"Captain, there's nothing you can do."

"Mr. Lekket, with all due respect, *shut up!*" The captain jabbed at her combadge. "Janeway to Security! Get Bolis back up here!" She spun toward Tuvok. "How long?"

"We have two minutes and sixteen seconds before radiation will cause widespread burns among the crew."

She took that information and thought for only a brief moment. Even brief moments were too long to wait. "Janeway to Engineering!"

"Engineering. Torres here."

"We need a radiation shield around the dorsal strut."

"We're trying, captain, but we don't have anything that strong."

"Reroute power through the warp engines directly."

"Aye, Captain, but we'll lose warp propulsion. We'll be as good as dead in space."

"Do it! If we don't get that forcefield up in less than two minutes, we'll be dead anyway."

"Aye. Engineering out."

The turbolift doors slid open and Bolis was dragged back

onto the bridge. He stared at Janeway, his eyes flat and meaningless. If he cared that everyone on board was in danger of dying, including himself, he didn't show it.

"How are you controlling the radiation?"

Bolis stared at her. There was a flicker behind those motionless eyes, perhaps a moment of decision. He needn't give Janeway anything if they were all going to die, and he knew it.

Continued silence seemed to be his verdict.

Janeway wanted to wrap her fingers around his neck. She wanted to squeeze until answers popped out of his mouth and eyes and nose and ears. She wanted it to be painful for him, as it must have been for the billions killed by the Gimlon.

Was he a Gimlon, or was he just a turncoat? It didn't really matter.

Seconds ticked by too quickly. She wanted a report from Torres on whether they could modify contamination fields through warp power, but wasting the time to find out could mean everyone's lives.

"Tuvok?"

Tuvok was next to Kim. When had he moved? "Radiation levels are still climbing, Captain. We have one minute, thirty-six seconds."

"Scan him for a transmitter. I want to know how he's doing it."

The Vulcan dabbed at Ensign Kim's console. "Scanning . . . no transmission devices."

Bolis looked toward Tuvok a moment, but his expression remained very blank. Almost distant. As far as he was concerned, Janeway was dead, and everything else was dead, too. That was his look. Dead.

Janeway wasn't going to accept death, even if it was a little more than a minute from her. She jumped past Bolis and toward the tactical station. "He had access to the computer. There must be a program that sets off the radiation if he doesn't stop it from happening at regular intervals."

The guard holding his arm, Bolis awkwardly turned toward Janeway. He pursed his lips slightly, in what might have been a tight smile. "You are correct, Captain, but there's no way to stop it now. Perhaps if you had three hours to break the encryption code . . . but you don't."

Three steps and she could be on him. But that would be futile. Normal containment fields would break down soon, and the flood of radiation would quickly burn the crew beyond repair, Bolis too.

The captain thumbed a control on the tactical board. "Torres, what've you got?"

"We're ready to try it now, Captain."

Janeway gestured to the helmsman. "Take us out of warp."

"Aye, Captain. We're out."

"Go ahead, B'Elanna."

The engines whined as if they were going to leap back into warp, but the sound was different than usual. The subspace envelope was not being created. Instead, the power used for that was being diverted to the containment-field system.

Lights dimmed. The console at Janeway's hands dimmed as well, then everything returned to normal.

"Radiation is blocked, Captain," Tuvok said, and even sounded a tad surprised.

Janeway took Bolis's gaze again, and he still seemed a dull palette of grays. If he was irritated he didn't show it.

"B'Elanna?" Janeway said.

"We're all here, Captain. I don't believe it, but the power is holding."

The captain nodded. "Excellent job, Lieutenant. To all of you." She turned her head to Tuvok. "Standard radiation decontamination procedures for everyone, Mr. Tuvok."

"Aye, Captain."

Bolis was still silent and Janeway's glance rested on him for a moment as she continued with her engineer. "How much time did we buy, B'Elanna?"

"That depends," Torres said. *"Several hours if we stay put."*

"And if we don't?"

"Captain, I'm not even sure we can get the engines to work in conjunction with the containment fields. We're pumping a lot of power through circuits that don't normally carry such a charge. If we go to warp by siphoning off the

energy from where we have it going, a spike to the whole system could blow out the containment fields, and we'd be dead in seconds."

"All right," Janeway said gravely. "Try to work it out. We can't sit here forever. Janeway out."

The last few words she said, Janeway said looking straight at Bolis again.

"Captain—" Lekket said.

She shook her head. She wanted to continue staring at the man who had managed to betray both herself and Lekket. She wanted to know what he was thinking—why he'd done this. How could he passionately talk about morality and values and pretend commitment to those things, and yet be complicit with a government that saw murder as a valid form of political persuasion?

He had fooled her. Fooled Lekket. And fooled the Edesian Fleet for a very long time.

But why wasn't he embittered? After all, he'd lost.

"I won," Janeway said finally.

Bolis shrugged slightly. Just enough to convey that he'd heard her.

"You don't think so?" Neither did she, not sitting here in empty space while two worlds tried to annihilate one another. But she wanted to know why he didn't think so.

"It doesn't matter what I think. You said so yourself."

She nodded. It didn't really matter why, she told herself. And yet it did. "I want to know why," she said after a pause.

When Bolis spoke, his tone was noncommittal. "Because it is my job."

Janeway felt her brow crinkle. "You did this for money?"

Bolis tried to take a step but his guard yanked at his arm and received a glare from the captured spy. "Money, power . . . it's much the same."

"On the contrary," Tuvok said. "Money is a tool. In a free market, a tangible result of selling one's time. Power is the ability to control, while money, in a free society, is merely an instrument with which to trade."

Bolis smiled thinly and shrugged. "As you wish. Since Gimlon does not have a free market, it doesn't really matter."

Janeway glanced at Tuvok; he accepted this with a nod.

The Vulcan's ability to attempt debate with a man who was a killer, and a cold-blooded one at that . . . well, it just amazed her. He'd heard a comment that he couldn't let stand on its face, so he didn't.

After a moment, her attention slid back to Bolis. "But now you won't get to spend what you've earned," she said.

He shrugged yet again, more with his brows than his shoulders. "I'm a professional, Captain. All business has risk."

Somehow, that infuriated her more. That this was only a job to him—not a passion, not a political goal, but a personal ambition to do his murderous job and do it well. . . .

He sickened her. Physically. She'd never condone his actions, but if he had murdered because he believed his way of life was in danger, or because he believed it was right within the bounds of his own warped sense of reality . . . that was one thing. It was another to murder because it was a vocational skill at which one excelled.

None of that really mattered, Janeway told herself. As she thought about this, and as she stared at Bolis's dry and hideously flat expression, there was a mass of Edesian ships headed toward the Gimlon homeworld. And toward Edesia moved the *Marauder* and its caravan of destruction. Those were the facts that mattered. That, and the reality that Janeway was stranded in the middle of enemy territory.

If she could get from Bolis the information she needed to turn off the warp-dampener's radiation field . . . she'd be a warp nine ship in a sector of warp five wannabes. She'd have a chance to stop the absolute destruction of two worlds.

Bottom line was, she had someone in her custody who had information she wanted.

"Mr. Tuvok, take him to sickbay. Have the doctor administer a . . . relaxing agent. Something that might get him to tell us that encryption code."

"Yes, Captain."

Even this didn't faze Bolis, and Janeway wished it had. Little goals—getting the man to lower his mask of horrible professionalism—seemed almost as important as the bigger goal of finding out what he knew and what he'd done to her ship.

She pushed that thought away as best she could. This wasn't a game, wasn't a battle of wits or personal goals. It was a battle for lives, not egos.

Tuvok took charge of Bolis from the security guard, and began to usher the prisoner toward the turbolift. This time the enemy issued no threat, and because he had last time, Janeway wondered if his warning that she would die a painful death was less an attempt at intimidation, and had been meant more as a warning—from one "professional" to another.

That didn't matter either. His thoughts, his feelings, her thoughts and feelings—it was all minutiae in a greater concern. People were going to die, and as of now, Janeway was helpless to stop it.

She couldn't let that happen.

"Janeway to Engineering."

"Torres here."

"I need that warp speed, B'Elanna. I need it soon."

"Seven and I are working on it, Captain."

"I know," Janeway said, barely loud enough for the comm to pick up. "Hurry."

CHAPTER

26

"How far off?" Paris asked the question somewhat breathlessly, as the massive *Marauder* and the other Gimlon ships headed toward their decrepit hijacked ship.

Painfully, Chakotay bent over the alien console and tried to glean some useful information. Life-support systems online meant warmer air, and for that his extremities were grateful, but his back was another matter. The pain in his back had finally been dulled by the cold. That protection was now gone, and he felt his tight, injured skin with every movement.

"I can't tell how close they are," he said after studying the screen a moment. "If we're seeing a one-to-one ratio on the viewer, they'll be here in a few minutes. That doesn't give us much time."

"To what? Pray?"

"No," Chakotay said, "to prepare to take over one of those escorts."

"Oh," Paris said flatly. "Of course."

"I'm not kidding, Paris. When they board this vessel, we have to be ready to take their working ship in exchange for this shell." Chakotay stabbed at the button to the comm system. "Bridge to Engineering."

"Chen here, sir. Still nothing to report yet on main power, sir."

"Change of plans, ensign. We need your group to fan out and find this ship's armory."

"Assuming they have one," Paris added.

"They have one," Chakotay said. "Find it, Mr. Chen. And meet us at the docking port as soon as you can. It's on the lowest deck."

"Aye, aye, sir!"

Chakotay nodded to himself and switched the comm back off. He felt Paris pull him gently away from the console.

"No matter how gung-ho that kid is," Paris said, "that doesn't mean he'll find a cache of weapons."

Holding Paris's gaze for a long moment, Chakotay finally decided to say nothing in response. Maybe Paris was right—maybe they couldn't find enough weapons in time. But they had four rifles. If all else failed, those would have to do.

Turning toward the sensor console, Chakotay pointed to an internal layout display of the ship. "We have to get here, without turbolifts. Any ideas?"

Paris grinned. "Turbolifts should be running," he said. "I didn't think we'd have time to use ladders if we got this tug running."

Chakotay felt his lips curl into a slight smile. "You never cease to amaze me, Paris."

"Finally, you're getting to know me."

"Yes, I . . ." His voice trailed off as he and Paris noticed the *Marauder* and her smaller escorts veering away from their position. "They're not stopping," Chakotay said.

"Finally!" Paris said. "Something's going our way."

"No, I *want* them to stop."

From his position just a few feet away, Chakotay believed he could hear Paris huff lightly under his breath. "You're kidding, right?" Paris said.

"No." Chakotay shook his head. "We have numbers on them, we have surprise on them, and if we find more weapons, we'll outgun them."

Whatever Paris thought behind his incredulous expression, Chakotay didn't know, and Paris didn't say anything more about it. He just shrugged his shoulders and turned toward the exposed panel on which he'd been working.

"You're the boss," he said. "But if they're not stopping for one of their own disabled ships, we'll have to get this one working."

Chakotay chewed his lower lip a moment. The ship they were on was damaged and they were having trouble repairing the systems without main computer help. They couldn't even read the sensors correctly without the computer to translate the Gimlon language for them.

"No," Chakotay said after a moment's silence. He was looking at the *Marauder* and the other Gimlon ships as they skewed away from their position so he could not see Paris's face.

"No? Don't repair this ship?"

"No. Don't," Chakotay said, his voice hoarse. "In fact, damage it. Take life-support back off-line. Maybe if they scan us, they'll send someone back to help us out."

"Or maybe they won't, and I won't be able to get life-support back on," Paris said.

Chakotay turned his head toward Paris. "You'll probably just amaze me with your feats of engineering."

Paris frowned, then slowly lowered himself into the access port/cubbyhole of circuits. "Tom, hurry up with the life-support," he mumbled. "Hey, Tom, forget it—turn that damn life-support off."

"I can hear you," Chakotay said.

This time Paris didn't mumble. "Good!"

"Commander, you're not going to believe this! Look at all this!" Chen had rounded the corner toward Chakotay and Paris, and as the rest of the crew followed the young ensign, it became very clear that the armory had been found—and emptied.

Each crewmember had one rifle in hand and two slung over his shoulders. Some wore helmets, some body armor, and others both. Ensign Chen was grinning widely, ear-to-ear—or in this case, rifle-to-rifle.

As soon as he had joined Chakotay and Paris, the ensign began handing the ranking officers weapons. He gave them each a rifle, and then, from a sack that hung in back of him, two round objects.

"Stun grenades?" Chakotay asked.

"I think so, sir." Chen sounded practically gleeful as he hefted his rifle farther up his shoulder.

Paris touched the rifle he held tentatively.

Chakotay noticed this. "Your fingers okay? Maybe you should hang back."

"No," Paris said. "I'll be fine."

They had become a hell of a team, Chakotay thought. But his thought turned dark. Perhaps they were all that was left of the *Voyager* crew.

Like trying to unring a bell, Chakotay couldn't ignore that real possibility, now that he'd thought of it. If Janeway and *Voyager* were gone, then he was charged with seeing the remaining crew to safety, if possible home to the Alpha quadrant. Something that wouldn't happen in their lifetimes in the warp-four-maximum Gimlon vessel that they might or might not be able to capture.

He shook his head to rid himself of the unwanted, unhelpful musings. It was more useful to assume they could find Janeway when they had the means to look.

"Before we left the bridge," Chakotay began, pulling toward him the attention of the Starfleet crew before him, "Mr. Paris and I cut off life-support systems all over this vessel."

As the crewmembers finished disseminating their new-found weaponry, a ripple of confusion swept across their faces.

"We did that so that one of the Gimlon vessels would scan us, see we were in severe need of help, and would come back to render that help. That plan has worked, and one of the enemy escorts should be here within the next few minutes." Chakotay paused, bounced the stun grenade in his hand a few times, then continued. "We're going to take their ship, because we have no other choice. Mr. Paris isn't sure he could get life-support back up again if we fail . . . therefore we can't fail. Captain Janeway is depending on us, and we're depending on ourselves to get out of this situation safely. We haven't lost anyone yet, and I don't want to. Be careful, but don't hesitate to take that ship as if you were defending your home—because you will be. That Gimlon vessel might have to be our new home for a while, and—"

Cut off by the sound of metal scraping against metal, Chakotay looked at the docking port at their feet.

"Out of time," he said quickly. "I want three people in each doorway alcove up both sides of this corridor. Paris, you and Chen take the farthest one. Lothridge, Holland, you're with me. Each take one of these stun grenades and be ready to drop them down the hatch when it opens. No one move until I say, or unless I'm killed."

Again—another scraping sound. The hatch was going to open.

"Move!" Chakotay whispered loudly.

When the hatch slid open with a loud hydraulic *shuggg*, most of the Starfleeters were only halfway into position. Chakotay pressed himself against the bulkhead on one side of the hatch, Lothridge and Holland on the other.

After a few long seconds, a Gimlon head rose from the hatchway opened in the deck.

The enemy looked at Chakotay, began to speak—his mouth opening in silent horror—as Chakotay took the butt of his rifle and swung it hard against the Gimlon soldier's face.

The Gimlon lost consciousness immediately, as well as his grip on the rungs of the docking-port ladder. He fell back down into the port and, judging by a grunt Chakotay heard, knocked into one of his comrades on the way down.

"Now!" Chakotay mouthed, and Lothridge and Holland dropped their stun grenades through the hatch.

Chakotay dove away from the hatch and the bright green flash, wanting to make sure he avoided any residual blast of the energy grenade, and from the corner of his eye saw Lothridge and Holland do the same.

Rolling onto his shoulder—which made his back scream with pain—Chakotay came up, his rifle leveled at the open hatch.

No Gimlon soldier presented his head to be shot off.

Chakotay, Holland, and Lothridge all elbowed their way to the open hatch and slowly peered down.

Below them, three Gimlon soldiers lay crumpled in a heap. Chakotay gave himself an approving nod, then called to the others to come from their alcoves.

"We go down in threes," Chakotay said. "If they have the same number of crew we found on this ship, we outnumber them significantly."

Lothridge and Holland went down, followed by another crewman. When they were to the left of the ladder, Chakotay motioned another three down. "Quickly. They might have scanned the stun blast."

In moments, half of the crew was still up top, with the other half holding positions in the airlock. Chakotay was down with the advance force. "Get them out of the way," he whispered of the stunned Gimlon soldiers as he stepped over them toward the door that led to the corridor.

There was no way to know who was beyond the door.

When he turned back to his people, Chakotay found the three Gimlon soldiers lumped awkwardly into one corner. "Three down, maybe twelve to go."

They nodded at him, ready to follow him into a small battle on a small ship for a big reward.

"Paris," Chakotay called up the ladder, "we're heading out in fifteen seconds. I'll leave two behind to guard the way. Follow us down and out in thirty seconds."

From above, he saw Paris accept the order with a salute of his rifle.

Adrenaline pumped through Chakotay's every fiber. The pain in his back was now barely noticeable as he shouldered the button to open the door and the corridor slid into view before him.

He nodded toward the hallway, and Lothridge tossed another stun grenade down the deck.

The globe rolled oddly, zigging one way then another. Chakotay closed the door, and just as the hall was shut away, he heard the grenade go off, zapping the hallway and any open door with energy.

When he opened the door again, he and his team swooped out into the corridor.

"Room by room," he said quietly. "By now they must know we're aboard. Be careful."

There was no one behind the first door Chakotay opened. Just an empty control room of some kind. The second door was more exciting.

A Gimlon soldier leaped forward.

Chakotay saw the flash of a blade in the man's hand. He didn't want to fire—he knew there was no stun setting on the weapon—but the Gimlon was aiming for his chest, for his heart or lungs. He slid back and the Gimlon's lunge missed. The enemy soldier faltered, fell.

Chakotay kicked at the man's knife hand and sent the dagger skittering across the deck.

The Gimlon raised himself to a crouch, ready to attack again. Chakotay led his full weight into a blow across the man's chin with the rifle. The crack of the soldier's jaw echoed in the corridor, and he toppled flaccid onto the floor.

"Four down," Chakotay said in a low tone. "Put this one with the others."

"I found two more, Commander," Lothridge called from up the corridor. "Both knocked out."

"Okay, six down." Chakotay turned toward the open corridor just as Paris, Chen, and the others were making their way into the hall. "Move out. Deck by deck. Teams of three. What I just did was stupid—if someone attacks you, don't do the same unless you know you can win. And I mean *know* it."

"Meet you on the bridge?" Paris asked, that weird little grin curling his lips.

"Actually, you and I and a few others are going there directly," Chakotay said.

Paris gripped his rifle and winced in pain. "Fingers, don't fail me now."

The lift door opened unexpectedly—but Chakotay should have been expecting it. Two Gimlon jerked their necks back in surprise as Chakotay, Paris, Holland, and Lothridge looked back.

Chakotay pushed both soldiers back with the long frame of his rifle, and Lothridge tossed them an armed stun grenade. As the lift doors closed, they heard the grenade go off.

"One of the other teams will pick 'em up," Paris said.

"Yeah, but that was our last stun grenade." Lothridge looked very disappointed.

"We do this the old-fashioned way, then," Chakotay said. "And we fire when we have to."

"Aye, sir."

Silence dominated, save for the hum of the lift as it sped toward the bridge. When the hum stopped, and Chakotay knew they had been moving long enough to have reached their destination, Chakotay thumbed a button that kept the door from opening.

"Holland goes left. I'll go up the middle. Lothridge, flank us on the right. Paris, stay back and cover us," he whispered.

They nodded to one another, and Chakotay released the button that held the door.

When the lift door was out of their way, the Starfleeters spread out onto the bridge.

Three Gimlon officers looked up from their stations. The captain of the ship turned in his command chair, and first showed an amazed expression—then an angry one.

"Don't move," Chakotay ordered, his weapon outstretched.

The Gimlon captain rose, slowly, his chubby body awkwardly pulling itself from the bridge's center seat.

"I assume you are why I have lost contact with half my crew," the Gimlon said.

"Step away from any controls," Chakotay said to the other Gimlon. "Let's not make this difficult."

The Gimlon captain nodded. "Of course not. However, I must tell you: Computer, initiate self—"

Chakotay fired, and his rifle's whine filled the bridge.

The Gimlon captain screamed, then his body seemed to collapse in on itself as he evaporated into nothingness.

Fool me once . . . Chakotay thought. "He shouldn't have moved."

The other Gimlon just stared, incredulous.

Chakotay shrugged and stepped down to the lower deck of the bridge. His bridge, for now.

"Who are you?" One of the Gimlon soldiers finally asked.

Chakotay paused, looked at Paris a moment, then back at the Gimlon. "A leader."

CHAPTER
27

"THIS IS ALL MY FAULT," LEKKET SAID, FOR THE THIRD TIME IN as many minutes, and everyone in Engineering, Janeway especially, was tired of hearing it.

Yes, it *was* mostly his fault. The warp-dampening device that was locked onto *Voyager*'s hull had been placed there by Lekket. And the radiation it gave off had always meant to be used as a threat against Janeway and her crew. Lekket may never have intended to actually use it to kill them, but his traitorous lieutenant had had other plans. Bolis had fooled both Lekket and Janeway, and had betrayed them both in turn. That made it partly Janeway's fault that they were in this situation—but as it was her ship is was *entirely* her responsibility, no matter where blame lay.

"I need you to think," Janeway said. "Does any member of the crew you stationed on this ship have detailed knowledge of the warp-dampening device? There must be another way to shut it off."

"No, Captain . . . I'm afraid not. Bolis was in charge of such things. The only way I ever controlled the device was through him." Lekket looked even more despondent.

Janeway sighed and looked to Torres and Seven-of-Nine. "Ideas?"

Torres shared a quick look with Seven, then looked back

to the captain. "We've run it up one way and down the other, Captain. There's just no way to change the laws of physics. We can continue to put all warp power to the containment system, which will hold for only about another four hours, or we can transfer the power to the warp drive— all of it—but I don't see a way to do both. Not if we want a smooth power drag. The spikes and drains that will occur if we feed both systems will overload containment for sure, and maybe even warp propulsion."

"No," Janeway said, shaking her head. "There has got to be another way." She touched one of the Engineering consoles and a schematic of the energy conduits appeared on the board. "What if you route power through the auxiliary power conduits—split up the energy between normal lines and the auxiliary lines?"

"That seems possible," Seven said. "But there will be risks to other systems."

Janeway looked at both of them and Torres picked up the details.

"We won't have auxiliary power," Torres said. "And the dilithium chamber isn't made to have two power sources spitting energy into it. We'll crack our crystals in a matter of hours, give or take a phaser shot. And I'm assuming you want weapons on-line."

"Yes." The captain pointed again at the schematic. "I want this done—fast. We'll risk not having auxiliary power, and we'll risk cracking our dilithium. But we can't risk billions of lives. Clear?"

"Yes, Captain," Torres said.

"Understood," Seven said.

"Keep me informed." Janeway turned on her heel and walked toward the doorway. "Come on, Lekket," she called. "Let's see what Bolis has to say for himself."

Sickbay was a hub of activity, which meant that the doctor would be annoyed.

"You're asking me to give precedence to an interrogation when I've got a dozen more crewmen with radiation sickness," the Doctor was bellowing at Tuvok. "And without Mr. Paris I've only got Neelix to lend a hand. Needless to say I'm still trying to determine if that's a help or not."

"He's not asking you," Janeway said as she strode toward them, Lekket still in tow. "He's ordering you, and that order comes from me." Bolis was lying on a bio-bed, she noticed as she approached. "What's the delay?" she asked Tuvok.

"The doctor is wasting time," Tuvok said flatly.

"Hardly," the doctor replied, turning toward Janeway. "Captain, I don't know enough about his physiology to start pumping drugs into him—"

"Assume his is close to Kes's. They look similar."

"I'm sure the captain is aware that one shouldn't judge a book by its cover. Many races can look similar for evolutionary reasons, but that doesn't mean they have similar—"

"We don't have time." Janeway cut him off with a wave of her hand. "Make the best guess you can, and use a zenogenic sodium pentathol-like drug. That tends to work well with most races." She only partly knew what she was talking about, but command officers were given updates on these things, drugs meant to relax a member of an alien race—almost a hypnosis inducer. She had no time to debate the medical ethics of testing such a thing on a non-Alpha-quadrant race. Too much hung in the balance.

The doctor seemed to sigh inwardly, then relent as he readied a hypospray.

Bolis lay motionless on the bio-bed. Did he care what was going on? If he did, he didn't show it. There was a restraining field around him, but perhaps it wasn't even necessary. A regulation nevertheless. Drugs meant to help in interrogation usually lowered inhibitions, and sometimes that meant violence. Restraining him was a necessary precaution.

Besides, he had proven to be traitorous. She should have had him in chains from the first moment.

Should've, could've . . . no sense looking back now. Twenty-twenty hindsight is very clear and very useless.

The doctor placed the hypospray on Bolis at the neck, and the drug hissed into the man.

"How long before it takes effect?"

"Approximately thirty seconds."

Janeway looked from Lekket, who stood silently behind her and to her left, to Tuvok, who had his hand on his holstered phaser. A few moments into their wait, Bolis became agitated. He was still silent, but now he shifted back and forth, not really testing his bonds, but certainly stretching against them.

The doctor was monitoring on his medical tricorder. "This is wrong," he said, and punched some buttons on the bio-bed. "He's having some kind of allergic reaction."

"How bad?" Janeway asked.

As if in response, Bolis grunted in pain and pressed harder against the field that pinned him to the bed.

"Tell us the encryption sequence," Tuvok demanded.

The Doctor was now injecting something else into the prisoner's neck. "His brainwave activity is very erratic. Some neurotransmitters are hyperactive, others are breaking down into their molecular bases." He looked from the patient to the medical diagnostic board on the bio-bed. "The antidote to the drug is not having an effect."

Bolis cried out in pain. His eyes bulged, his muscles were taut and straining. Blood vessels rose on his neck and forehead.

"Tell us," Tuvok said, stepping toward Bolis's writhing form. "What is the encryption code?"

The Doctor stood incredulous, staring at his monitor. "This isn't possible! This drug couldn't cause this. His brain is breaking down—and those brain centers that are active are telling his body to shut down!" He kept resetting the hypospray, trying first one potion, then another. He attached a cortical stimulator, but to little effect.

After a long moment of terror on Bolis's face, the Doctor stopped his attempts at revival. "There is nothing left of him. His mind is gone."

The captain looked at Bolis, now lying silent, eyes rolled back in his head. If there was breath left in him, she didn't see evidence of it.

"He's dead, Captain," the Doctor said, and the words hit her like a million torpedo blasts. He shouldn't have been dead. She'd made her doctor kill someone.

"How?"

"It will take time to find out," the Doctor said, his hand gently closing Bolis's eyes.

"I am sorry, Captain," Tuvok said. "I was not able to retrieve the information we need."

The captain gripped the Vulcan's shoulders, then patted him on the arm. "We have people working on the encryption code. Last report we had twelve of the seventy-three characters decoded." She tried to smile at him, just a little—as if a Vulcan would care. "He fooled me too."

Tuvok nodded, and for the first time Janeway shifted her gaze toward Lekket.

The Edesian commodore stood, still staring at Bolis's lifeless form. Lekket's face was ashen, his eyes bloodshot. Not from tears—from horror.

"Lekket?" Janeway prodded lightly.

"I—I'm fine, Captain. I knew him, his family . . . I'd come to hate him in the last few hours . . . but I knew him . . ."

"I understand," Janeway said, although she didn't give it enough thought to do so.

Lekket nodded, lowered his head, then looked toward the other end of sickbay, where his soldiers were still held behind containment fields. "They trusted him as well . . ."

She knew he wished his men freed, but Janeway still wanted to be cautious about that. "I know," she said, then spun back to the doctor and hoped Lekket's silent inquiry would remain unspoken.

The doctor had his head lowered over the bio-bed console.

"Doctor?"

"I cannot be sure, Captain," he said, "but I don't think his death was an accident. There is a very odd enzymatic residue that none of the other Edesians seem to have."

"Perhaps he's a Gimlon," Tuvok offered.

"Unlikely. Unless their DNA structure is identical. However, if I test his mitocondrial DNA with that of the others, we might know more."

Janeway shook her head, pushing away the familial connection. "I don't care about that. What killed him?"

"Perhaps he killed himself. Or someone did," the Doctor said. "His body may have had within it an enzyme that would destroy him if a drug such as we injected came into contact with his bloodstream."

Janeway was aghast. Was Bolis a fanatic, or just a professional? "A personal self-destruct device?"

"It is not unheard-of," Tuvok said.

The captain stared at Bolis a long moment. "Maybe he didn't even know it was there," she whispered. "Maybe Gimlon spies are never meant to talk."

"We've never captured one," Lekket said. "The few times we've been in a position to, they've destroyed their vessels. Usually attempting to take our ships with them, if they can."

Lekket sounded tired. Janeway felt the same fatigue.

And *Voyager* felt it too. The engines whined, and Janeway sensed their light vibration under her boots with every step she took—even though the ship sat immobile in space. A starship was a powerful thing when it could zip into action. Stagnant, it was a giant space-paperweight, useless and exposed.

The captain tapped her combadge. "Janeway to Torres. I need that warp speed now," she demanded.

"One moment, Captain."

What if demands couldn't make the impossible possible this time?

What of the Gimlon and the Edesians if she couldn't stop them both?

"I'm out of ideas," she whispered, and Lekket overheard her.

"You did your best, Captain. Despite my foolishness and all I've done to you, you still tried your best. This is not your fault or your responsibility. It never has been."

Janeway shook her head. "My best . . ." She scoffed at herself. "I had the chance to stop all of these deaths . . . and I—"

"Captain," Torres said over her comm, *"we can take it to warp four on your orders. That's all we'll be able to do, and even that might blow every circuit we're using. We can sustain this for a few hours, or until we run out of dilithium replacements—whichever comes first."*

The smallest of chuckles catching in her throat, Janeway turned toward the door and set off for the bridge. "It's better than sitting here, B'Elanna. Janeway out." She looked over her shoulder as she strode out the door. "Mr. Tuvok, Mr. Lekket. Come on. We have a *Marauder* to catch."

CHAPTER

28

"STATUS REPORTS." CHAKOTAY SWIVELED AWAY FROM THE Gimlon computer console he'd been studying. "Holland?"

"All Gimlon prisoners are accounted for and secured in the cargo hold, Commander. To make room, we had to move what cargo they had to the disabled ship."

"Good. Let's find out what the cargo is. Chen?"

"Sir, we have access to all the ship's systems. Sublight and warp drives are nominal. Weapons array, communications, all primary systems and secondary backups are on-line and nominal. We've boosted their minimal shields some—we might get a little more protection out of them."

"Run through a few damage-control drills. If we take this ship into battle, we'll need them."

"Aye, sir."

"Lothridge?"

"Sensors are now on-line, and the computers are under our control, sir. I've used communication logs and library archives to craft a translation module. In about two minutes, all screens and readouts will be in Federation Standard Language, sir."

"Great. Paris?"

"Helm responsive, navigation ready, fingers still hurt."

"Understood. Excellent job, people. Prepare to be underway in fifteen minutes. We don't want to look suspicious to the other Gimlon. We're going to fall right back into their formation, understood? Dismissed."

They nodded their salutes and disappeared into other parts of the alien ship, except for Paris, who was learning a new helm console.

Had the Gimlon vessel possessed a sickbay, Chakotay would have liked to get a dermal regenerator working on his back, assuming the technology was available. Since they hadn't found a medical bay of any kind, even old-fashioned aspirin would have been welcome.

Glancing at Paris, who had moved from the helm to one of the computer consoles, Chakotay noticed a sour look on the man's face.

"Something wrong, Paris?" As he rose, the sores on his back, which were dry now, cracked with pain.

"Chakotay, I think you better take a look at this."

"What's wrong?"

"Everything." Paris's tone was clipped, his face tight and pale. "This is amazing. This is unbelievable. These people—"

Paris let his voice trail off. He didn't have the words. But as Chakotay gleaned the information scrolling slowly across one of the Gimlon computer monitors, he gathered the right word.

Official files of the Gimlon war effort read like propaganda—proud reports of mass murder, forced slavery, depraved methods of torture to gain information already known. The Gimlon were indeed Nazi- or Cardassian-like in their methods of terror. The database Paris had found showed evidence—boastful details, in fact—of Gimlon attempts to destroy their enemies in some not necessarily unique but certainly gruesome ways.

The Gimlon had been at war not just with Edesia but with every other race that had had the misfortune to share their borders. Two other governments were allied against the Gimlon on the opposite side of their space from their current war with Edesia. Gimlon was winning those battles, according to their own reports, but even they admitted the personnel cost was high. "The weapon" (apparently the

Marauder) had destroyed the planetary defenses of a number of worlds, and now billions of Gimlon troops were spreading out to secure those planets.

Forced famines, giant "work" camps where the goal was really death—and more often than not simple lining up and vaporizing of entire towns—all were used as methods of conquest.

Every planet that reached civilization had dealt with their share of tyrants who killed for power or even pleasure.

But the Gimlon really stood out. And they were winning their wars. Only Edesia had blocked their way, which was why they had sought simply to destroy the Edesians. Conquest of *their* worlds didn't matter anymore—so long as they were defeated such that no one would again bar the Gimlon's path to victory.

"The word you're looking for," Chakotay said finally, a slight rasp to his voice, "is evil."

"If not," Paris said, "that's close enough."

"It explains a lot," Chakotay said, leaning against the console. He felt so . . . spent. As if the revelations had been a punch in the gut that had taken in breath. "Now we know why the Edesians fear them so . . . and why *this* ship is mostly automated. . . . They have an enormous occupation force on dozens of planets on the other side of this sector. They can't afford to man this vessel at specs."

"But they have the resources . . . and the slaves to build weapons from those resources."

Chakotay nodded, and wondered if he looked as pale now as Paris did. "What about the *Marauder?*" He leaned back over Paris's shoulder. "Anything on how to defeat it?"

"No information on it at all under that name. They call it 'the weapon,' if the translator is right. Not much about it other than its use for the destruction of anyone who stands in their way. There are some classified files on it, but they're heavily encrypted. From what I've read, they use the *Marauder* to destroy a starsystem's main hub of economy and industry. Then they send in their normal vessels, then their troops." Paris looked somber, of course, but for him to say anything without a glint in his eye or a laugh just under his breath was very unusual.

There just was no glint that could live in the shadow of the Gimlon destruction. Their willing and jovial annihilation of billions of lives . . . Billions upon billions, when one added up the decimation. Perhaps only the Borg had murdered more.

"We have to stop them. Or at least try," Chakotay said quietly.

Paris nodded his silent agreement . . . then, after a few moments of staring at the computer console, he began tapping furiously and said, "Why didn't I think of this before?"

"What?" Chakotay asked.

"Searching for information on *Voyager* . . . got something!"

> *Data entry 033512A884*
> *Vessel: Voyager*
> *Origin: Unknown government referred to as "United Federation of Planets." No further information on this government body.*
> *Class: Unknown. Weapons graded as high to superior. Contemporary power source but higher yield through unknown methods.*
> *SPECIAL NOTE: This vessel should be captured if possible and delivered to Ministry of Alien Technology.*
> *Status: Sabotaged by Agent D76QPL*
> *Last report: Alien captain captured Edesian commodore and crew with help of Agent D76QPL. Agent believes alien captain will pursue hostile activity with Gimlon fleet and attempt to attack the weapon regardless. Agent ordered to disable or destroy vessel Voyager. Five Dalga Class vessels sent to intercept at Ja'len Nebula. Communications lost with all five. Search party will not be issued.*

"She's out there," Chakotay said, and almost felt like smiling.

"The captain probably thinks we're dead," Paris said. "The planet we were on before we were herded into transports was destroyed by the *Marauder*."

Chakotay nodded again . . . this was a lot of information,

and his stomach was now twisted as badly as his back ached. "What about getting a message to her? Didn't Lothridge say that they have a focused pinpoint method of secure communication?"

"They do," Paris said. "But that doesn't help us. We'd need to know *Voyager's* exact coordinates. Otherwise we have to send something wideband, and even coded it would raise suspicion."

Neither man said anything for a long time. There were alien sounds on this alien bridge, and Chakotay found them unnerving. Where he kept expecting a certain whistle or a particular creak, there was a different noise. He felt out of place, disoriented. When the lift hatch opened and Chen entered, both Chakotay and Paris seemed to snap out of their forty-five-second trance.

"Commander," Chen said as he approached. "Ensign Holland found out what's in all those cargo containers."

"Something good?" Paris asked.

"Antimatter, sir."

Chakotay shared an approving glance with Paris. "How much?"

"In all?" Chen asked. "About half what it would take to run a ship like this. That's between the cargo containers of both ships. Separated into fifty equal containers, each with their own power supply for their respective containment-field generators."

"They could be used as weapons," Paris said.

"Delivery is the problem." Chakotay looked to Chen. "Could you rig all of them to lose their containment fields at once?"

"Easy, sir. Each has a computer—just program them to go off at a certain time."

Making his way back down to the Gimlon bridge's command chair, Chakotay considered their options. . . . He couldn't count on *Voyager* because contacting her meant giving up their advantage of surprise. He couldn't defeat the *Marauder* alone, even with surprise on his side. And he couldn't transport his bottles of antimatter into the *Marauder,* because the Gimlon ships didn't have that ability. "I don't suppose we can push these things into a shuttle and send it into the *Marauder,*" he offered.

"No shuttles on this ship. There probably were at one time, but not now," Paris said.

"Taken for the war effort on their other fronts. Why not just build a fleet of *Marauder*s and take over that way? Use them as a threat."

"These folks seem to be the type who don't threaten— they just do," Paris said.

Chakotay swiveled in the command chair and faced Ensign Chen. "Can you rig those antimatter containers to go off when we flip a switch up here?"

"Aye, sir. A computerized switch could be flipped from any console."

"Do it. Fast."

Chen turned on an enthusiastic heel and left the bridge. To him this was probably exciting. He didn't know about the large moral debts the Gimlon had racked up, but those he did know about he felt would be paid. After all, his commander was in charge of an enemy ship and had the upper hand now, right?

Inexperience was bliss.

Things didn't look quite so good to Chakotay, and when he and Paris were alone again, Paris voiced the big question that Chen was too green to ask.

"You got a plan?"

"Same plan you had all day."

"I sense we're in trouble."

"Ummm," Chakotay said. "Can you maneuver this ship with any skill?"

Paris nodded. "Some. I won't know for sure until I have a chance to work with it. Every helm is different."

"You'll get your chance," Chakotay said. "We're going to attack the *Marauder*, and with any luck—destroy it."

"I'm with you," Paris said. "Even though that's more of a goal than a plan." Just a dab of lilt was back in his voice. "We *do* have an extra advantage, you know."

Chakotay would've liked to think there was something other than surprise on their side. "Yeah? What's that?"

"We have a crew on this ship. The other Gimlon ships have mostly automation."

That was true, but would it help? "It's not the little ships we'll be going after. It's their supership. Their 'weapon.'"

"Have you thought about how to deliver the antimatter?" Paris asked as he slipped into the helm seat as if he'd been there forever.

"I've thought about it," Chakotay said, and mused to himself that thinking was all he'd done—he hadn't actually come up with anything. "Any ideas?"

"Not a one," Paris said.

"Chen to bridge."

Chakotay thumbed a button on the console next to the command chair. "Bridge."

"The antimatter containers are now computer-controlled, Commander. Call up the cargo manifest on the monitor, and there's a setting to detonate. No delay."

"Good work, Chen. Report to Engineering and lend a hand there. Bridge out."

An explosion of all that antimatter would provide nice firepower. It wouldn't mean much, however, if they couldn't actually hit the *Marauder* with the blast.

Certainly before they were actually within range of the *Marauder,* a plan would present itself, Chakotay figured.

Hoped.

Prayed?

"We ready?"

Paris checked the helm console. "All stations report ready. I've got helm and navigation. You want to take tactical, or call Holland or Lothridge up here?"

"I'll take it. I want as many people in Engineering as possible. If the enemy gets some shots in, that's where it will hurt us." Chakotay left the command chair—unnecessary with such small numbers manning the needed stations—and sat himself before the console that had sensor control and tactical computer consoles.

He dabbed at the panel before him and put a grid of the sector up on the main viewer.

"The *Marauder* is a little over four minutes away at maximum warp," Chakotay said. "They're traveling at just below their maximum. Saving themselves, I guess. I'm sending coordinates to your console."

"Got 'em. Course plotted."

"Paris, is there a way to address the crew?"

"Part of communications. Panel to your left—upper controls, first three buttons."

Chakotay looked and switched the buttons on. "This is it, people . . . We're plotting a course toward the *Marauder*. We're going to make the most damage we can, and then attempt to rendezvous with *Voyager*. I know this has been a . . . *hectic* twenty-four hours. I know you're working with alien technology, on an untried ship . . . but I have faith in you all. In four minutes I'm going to ask more of you than anyone has before. But you'll come through . . . because just causes, whether you were Starfleet or Maquis, is what you're all about. This is one of those causes . . . and the fate of billions now depends on our actions in the next few minutes." Chakotay wasn't good at this—he hoped he sounded inspirational. "Let's make Captain Janeway proud . . . wherever she is."

He clicked off the comm.

"Engage maximum," he ordered, and Paris pushed their stolen Gimlon ship forward.

As the stars began to fly by across the forward viewer, Chakotay felt the chair under him and the console at his fingers starting to shake.

"What's wrong?"

"Nothing," Paris said. "Just having to compensate for the derelict vessel docked to us. No problem."

After a moment, the shudder subsided. Power readings on Chakotay's sensor console leveled off. He wondered if it would look suspicious to the Gimlon that both vessels were remaining locked together. It was probably Gimlon policy to rescue personnel, perhaps cargo, but not ships themselves. At least not when they were part of an attack squadron.

If they noticed, Chakotay hoped it would be too late.

The *Marauder* grew steadily in the center of the forward viewer. Four minutes wasn't long, and before Chakotay knew it the enemy "weapon" loomed large across the screen.

"Fall into their formation," Chakotay ordered. "We're just one of the guys."

"Is there a reason we're waiting?" Paris asked.

"Yes." A good reason too, Chakotay thought. He was

waiting for that plan to kick in. Whatever it was. "What about shoving those containers of antimatter out the cargo holds? Tractor beam them into the *Marauder*—like we did on the Edesian transport."

"I thought about that," Paris said. "Easy to do at impulse speed . . . just about impossible at warp. Not with fifty of those containers."

Chakotay's back still hurt. And his stomach was still churning from learning all that the Gimlon were—to their enemies, and probably to their own people as well.

Something had to be done, and it had to be done *right*.

"Stand by to come about on a course that takes us directly behind the *Marauder*," he ordered Paris. "Can we detach the derelict ship from here?"

"I'd think so," Paris said, plotting the course. "Just a set of docking clamps reinforced by structural integrity fields. All computer-controlled."

"That's what I think," Chakotay said hurriedly. "And so I think I've found that plan." He almost pounded at his controls. "We have to time this just right." A diagram of the *Marauder* flashed across his screen, and he verified that its armor was, in fact, weakest at the aft plasma vents.

"What?" Paris asked. "What are we timing?"

Looking up only a moment, Chakotay allowed just a touch of grin to pull his lips. "Delivery of those antimatter canisters—*in* the disabled Gimlon ship. We're going to ram it right up the *Marauder*'s tail."

His eyes back on the information that skittered across his display, Chakotay couldn't see Paris smile, but he could hear it in the man's voice.

"I love it," Paris said. "It takes you a while to come up with a plan, but when you do—look out!"

"It might not be enough."

Paris shook his head. "Oh no. This is gonna smart."

"Set the course I'm sending you," Chakotay said, still hanging over the tactical console. "I need a clean shot at those plasma vents."

Chakotay pulled in a deep breath and held it a long moment. Everything rode on this, he thought. Everything for parsecs and parsecs of inhabited space. His speech to his fractured portion of *Voyager* crew hadn't been just words . . .

but he also hadn't felt what was behind those words as he did now.

"Uh-oh . . ."

"Uh-oh?" Paris asked. "I don't like the sound of that."

"They're hailing us," Chakotay said. "Asking us why we're pulling a dead vessel with no crew into battle."

"Uh-oh."

Chakotay didn't send a reply. Instead, he brought up the controls that would release the docking clamps. "Go, Tom—now!"

Their Gimlon ship turned out of formation, her engines whining with the strain of a maximum warp maneuver. Had it been a steam engine, rivets would have popped and steel would have melted. Instead, structural integrity fields taxed the ship's systems, and coolant-leak warnings spotted Chakotay's alert console.

A communications alert flashed too—the Gimlon were now demanding to know why one of their own was suddenly acting on unknown orders.

Paris brought the ship around and straight up toward *Marauder's* aft. Too late, the *Marauder* began to turn. In its immense bulk, the maneuver was grindingly slow.

The other escorts peeled away from the giant weapon ship, but they were too late as well.

As the *Marauder* slowed to turn, Chakotay pounded at his console, releasing the derelict, antimatter-filled vessel. Inertia carried it forward, ramming it into the sluggish Gimlon supership. Metal clashed with metal in a molten flash and an accordionlike crumple tore forward from *Marauder'* aft.

Chakotay fumbled with the Gimlon computer controls before him—where was the cargo console? Where was the detonation button for those canisters? *Where?*

Finally he managed to call up the screen, then jammed his whole fist unnecessarily hard on the computerized button. He looked up—and watched as the *Marauder* was masked by white-hot explosions of energy.

"Shockwave!" Chakotay called. He knew there would be one. No sensor needed to tell him the consequence of mixing matter with antimatter. "Paris, get us out of here!"

Harsh rings of subspace disruption washed over their

hijacked Gimlon ship as it tore away from the erupting mass of the *Marauder*'s aft. The lights dimmed as power was automatically diverted to the systems that struggled to hold the small vessel together.

Chakotay glanced at the main viewscreen only another moment. Past the expanding shockwave, he saw a glint of a section of the *Marauder*'s armor careening off into space. Then another explosion—and as the flash dissipated, he saw that a giant gaping hole had been blasted from the supership's armor—where its *propulsion* had been. *Marauder* was drifting fast and out of control, her aft section open and damaged.

Their small vessel shoved itself away, bouncing across the swells of energy that radiated from the explosions.

"Paris?"

"I'm handling it!"

The ship felt as if it was being torn apart. *Voyager* could have handled the shockwave, but these low-shielded, heavily armored Gimlon ships weren't made for such deluges of raw energy.

Their hulls couldn't take the stresses. "We've got breaches!" Chakotay yelled as he struggled to order the computer to seal off exposed sections. He hoped he was working the controls correctly—these panels were alien to him. The ship was still one big unknown.

More alert beacons flashed across the sensor panel. Chen's voice could be heard on the Engineering comm. "We're losing warp power," Chakotay said, trying to take in all the blinking messages and warning flashes.

A sizzle cracked the air and Paris grunted as his helm console burst into flame before him. Puffy foam fell from the ceiling, putting out the fire and sending black smoke curling around the bridge.

White suds covered his head and his tunic, and as he turned toward Chakotay, Paris looked grim. "Warp power won't mean much—we just lost the helm."

"How bad?"

"Bad," Paris looked at his dead console. "We're out of control."

Chakotay looked from one sensor monitor to another. The *Marauder* drifted in one direction, vectoring helplessly toward open space, while Chakotay and his stolen ship spun in another direction, helpless and powerless.

The beast had lost its legs, but they'd sacrificed their own limbs, perhaps their lives, to do it.

"Heaven help us now."

"Amen."

CHAPTER
29

"WE'RE LOSING MAIN POWER," PARIS SAID, STATING THE OBVI-
ous as the lights flickered, flashed, and dimmed. He'd fled
his charred navigational console for one of the engineering
stations. "Chen and the others are having to evacuate
Engineering. There's a plasma leak. Everything is dropping
off-line. Communications, life-support, and structural-
integrity fields are on batteries, but not for long. I'm trying
to use manual thrusters from here—see if I can keep us
from drifting."

Chakotay nodded and struggled with his controls. He'd
made a record of everything he and the others had learned
about the Gimlon and their ships, everything from the
Gimlon library computer and everything they'd learned
about the automation of the small Gimlon ships. If he could
just add the *Marauder*'s status, and their own, and get it
broadcast to *Voyager* before they lost power . . .

It didn't matter now if he sent out a wideband broadcast.
Let the Gimlon know. What could they do?

"We've got hostiles," Paris said, pointing to the dimming
main viewer. "Isn't that tactical display working at all?"

"No," Chakotay said, trying frantically to send out
the supercompressed hypertransmission. He glanced up a
moment, watched as four Gimlon escorts headed toward

229

them, then suddenly turned away—back toward the *Marauder.*

"Where are they going?" Paris asked. "Not that I'm complaining."

Chakotay didn't answer. He waited, rerouting all available power to communications so that he could send all the data in a single fast burst.

"Look at that," Paris said. "They're tractoring the *Marauder.* Pulling it back on course."

"Damn!" Chakotay allowed that news to stop him. "It's not as damaged as we thought. Their weapons system must be completely separate from propulsion." Quickly he plotted their course from current trajectory, and added that info into the report.

Again the lights and panels dimmed. Chakotay saved the information, called up the last of the communications power, then sent the transmission, broadcasting it on a Starfleet frequency. Maybe the Gimlon wouldn't even be listening to such a high subspace channel.

Suddenly, the power dropped off. The lights flashed and then were gone. Emergency light beacons lit up, but they were dim and everything was cast in shadow.

"I don't know if it got through," Chakotay said, feeling defeated. "Any chance we can get some power here?"

Paris shook his head. "We're pretty good at disabling these Gimlon ships. Too bad it's always from the inside."

Chakotay shook his head and chuckled darkly. "If the *Voyager* has been sabotaged, and doesn't get that message . . ."

"Yeah, I know," Paris said. "We're dead . . . again."

"Captain, we're back up to warp four point six-two."

Janeway nodded. She felt like she was riding in an early-model solid-fuel low-atmosphere shuttle. Her uncle had several in his collection and he'd taught her to fly above the fields of his property. Sometimes they'd even go into town, and people with modern flitters would wave and come up to see the old-fashioned vehicle. Occasionally they'd go to an antique shuttle show together.

That's what her state-of-the-art ship reminded her of—an old Oldsmobile shuttle running out of gas but never quite going empty. *Voyager* surged forward at warp five with a gush of energy, then slowed to warp three as power sagged back to a level the energy conduits could really handle. When Torres had told Janeway she could have warp four, the captain didn't think that would mean their *average* speed.

"What will you do, Captain?" Lekket said softly from next to Janeway. He sat in the seat usually occupied by Chakotay. "If we find the *Marauder* . . . in your weakened condition, what *can* you do?"

That question had been gnawing at her since they'd been underway. The *Marauder* was slow, but warp four was its maximum. If *Voyager* could inch out just a little faster, they might catch up with the *Marauder* before it got to the Edesian homeworld. And if that happened, and if *Voyager* could stop the *Marauder,* then Lekket could have the Edesians call back their fleet, which was on its way to destroy the Gimlon homeworld.

A pile of "ifs." Not a strong foundation for a plan.

However, Lekket's question wasn't what would she do. It was what *could* she do. She could exhaust the *Voyager's* weapons, for one. That might do it. Might.

"We're back down to warp three point three, Captain," the helmsman said.

Janeway finally turned to Lekket, groping for an answer to his question. "They've found nearly half of the encryption code Bolis placed on the computer control of the warp-dampener. If we can get full power . . ."

It was a half-hearted answer, and the chances were they would not intercept the *Marauder* before it arrived at Edesia. That was the gamble Janeway was taking. She didn't want to anticipate the *Marauder's* path toward the Edesian homeworld. Edesian intelligence didn't know what course their enemy was taking toward them . . . and Lekket wasn't sure where the *Marauder* would come from. As far as he was concerned, its ability to disappear was still near-magic. She'd decided to try and head the *Marauder* off at the pass, and she just hoped she'd get the *Voyager* to Edesia before the Gimlon destruction force arrived.

"Warp three point six, Captain."

"Mr. Tuvok, what's the average?"

"We've been averaging warp three point seven-five, Captain."

Not good. Not if *Marauder* was heading toward Edesia at warp four—and the *Marauder* had the advantage of a head start.

"Captain . . ." Harry Kim's voice.

Janeway swiveled toward him. "Mr. Kim?"

"I'm picking up a hail—on a Starfleet frequency!"

Moving quickly from her chair to Ensign Kim's side, Janeway wanted to see this for herself.

"From where?"

"This sector," Kim said. "A small burst of activity on that channel, now nothing."

"Chakotay?" Janeway looked over to Tuvok who was suddenly bent over his sensors.

"Ensign," Tuvok began, "please transfer the data from that transmission to my station."

Kim nodded and dabbed at his console. "Aye, sir."

After a moment's study, Tuvok looked up at Janeway. "I believe we can assume from this that Commander Chakotay is alive."

Chakotay *was* as good as dead, and he knew it. They'd lost everything but the dim emergency lights, and had they not rerouted the Gimlon automation, they wouldn't have even had that.

Time had passed slowly, and the air was very thin. Both men were feeling sleepy, and while Paris kept himself busy fiddling in one of the bridge access panels, Chakotay just sat, running through in his mind what he could have done differently that might have saved their lives.

There must have been something.

"Paris?" Chakotay's voice echoed slightly on the quiet bridge.

"Yeah?"

"What are you doing over there?" Chakotay could barely see him.

"Just looking. Feeling around is more like it." Paris coughed. Gasped for breath a little. "Maybe . . . maybe we can get battery power on-line again. Life-support . . ."

For all his complaining, Paris was more than just a guy

with a smirk and a glib comment. He *was* that, of course, but he was also an optimist. Not just a wiseguy, a never-say-die guy. Chakotay admired that, and wondered why he sometimes forgot it.

Right now, Chakotay was feeling anything but optimistic. If his message had gotten out, there was no guarantee *Voyager* would pick it up, and even if *Voyager* did get the message, maybe she was already sabotaged beyond repair.

He should have risked sending the message as soon as it was possible. So what if that would have given him away to the Gimlon? Had he sent the data an hour ago, he'd be just as dead, but Janeway would have heard the message and maybe saved *Voyager* and the Edesians both.

Chakotay pulled in a deep breath . . . noticed the air was getting thicker with soot and thinner with oxygen. Hull breaches . . . no power to life-support . . . plasma leaks . . . coolant leaks . . . toxic smoke . . .

"You think the others made it out of Engineering before the plasma spread?" Chakotay heard himself ask this, and thought his voice sounded thick. His back was in pain again.

"Yeah, they probably got out."

"No one's tried to make it up here."

"Might be trapped between decks. Debris, or a breach stopping them from getting here," Paris said, grunting as he continued to work.

"What are you doing?" Chakotay asked, then realized he'd asked the same just a few minutes before.

He coughed. He'd taken in so much smoke. The air was so thin . . . so dirty . . .

"Paris?"

"Yeah?"

Chakotay never says this. He should say it. Now. Before it was too late. "I think you're . . . I like you, Tom."

"You're not going to kiss me or anything, are ya?"

The darkness hid Tom's smile, but Chakotay knew it was there.

Chakotay smiled back, into the shadows. "Not even to save my life. But . . . I—I just didn't want you to think we weren't friends."

There was a pause. Or maybe there wasn't. Everything seemed very slow.

"I never thought otherwise, Chakotay," Paris said. "I always just figured that you were my hard-nosed, moralistic, mostly humorless friend, and I was your sarcastic, sometimes-insubordinate, kinda-jerky friend."

Chakotay felt himself chuckle, and the motion sent a dull pain down his back.

The air was so thin . . .

Hull breaches . . . coolant leaks . . . no life-support . . .

Janeway . . . B'Elanna . . . Seven . . .

Harry . . . Tom . . . Neelix . . .

Tuvok . . . the Captain . . . B'Elanna . . .

Toxic smoke . . . Chen and the others . . . Did they make it out of Engineering?

Sure they did. Didn't they? Chakotay's back hurt and he heard Tom say something. Shadows swirled around him. He was so sleepy . . . the air was so thin . . . and the dark was now so dark . . .

"Paris?"

"Yeah?"

"What are you doing over there?"

"Nothing, Chakotay . . . nothing."

CHAPTER
30

"How is he?"

Dark as pitch at first, the universe bubbled only black.

"Ready to come out of it soon."

Voices bounced across the darkness as the black melted into a gray palette with small flashes of light, even some color.

"How badly was he hurt?" That voice was soft, caring, worried, yet also strong, and it held a ring of familiarity so great that the darkness was pushed even farther away.

"Worse than the others. His back was injured—the lacerations were infected, and he also had two cracked ribs."

His back, yes . . . the pain was gone now. The sting had been so constant that he'd thought it a part of his soul. One of the voices had healed him—the male voice.

"He'll be fine in a few moments, but I would say you beamed them out just in time."

Chakotay tried to raise his head, open his eyes. Nothing happened.

"He's wheezing," the female voice said.

Were they talking about him? He didn't think he was wheezing. It was then he recognized his own heartbeat, slow

235

and steady, and over that, the slight wheeze the voice mentioned.

"That's normal," the male voice said. The doctor—he was in sickbay—on *Voyager*. He'd heard all their words but hadn't placed the voices. He was waking up, inwardly at least. He was beginning to realize—he wasn't dead!

"I had to clear some carbonaceous sputum," the Doctor said.

"And that is?" Janeway's voice.

"Black soot in the back of his throat. Upper respiratory burns. He also had some conjunctival irritation and acute laryngeal edema. As I said, you beamed him out with only moments to spare. The first tricorder reading we took showed an eighteen percent carbon-monoxide blood level. All of them needed a hemoglobal injection to increase the oxygen content of their blood."

The male voice babbled on like that for some time, and Chakotay allowed himself to ease back into the darkness. He didn't try to rise again, didn't struggle with the dark. He let it envelop him like a cocoon, warm and restorative. The voices continued, for how long he wasn't sure, but they were warm too, and in their way, also refreshing.

A hiss—near his ear—and suddenly the dark evaporated completely. The universe was too bright now, even through his closed eyelids. Inwardly, perhaps outwardly as well, he cringed.

"Chakotay?" Janeway whispered close to him.

He tried to nod, tried to speak. His neck was stiff and his throat was very dry.

"Cap—tain . . ."

"Save your voice, Commander," the Doctor said. Chakotay opened his eyes a slit and looked up, but the light was too bright and he quickly jammed his eyelids shut again. "Your larynx was swollen—the heat and smoke inhalation. You'll be a little hoarse for the next few hours."

Chakotay managed a short nod, and this time felt his head bob against the bio-bed. His voice sounded old and rough when he said "I . . . understand."

Struggling against the glare of harsh sickbay lights, Chakotay managed to flick his eyes open slowly.

"Good to see you," he told Janeway, and she smiled back at him. "The others? Paris? Chen?" he asked, still not believing the voice with which he spoke was his own. It sounded more like his grandfather's.

"All fine, Commander," the Doctor announced with some pride in his tone. "Most have returned to quarters, a few to duty at their request, the captain's approval, and against my recommendation. I do hope you'll be wise enough to take your doctor's advice and return to your quarters for some much needed rest."

Chakotay nodded again. Maybe he would, maybe he wouldn't. He could handle the light now, and he cautiously eased himself into a sitting position, swinging his legs off the bed so that he could face the captain. "Where are we?"

Janeway put out her arm to steady him, and even though as every moment passed he felt stronger and stronger, he leaned into her support.

"We're about thirty minutes from where we picked you up," Janeway said. "That puts us between seven and thirty-three minutes from the *Marauder,* at current speed."

"Seven to thirty-three?" His voice was gravel. He tried to clear his throat, and while that didn't hurt, it didn't help the dryness.

"Commander, can I get you some water?"

Chakotay turned toward that voice, and saw Neelix, bright and happy, at the head of the bio-bed.

With Chakotay's nod, Neelix smiled, spun around, and headed for the nearest replicator.

"Not icewater, Mr. Neelix," the Doctor called after him. "Ten degrees, no less."

Chakotay nodded again, accepting that he couldn't have a cool drink, which was regardless what he craved. "Sabotage?" he asked Janeway.

"Bolis," the captain said, her voice bitter, and in a few sentences filled Chakotay in on what had happened since she thought he and the others had been killed.

"Now," she said, "we're having trouble maintaining warp four. We have two-thirds of Bolis's encryption code broken, but I doubt we'll have it all before we meet up with the *Marauder.*"

"We could wait," Chakotay offered, speaking slowly, unsure of his speech. "How soon until they would reach the Edesian homeworld?"

"Another two hours. The escorts towing the *Marauder* can only manage warp two now," Janeway said. "Our other ticking clock is what's left of the Edesian fleet. The Edesians are headed toward the Gimlon homeworld. They'll get there within the hour, and will threaten to destroy the planet if the *Marauder* isn't called back."

"They won't call it back," Chakotay said.

Janeway frowned. "I know. And the Edesians will follow through on their threat. They believe they'll be saving the galaxy—keeping the Gimlon from making war for at least a few hundred years."

"I'm not sure they wouldn't be wrong." The cloudy haze that blanketed Chakotay's mind was peeling back somewhat faster now, and he slipped off the bed and stood firmly on the deck as Neelix brought him the glass of water. He took it and drank greedily. Every mouthful tasting better than the last. As he lowered the glass from his lips, he glanced around sickbay. Crammed behind a containment field to his left was a large group of Edesian soldiers. Standing confined to the right, the Gimlon soldiers he'd captured from the second Gimlon vessel he'd acquired.

"Captain," he ground out finally, "the data we sent—on the *Marauder*—the Gimlon . . . they're running a three-front war. They won't need their own homeworld—they'll use someone else's and rebuild there."

"We got your data," Janeway said, nodding her agreement. "It's what led us to you. But while you and I know about the three-front war, the Edesians didn't. Lekket was surprised. All he knew was that Edesian trade terminated with the one starsystem, they thought for internal reasons. They didn't even know about the existence of the other culture the Gimlon are destroying."

"Contact them." Chakotay handed Neelix the glass and smiled a thanks. "Tell them—"

"They won't listen." Janeway waved the idea away with her hand. "Lekket was told to maintain radio silence. They won't answer hails now. If we can stop the *Marauder*—stop this before more billions die . . ."

Chakotay nodded a salute. "Permission to report to the bridge, Captain?"

A slight smile tugged at Janeway's lips. "Doctor?"

The Doctor sighed. "Does it even matter what I recommend?"

"Not really," Chakotay said huskily. "I feel fine."

"You feel fine because I've injected you with biochemical confections that *make* you feel fine."

Chakotay cocked his head to one side and looked at the Doctor with eyes that tried to appeal to a holographic and computerized conscience. He was home, he was alive, and *Voyager* had a job to do. He needed to be on that bridge, and the doctor knew that.

"Fine. Go. Get out," the Doctor said, motioning Chakotay and the captain out the door. "But when you come running back because you're exhausted, don't expect my normally genial, even-tempered bedside manner."

"I won't, I won't." Chakotay, his captain at his side, headed for their bridge.

As the door closed to sickbay, Janeway whispered to him, "Even-tempered?"

"Normally genial?"

Janeway shook her head. "If that's what he's like when he's genial . . ."

CHAPTER
31

"CAPTAIN ON THE BRIDGE," PARIS CALLED AS CHAKOTAY AND Janeway marched from the turbolift.

Janeway slid down to the command deck, greeting Lekket with a nod. "Mr. Paris, looks like you're feeling better."

Paris held up his fingers, wiggled them, then nodded his own approval. "Yes, ma'am. I certainly am."

Janeway felt her brows knit.

Chakotay slid into his seat next to the command chair, and leaned toward Janeway. "Paris burned his fingers pretty badly. The doctor probably had to repair some nerve damage."

"I see," Janeway said. "Mr. Paris, did you get too used to that Gimlon ship, or can we count on you to remember how to pilot *Voyager?*"

Paris turned back, his hands gliding over his console even with his eyes turned away. "Amazingly, Captain, everything is right where I left it."

"Mr. Tuvok, is the *Marauder* still on sensors?"

"Affirmative, Captain. At our average rate of speed, we will intercept within fourteen minutes."

She eyed the viewscreen with caution, and regarded the small dot that was the Gimlon's *Marauder*. "Do they read us?"

"Unknown. At this range I cannot determine."

"Status on the encryption code?"

"Fifty-six of the seventy-three characters have been determined."

"Not enough. I wish we had had a chance to at least try a Vulcan mind-meld before Bolis self-destructed."

"I don't understand," Chakotay said.

"Bolis, maybe even without his knowledge, had some kind of implant in his brain. When we introduced a chemical to loosen his tongue . . . the device killed him—painfully."

Chakotay nodded. "That sounds like something the Gimlon would do." He looked at Lekket, who sat in the seat farthest from Janeway—the only other seat that was available. "Mr. Lekket," he greeted.

"Commander . . . I am sorry for your injuries. I trust you had no casualties—"

"None, thankfully."

Lekket nodded his somber approval.

He'd been a different man, Janeway thought, since he'd learned his own people were now only fighting for revenge.

"They'll listen," Janeway said to him. "They'll have to."

"With some luck, yes," he said. "You're our only hope, Captain."

Unfortunately, that was probably true.

"Weapons status?" Janeway asked, turning toward Tuvok.

"All weapons on-line. Phasers ready, but with the drain on warp power we can only manage a forty-three percent charge."

The captain turned her gaze back toward the forward viewer. "It'll have to do."

"Captain," Paris pulled her attention. "We're speeding up—warp four point seven."

Tuvok only checked his board for a moment. "That will bring our IP with the hostile to ninety-three seconds, Captain."

"Better to take them by as much surprise as possible. Maintain speed as best you can, Tom." Janeway thumbed a control on the arm of her chair. "Battle stations, all hands."

All hands . . . at least she had all hands back on board.

Only now to lead them to their deaths? Not if she could help it.

"The *Marauder* is weakened," Janeway said. "Go after the small escorts first. Get them out of the way. Target their automation centers—and make every blow count."

"Targeting," Tuvok said evenly. "Intercept with first escort in sixty-eight seconds."

"Attack pattern delta, Mr. Paris."

"Aye, Captain. Delta pattern."

Sixty seconds became sixteen, then six, and the *Marauder* grew large on the forward viewer, then spun out of view as Paris maneuvered *Voyager* in a large loop, swinging itself toward one of the middle Gimlon scouts that were towing the *Marauder* into battle.

All five Gimlon escorts dropped their tractor-beam connections to their supership and turned toward *Voyager*.

"Get them out of the way, Tuvok," Janeway called as Paris jumped the ship around Gimlon disruptor blasts.

Chakotay turned to the console next to him and pulled up a tactical display. "Automation systems running on all those ships."

"Already targeted," Tuvok said . . . and at Janeway's order, *Voyager* fired.

Long bars of phaser energy slammed into one Gimlon ship, then another.

"Direct hits—" Harry Kim called excitedly.

"Those two are breaking off attack. Drifting," Paris said.

"They've lost main power," Harry said.

"Three more coming in." Tuvok pressed his controls. "Phasers, locked."

"Fire at will." Two Gimlon escorts had dropped out of the battle with only two phaser shots. Chakotay's information on their internal systems was a godsend. Perhaps they'd make it through this after all.

Lekket, too, looked somewhat more convinced that the war wasn't over. He leaned forward in his chair, and watched Chakotay's tactical display with concentration.

As her ship sliced out into cold space with hot power, Janeway saw triumph in a plan, even as two of the three shots *Voyager* fired did only minimal damage to the Gimlon escorts. "Tom, alter course. Push us as close to the *Marauder* as possible."

"Aye, aye."

"All three Gimlon are trying to protect their automation centers," Harry reported.

"They're firing—"

The ship quaked. The shields had let a lot of the energy from the Gimlon disruptors through to the hull.

"Evasive against the *Marauder*, Mr. Paris. Stick close and let them miss us and fire right into the ship they're trying to protect."

Voyager launched six fast shots of red-orange phaser fire at the three escorts. One more ship bounced away, limping, electrical flame dancing across its armored hull.

The enemy fired, raking its salvos against *Voyager*'s shields. Janeway gripped the arms of the command chair.

"They're trying to knock out primary phasers," Tuvok said. "I believe we can assume they have a detailed schematic of our vessel."

No doubt thanks to Bolis. Even in death he hampered them still.

"Torpedoes, Mr. Tuvok. We need a clear shot at the *Marauder*."

"Aye, Captain."

Red bulbs shot forth from *Voyager*'s torpedo maw—and swiftly connected with the two remaining Gimlon escorts.

Each enemy ship exploded into its own orange-white bubble of fire.

Their debris tumbled helplessly into space, cooling as it went, until only dark cinders toppled end-over-end into the emptiness.

The *Marauder* was alone. Motionless. Unable to run.

The supership tried to turn, too slowly, like a beetle trying to outmaneuver a bee.

"Mr. Chakotay disabled its propulsion—now let's disable its weapons," Janeway said, inching out of her command chair. "Point blank and fire, Tuvok."

Phasers sliced into *Marauder*'s armor, etching fire into lines plowed apart by *Voyager*'s angry energy.

Torpedo blasts exploded over the enemy supership's skin, pocking it and making it bubble molten ore.

The *Marauder* struggled to roll toward them, so that its forward weapons might strike out. Janeway didn't let that happen. She ordered Paris to ride the *Marauder's* back, and Janeway could almost feel the frustration of their Gimlon captain.

He was helpless, and she had the upper hand.

Finally.

"Captain, we have an overload in conduit thirty-seven gamma," Harry Kim said. "Engineering is working on it."

"Reroute." Janeway swiveled from him to Tuvok. "Maintain fire."

It wasn't the way most battles went. Enemies usually didn't sit and allow you to destroy their systems. But Janeway felt no pity. Only hate. Three billion lives. And how many other billions in the two other wars the Gimlon were fighting?

She realized she was gritting her teeth as she watched the *Marauder's* armor crumble and crack, then blast away under the force of *Voyager* onslaught.

The structure beneath the enemy's armor was showing through the cracks and chasms. A *solid* structure.

Her jaw aching from her unconscious teeth-gritting, Janeway spun toward Harry Kim's station. "Scan that. Is that a solid hull *beneath* the *Marauder's* armor?"

"Scanning—"

There was too long a pause. Janeway glanced at Tuvok, who was consumed with his task of breaking through the rest of the *Marauder's* armor shell.

Shell . . . was it just that? Just a shell?

Or was there even more armor under this?

"Captain," Harry finally said, "I can't scan the structure beneath. Sensors are being reflected back."

"Reflected back?" Incredulous, Janeway turned her head toward the viewscreen—toward the *Marauder* as it lost its blanket of armor, only to reveal an inner vessel.

Pushed down by the force of *Voyager's* attack, the *Marauder* drifted beneath them, shards of armor now peeling off and careening into space.

Below the last remnants of protection that had been the

Marauder's outer skin, was a vessel of such . . . beauty, such smooth design, that Janeway couldn't imagine it was made by the same Gimlon designers who had manufactured the bleak and colorless *Marauder*.

Golden and gracefully curved, the inner *Marauder* was also missile-shaped, but much more fluid and elaborate in its line and cut. The *Marauder* had been slow and looked fast. This new vessel, now out of its armor cage, looked faster and sleeker than anything Starfleet had ever designed.

"Tuvok? Harry?"

"Energy readings are off the scale, Captain," Tuvok said.

Harry Kim sounded as uncertain as his readings. "Still unable to penetrate . . . *that* with sensors. Hull composition: unknown. Power source: unknown. Weapons: reading the massive weapon the *Marauder* used to destroy the Edesian colony."

"It's not their technology," Janeway said, standing, still glaring at the "new" *Marauder*. "That's why they have only one. They didn't design this. They never had this much power."

"That is possible," Tuvok said. "It has no propulsion. Perhaps it is a part of another vessel."

"It can still do damage, and can still be towed into battle," Janeway said, leaning over Paris to dab at a button on his console. "Target the—"

"Captain—I'm reading an energy buildup on the alien vessel!"

She turned to Harry. "Its cloak?"

"Has to be, Captain."

Janeway twisted toward the tactical station. "Tractor beam—*now*. Wherever it goes, so do we."

The alien vessel began to quiver on the viewscreen—and then the *Voyager* along with it.

"I cannot guarantee power will hold—"

"Transfer all avail—"

"Brace for energy wave!"

Craaaack!

The universe snapped. Janeway grabbed hold of Tom's chair and held on as *Voyager* was crushed by the laws of physics in action—then reborn a moment later with the silence held by empty space.

Janeway staggered toward her command chair, feeling drained and a little dizzy. "What happened?"

"Unknown. Shields holding. Tractor beam intact. And we have seven hostiles, Captain," Tuvok said, a bit amazed. "E.T.A. thirty-three seconds."

"From where?"

"Captain—" Harry Kim sounded a bit dizzy himself. "We've moved thirty-six thousand, four hundred sixteen kilometers from our last position."

Janeway looked toward Lekket, who sat dazed, staring at the forward viewer. At the *Marauder's* inner-self, and at the seven Gimlon escorts that approached.

"That's not very far for an escape," Paris said.

"Disengage tractor-beam. Mr. Paris, come about. Prepare to engage the escorts." The captain swiveled toward Tuvok. "Where did they come from?"

"They didn't," Tuvok said, looking up from his console. "According to our relative position to the nearest star and the positions of its local planets, we have moved forward in time approximately forty-three minutes."

Janeway's jaw was tight and for a moment she didn't quite grasp Tuvok's statement. They'd been right—and wrong. "We were right. It's not a cloak. But they don't escape to another *place*—they escape to another *time.*" She turned to Lekket. "Not magic—"

Harry Kim cut his captain off. "Five more hostiles are approaching. Twelve ships in all now."

Janeway nodded toward the forward viewer. "Mr. Paris, full impulse attack. Dance around their fire."

Paris's fingertips drummed at his naviconsole. "Aye, Captain," he said . . . and sent *Voyager* plunging into the cotillion of fire and power.

Last dance, Janeway thought. *Better make it count.*

CHAPTER

32

"TACTICAL REPORT," JANEWAY ORDERED.

"The first seven ships are engaging us," Tuvok said. "The other five have taken the *Marauder*'s inner device in tow."

"Smart," Janeway said, spitting the thought in anger. "They called enough reinforcements to handle us *and* continue their mission."

Voyager glided one way, then another. The Gimlon escorts surrounded her, swarmed her, protecting their underbellies where their automation centers were.

"Why seven? Why not seventy?" Paris asked, wrestling with his controls, making their ship loop and spin and sway its way around Gimlon plasma bolts and disruptor shots.

"They have limited resources with a three-front war," Tuvok explained. "They did not expect us to stand in their way."

Paris nodded. "Neither did we."

True. Six days ago *Voyager* had been battling four Aakteian War Raiders and had barely left Aakteian space with their ship intact. Five seconds ago, twelve Gimlon escorts had swooped down from fate and meant to destroy *Voyager* and her crew.

But Captain Kathryn Janeway wouldn't let that happen.

She hadn't let it happen at the hands of the Aakteian, the Borg, and the Kazon—and certainly wouldn't at the hands of the Gimlon.

Twenty-four hours ago, this hadn't been her war to fight. Now it was. The Gimlon had technology they shouldn't and were using it to fight a war of conquest that they would expand as far as possible.

Today three neighboring starsystems—tomorrow, the quadrant. They had murdered billions, and intended to murder billions more.

The Edesians, in revenge, in terror, would destroy the Gimlon homeworld. That might end the Gimlon's ability to make war—but how many innocents would die in that battle?

If Janeway let it happen.

She could not . . . and if she was somehow unable stop it all from happening, she would die trying. *Voyager* and its crew would die with her.

"The *Marauder* was just taken to warp," Harry announced. "Warp two point two-one-five." It was headed back into battle, tugged by five Gimlon escorts toward the destruction of entire planets.

"We don't have time for this," Janeway said, rising from the command chair and stalking toward Tuvok's tactical console. She glared at the schematic of one of their ships. Small flashes showed places of damage. "Protecting their underside leaves their impulse reactors open," she said, pointing at the display. "Phaser their propulsion, then move around and target those automation centers with a torpedo."

Tuvok nodded. "Aye, Captain."

"We keep using them at this rate, eventually we'll run out of torpedoes," Paris said, grunting as he struggled to be fast enough on the helm to keep ahead of the Gimlon's salvos.

"Then we run out," Janeway said, coming back down to the lower deck and setting herself back into the command chair. "So long as we stop this insanity."

Voyager's crew acted as the team they were. Paris maneuvered in and out of the line made by the seven Gimlon ships. Tuvok targeted the enemy's impulse drives, and when those were skewered with phaser shots, the vessels slowed to thruster maneuvers.

Plasma from seven leaking impulse drives filled the vacuum around them, making space sparkle. Had not so much death hung in the balance, the sight would have looked almost pretty.

The ships slowed, but they hadn't stopped. The enemy seemed more frantic in their attack pattern. Some of their shots began to connect.

"Spin around them, Tom. We have to stop their ability to achieve warp speed." It wasn't enough to disable their impulse capability. Janeway couldn't let them follow her into final battle with the *Marauder* weapon.

Voyager fired two torpedoes, then another two, and finally one more. The orange globes spread out. All but one connected with their targets.

Four of the Gimlon escorts sputtered at odd angles away from *Voyager*. Inertia carried them out of weapons range. "Four hostiles disabled, Captain. One remains, bearing one-five-five mark three."

"Target and fire."

"Captain, the remaining Gimlon is moving off . . . heading into warp."

Janeway felt her brows pull together in surprise. "Running?"

"I don't think so," Chakotay said. "That's not like them."

"Pursuit course, Mr. Paris . . . take us into warp."

"Warp engaged, aye."

"I cannot believe they are running, Captain," Lekket said, his voice both surprised and elated. "You have them on the run!"

Harry Kim had the answer from his Ops station. "He's taking a course toward the *Marauder*, Captain. And the *Marauder* is stopping and turning around."

"No!" Lekket slumped back into his seat, his spirit dashed.

"They know we can outrun the *Marauder*'s weapon," Janeway murmured. "Why—"

"Captain, we're falling out of warp!" Paris stared at his console as if the ship had lost its mind.

Janeway struck her combadge. "Bridge to Engineering. What's going on?"

"Torres here, Captain. The warp-dampener has activated. We can't maintain a warp envelope."

Bolis—again from beyond the grave. Not only had he programmed the warp-dampener to irradiate the ship, but it was programmed to disable their warp drive.

"Why now?" Janeway asked herself, but Tuvok answered. The Vulcan shook his head and rechecked his console. "We just found the sixtieth character of his encryption code. That seems to have triggered the warp-dampener. The radiation level is declining, but in response the dampener is not allowing us to maintain warp speed."

Bolis had planned well. Thinking it possible that Janeway would be able to hold off the radiation for long enough to find the encryption code, he had rigged it so the warp-dampener would kick in if enough of the computer code was decrypted. Smart.

"We're sitting ducks again," Janeway said, edging toward the helm. "Impulse evasive. Best possible speed."

"You cannot escape at sublight speed," Lekket said, his voice once again reeking of self-pity and despair.

Janeway did her best to ignore him. "Torres, we can't create a warp envelope, but warp power is still available, right?"

"Yes, Captain."

"Transfer from the containment fields—since we don't need them right now. I want all available power to the shields."

"Aye, Captain."

"Bridge out." Janeway pivoted toward Ensign Kim. *"Marauder* status?"

"Building up their main weapon. They're at impulse and closing to weapons range." Harry's tone was calm in relation to Lekket's. Then again, anyone's would be.

"Can we outmaneuver that beam of theirs?"

"Unlikely," Tuvok said gravely. "Not without warp speed."

Harry braced himself, his fingers pressing hard into his console. "Captain, they're within range!"

"Tuvok, fire at will! Try to disable the escorts pulling the *Marauder*. If we can immobilize them—"

What was left of the *Marauder*—really just a few shreds of armor over the glistening technology that was surely not the Gimlon's own—loomed forward, the maw of its weapons port glowing in malevolent anticipation.

Voyager slung torpedoes at the giant, her captain hoping that all Davids had a knack for downing relative Goliaths. Three globes of fire hit the *Marauder* dead on. Two jammed themselves into the Gimlon escorts.

The escorts staggered, shuddering in space, their tractor beams wavering for a moment but holding. They continued forward, pulling the *Marauder* with them. Apparently the Gimlon had diverted some of their ships that did not use automation. They were probably fully staffed vessels— much to Janeway's dismay.

"They're firing," Tuvok called, and every muscle in Janeway's body stiffened.

There was a flash, and the view on the forward screen dimmed.

"Subspace disruption off the scale, Captain—"

How could she fight a beam that could vaporize an entire ship in an instant, and destroy an entire planet—ripping it to shreds—in an instant more?

The impact felt like a sledge hammer to her gut, and there was a loud crack that Janeway felt in her bones. An overload caused a console to port to smoke and spark. The ship creaked, rumbled—a support strut clattered from the ceiling to the deck behind her, bringing wires and computer components down with it.

Last time the *Marauder*'s heavy weapon beam had pushed *Voyager* into warp, this time there was a difference. *Voyager* shook and quaked and unhinged some—but she didn't fall into warp. The enemy stopped firing, and while the ship was tattered, and the worse for wear, she was nevertheless intact.

Everyone unclenched just a little—Janeway could feel a collective sigh of relief.

"We survived," Paris said, amazed, and he spoke for the entire bridge.

"They're retreating, Captain," Harry Kim said. "Pulling out to just outside our weapons range."

"Pursue, Captain?" Paris asked.

"Not yet." Janeway didn't think that their weakened state would hold up. That it did had to be more than luck—there was a reason, and she wanted to find it.

"Tuvok?" She prodded him for an answer to her unasked but obvious question.

"Yes, Captain, I am doing some calculations . . . Perhaps we damaged them more than we thought."

"Hurry."

Somewhere there was an answer, and with Tuvok's help she had to find it. She'd been hampered at every turn . . . If she'd had just one other ship with *Voyager*'s power . . .

But she didn't have another ship—and she had only the technology *Voyager* brought from Alpha quadrant.

No . . . that wasn't quite true. She had some technology that wasn't hers at all.

Janeway leaped up to the tactical station. "Tuvok—the warp-dampener! It's dampening their beam. Of course—we knew it was a subspace beam."

Janeway chided herself. She had never thought to use the warp-dampener as a defense—she had only considered it a ball and chain around her ankle.

Tuvok paused in his calculations—or just continued them in his head, Janeway wasn't sure which. After only another moment, he called up more data on his console and went through it at furious speed.

"You have something." She leaned across the tactical console, hoping that he'd found their answer.

"I have," he said, with just a dash of excitement in his tone. "This vessel—the advanced technology they are using—is essentially a subspace amplifier with a method of applying that power to an object—us, a planet . . . I have looked at the data from their destruction of the Edesian colony, and should have seen this as the dynamic in use before. For only a brief moment, their beam actually caused a large amount of that planet to travel forward in time. When it reappeared just a moment later, the rest of the planet had moved forward in space as well as time. The two sections of planet were reunited, and the force of that explosion was massive—and fatal. They did not wink part of the planet out of existence, or even move it in space. They merely moved it forward a split-second in time."

Janeway nodded her understanding. "And when that beam struck us, most of the subspace force was canceled by the warp-dampener. Allowing us to survive."

"Indeed," Tuvok said. "When they have previously used it on vessels it most likely overloaded a ship's warp engines and caused an immediate warp-core explosion."

"My soul!"

Janeway spun toward Lekket, who now stood rigid in awe and horror. "We had the answer all along," he lamented. "We could have . . . we could have saved them all!"

"No time for hindsight," Janeway said, and she turned back to Tuvok. "Before they have time to repower fully— give me a way to use this."

"Placing a series of warp-dampeners on the *Marauder* would probably cancel its power," Tuvok offered. "But I do not believe we have those resources or the time to gather them."

The captain shook her head. "Then don't mention it. There must be a way—"

The thought struck her like a bolt of lightning. She stared at Tuvok's face—past him really, straight into her idea.

"Captain?" the Vulcan prodded.

"Yes, Mr. Tuvok. Hold on." Janeway stepped toward Tuvok's console. She leaned over the station behind him, punching up the data she thought would help.

She tapped her combadge. "Janeway to Torres. I'm sending some data to your station. Can we do what I want?"

There was a pause, as Torres probably scanned the data and gathered her captain's idea. *"Captain, I can do it—but we won't survive it."*

"How long will it take you to hook the warp-dampener into our shields?"

"It's just a matter of matching its frequency and modulation, I'd think. Reconfiguring the deflector array might for that much output, however . . ."

"Don't reconfigure it. We don't have time. Just tell me when the shields have been modified. No more than five minutes, B'Elanna. It's all we can spare."

"You can have it in three, Captain."

"Stand by to engage on my mark. Janeway out." The captain marched down to the command chair, but did not sit. "This might not be total protection, people, so we want to move fast and try to avoid that beam as much as possible."

"What exactly are we doing?" Harry asked.

She cocked her head toward Tuvok. "We can't destroy that thing with conventional weaponry, right?"

"I do not know, but I would surmise that we cannot," Tuvok said flatly. "The hull is of unknown construction but what readings we can get show it to be very dense."

Janeway's throat felt very dry and she suppressed a gulp. "What if we got it to fire on us, with our shields running through the warp-dampener?"

"Their weapon would be almost completely ineffectual," Tuvok answered.

Janeway lowered herself back to the command deck. "And if we enveloped the *Marauder* with our shields?"

Tuvok paused. He took in the ramifications of that idea, then slowly gave his reply. "The subspace disruption beam would be trapped within the shields. The power would build to unmeasurable levels . . . perhaps."

"If we can't destroy it," Janeway said, "maybe we can get it to destroy itself."

Tuvok nodded. "I would not put it in such colorful terms, Captain, but that is essentially the idea."

Chakotay, silent for the last few minutes except when giving orders to the damage-control teams, turned to Janeway. "We're going to have to get very close to it to put shields around such a large vessel, Captain."

"I know," she said. "Let's hope we survive anyway."

"Will this work?" Lekket asked Chakotay.

"Maybe," Chakotay said. "If we're lucky."

Lekket frowned. He had never seen himself as lucky, Janeway realized. "Will we survive?" he asked. He didn't sound much like he cared.

"Maybe," Chakotay said again, and Janeway wondered if he believed it. Did she? Lekket didn't even sound like he wanted to survive. Was that why he asked? Not out of cowardice, but in the hope that his life would end?

No time to weigh that either. "Paris, set the course," she ordered. "Straight up and on them. Make them fire at us, but not until we're within . . ." She leaned over his station and punched a coordinate. "This distance."

He nodded. "Understood. Put my head in the tiger's mouth. Got it."

Paris was flip, but essentially correct. And they weren't even sure this would damage the enemy sufficiently.

"Engineering to bridge. We're ready, Captain."

Janeway lowered herself into *Voyager*'s command chair, perhaps for the last time. "Engage, Lieutenant."

The ship sounded no different, except for a slight drag in power as energy was transferred from wherever to the shields.

"Full impulse, Mr. Paris. Stand by."

"Full impulse, standing by, aye."

"Mr. Tuvok—as soon as we're in range, fire torpedoes as fast as we can load them. I want to distract them. Get them to fire on us again." Janeway grabbed the arms of her chair and held on for dear life. "Let's hope they've recharged enough to do it."

"Target locked, Captain," Tuvok said, his voice still a pool of calm in these choppy seas.

"All ahead full, Tom—and hold us together!"

Voyager pounced forward, and as she did the view of the *Marauder* jumped closer on the forward screen.

The Gimlon escorts broke away from tractoring their superweapon, diving toward *Voyager* and firing as they plunged.

Janeway was buffeted from one side of her chair to the other as the ship jolted around her, twitching and jumping under the concussions of the Gimlon disruptors against *Voyager*'s shields.

"Reduce magnification," she ordered through gritted teeth, and her view of the *Marauder* was less overwhelming—now it took up only half of the main viewer.

The shots rang through her ears as *Voyager* fired torpedoes one after another, all over the *Marauder*'s escorts.

Two torpedoes, then four, then six . . . bolts of energy that pounded into space—sometimes connecting with the Gimlon escorts, sometimes not.

The enemy ships abandoned their fire and tried to get back to the *Marauder* to pull her around for another attack at *Voyager*.

Janeway accommodated them and started to move close to *Marauder*'s bow.

Twelve torpedoes, fourteen, sixteen—one on top of another, over and over. Explosions ripped into the escorts, into the *Marauder* . . . everywhere.

Whatever she was made of, the *Marauder* was tougher than *Voyager*'s hull. Without armor, without shields, any other ship would have been destroyed.

"Captain—" Tuvok's voice. "We have only eight torpedoes left."

"Use them! I don't want those escorts pulling the *Marauder* away."

Hurling her last remaining torpedoes forward, *Voyager* sped on closer to the *Marauder* and the massive forward opening that was her target.

"Reading an energy buildup on the *Marauder*, Captain—" Harry Kim—holding up well under the strain. "They might be ready to fire!"

As the last explosions from the photon torpedoes gushed energy into the *Marauder*'s escorts, the enemy ship's weapon began to glow harshly.

"Ready on the deflector, B'Elanna!"

"Ready, Captain."

This was it . . . this was the last ditch effort. They might not win, but they damn well wouldn't die on their knees either.

Marauder heaved forward, ready to fire, and as *Voyager* swooped close, Janeway gave the order. "Now, Torres! Get our shields around it!"

Voyager shuddered as it massed power away from its own skin. Space, for all its vastness, seemed small as Janeway's ship tried to bear-hug the enemy.

Marauder fired and its beam pounded the shield bubble all around it. The white plank of energy bent back on itself and bounced within the shield globe, filling the subspace dampening cocoon *Voyager* had woven around the Gimlon supership.

Janeway felt the surge of power that space itself had taken on.

The *Marauder* was buffeted within the trap, and quickly became wrapped in its own energy discharge. The enemy ship began to glow—first red, then orange, and then a dull white.

The main viewscreen flashed brightly, and a snap vibrated through *Voyager* and her crew. The captain felt it in every cell—a ripping feeling, as if she was being torn apart then smashed together again in less than a microsecond.

Janeway lost her grip on the command chair and was yanked forward, thrown up against the main viewer, then slammed again into the deck in front of the navigational console.

"Sh—shields col-lap-p-p-sing, Capt—"

She felt it all—the insanity that was a universe turned in on itself. They were dying . . . being crushed by the power of—

Suddenly the feeling was gone.

When the viewscreen winked back on, the Gimlon escorts were just a debris field pushing out in a ring of high-speed flotsam.

The *Marauder* was absent—again.

Janeway staggered, pulled herself up and leaned in front of Paris's station.

"Tuvok?" she rasped.

"Hostiles do not register, Captain. Debris ring expanding at warp one point five and slowing. Sufficient debris to account for the Gimlon escorts."

"And the *Marauder?*" She staggered forward, closer to the viewer. Had the damn ship escaped again? Disappeared to a different time? Minutes from now? Hours?

Before her, space opened up for a moment, deposited a chunk of gleaming goldish wreckage, then closed again. The fragment drifted toward them.

"Scanning," Tuvok said. "Composition unknown. Heavy subspace residue. This entire area of space is temporally unstable, Captain. I recommend we pull back to a safe distance."

"Pull back, Mr. Paris." Janeway inched around the helm

and toward her command chair. Her every muscle ached. "Why? What's happened?"

"We are in the presence of an unstable subspace phenomenon," Tuvok said, and as he finished that sentence space erupted just a speck and spat forth another slab of debris.

"We destroyed it," Janeway whispered.

"Apparently," Tuvok said. "And the debris will be scattered across not space . . . but time."

Before them, as *Voyager* slowly backed away, the fabric of vacuum flickered again, and more rubbish from *Marauder*'s form appeared, then disappeared. An eerie monument to the power that destroyed billions of lives.

"Communications?"

"Working, Captain," Harry said.

"Send this message to the Edesian government. Mark it urgent. "You have your revenge. The *Marauder* is dead. Your homeworld is safe. Come back home." Janeway stared at the screen . . . at the debris of the *Marauder* as it continued to bubble into existence and then disappear before her eyes. Without turning to Lekket, she spoke to him. "Convince them. It's over."

Lekket nodded. "Thank you, Captain. I just—there aren't words."

She glanced at him and found he was crying.

"Find the words to stop your people from killing anymore," she said. "And then we'll talk about the rest."

EPILOGUE

"IT IS A BEAUTIFUL PLANET. YOU REALLY SHOULD SEE IT," Chakotay said.

Janeway viewed the planet from her office window as it spun slowly below her—and felt like that was enough.

"I can see it from here," she said finally, absent-mindedly trying to do the shoulder exercises the doctor had recommended. A week had passed and she was still stiff. Probably tension—but she wasn't about to tell the doctor that. He'd find a way to order her to the planet for R and R, and she didn't want to be there.

Chakotay stepped closer into the room and laid a data padd on her desk. "I think I understand," he said. "I haven't actually spent much time down there either, except to debrief some of the Gimlon captures. Looks like we were right about the *Marauder*'s core being alien technology. Apparently the thing appeared in Gimlon space a few months ago. They discovered its power, and began their war of conquest. Its debris is still appearing in and out of space in that region. Tuvok says it might indefinitely."

She nodded, still staring at the planet below. Three billion people died on a similar planet—all Edesians. To see those who survived, even at her hand, would only remind her of those she couldn't save . . . didn't save. "How's the refit going?" she asked on the trail of a sigh.

"Fine. The Edesians are better hosts than taskmasters. We're almost completely repaired. The warp-dampening device is finally off the hull, and the hull plates are being repaired." Chakotay motioned toward the padd as she turned from the window. "With the Edesians' abundance of antimatter and their ability to duplicate our torpedo containers, we have a full complement of working torpedoes again."

"Unfortunately, we'll have occasion to use them," she said, and allowed just a little too much bitterness to tinge her voice.

"Captain," Chakotay began slowly, stepping closer to her desk, "you saved many more than those you couldn't—"

She lowered herself into her desk chair and dismissed his comment with a wave of her hand. "I know, I know." And yet somehow that didn't matter.

The chime at her door sounded.

"Come," she said.

Tuvok stepped into her office, Lekket behind him. "Commodore Lekket would like to see you, Captain."

She nodded, and the Vulcan led Lekket in.

"Commodore," she greeted, and gestured him to a chair.

Lekket spoke. "Mr. Lekket," he corrected. "Not Commodore. I have returned to my duties as husband, father, and grandfather . . . and I found out yesterday—greatgrandfather."

"How old are you?" Janeway asked.

"Will your translator convert the years? I am eightythree."

He wasn't young . . . he only looked it. Here she thought he might be like Kes, only a few years old. No accounting for looks—Lekket looked twenty-five and had greatgrandchildren.

"Congratulations, Mr. Lekket," Janeway said, but found it difficult to smile. "I thank you for your appeals to the Edesian government not to destroy what is left of Gimlon. I hope that standard is maintained."

"It is my hope as well," Lekket said.

He seemed a different man. He was a grandfather. A

great-grandfather . . . not a soldier, and suddenly he seemed more natural, more at peace with himself.

Janeway hoped her peace would return soon.

"Captain," Lekket said as he stood. "I wanted to see my great-grandchild first, and I have done that. Now I wish to offer myself to you, and the authority of your government, for my crimes against you and your vessel and her crew. I alone wish to represent the Edesian government in this matter."

The captain looked at him, head to toe, then looked into his glistening eyes. Something within her said that he had petitioned his government to do this—that they neither required his sacrifice nor sanctioned it.

"My government is sixty years from here," she said. "You want to be locked in this ship's brig for sixty years?"

Lekket looked back into her eyes. "Yes, Captain. I am prepared for that."

And he probably was. She believed him now. He was a man of honesty, thrown into a position he had not enjoyed and had not thought himself worthy of, by a war he didn't want to force others to fight.

"Prepare yourself for this," Janeway said, standing. "I'm placing you on parole. I want you to stay, and protect your family and your people from another war with the Gimlon, which I would expect to happen if nothing changes in the way the Edesians deal with their enemies."

Lekket looked perplexed. "I'm not sure I understand."

"When we first met you said we were all animals, Lekket. You said we only play at civilization. Maybe you have been—but I haven't. And I want you to stop," she said, flattening her hands on the desk and leaning toward him. "We're not animals, and neither are you. We have volition, Lekket. We can have control, and I want you to change things for your people. I want you to make sure the Edesians don't punish the Gimlon people for a war their leaders waged. I want you to fight for a legitimate government for them—not just for you. They have the right to liberty—just like you, and just like me. Freedom isn't just for those with the power—its for those without the power as well."

She glanced at Tuvok a moment, then caught Lekket's eyes again. "A friend and I once debated the idea that right and wrong—and liberty—might depend on the culture and perhaps didn't apply to all sentient beings. I don't believe that, and I don't think you do either."

"I . . . I have never thought about it," Lekket admitted.

"Start thinking," Janeway said, straightening.

Lekket lowered his head in a slow nod. "I was wrong to take your freedom from you, Captain. I do realize that, and I *am* sorry."

"Prove it to me, Lekket. Change your people's ways. Make sure it doesn't happen again. Fight for *your* liberty, yes—but fight for mine as well, and for the Gimlon's . . ." She motioned with her hand, taking in Chakotay and Tuvok and her entire ship with one gesture. ". . . as we fought for yours."

"I will try, Captain," Lekket said sincerely. "But I am one man and my people are stubborn."

"You're one man," Janeway said. "Now go convince a second. And a third. And the three of you—go convince others. All you need is one man with an idea, with reason on his side . . . and with liberty as his goal. Fight for it, Lekket. Teach it to your children, and grandchildren, and great-grandchildren. And for pity's sake . . . teach it to the Gimlon. They'll grasp it. All you have to do is ask them to think. And they can do that—we all can. We wouldn't have the ability to be out here if we couldn't."

Lekket nodded again, very slowly, but very deliberately. "You are most wise, Captain."

"No," she said. "I just use my reason as best I can. Your sentence . . . is to do the same. And to make others do that as well."

The Edesian held out his hand. "I will, Captain. You have my word."

Janeway took his hand and held it firmly. "Good luck, Mr. Lekket."

"Thank you, Captain. For everything."

He released her hand and Chakotay saw him out the door.

Tuvok remained a few feet from Janeway's desk, and she looked up at him after a moment. "Something wrong, Mr. Tuvok?"

The Vulcan, hands behind his back, walked smoothly toward her desk. "I am impressed. You have been just, and in doing so might just spread that justice to two peoples who otherwise would have extinguished one another. You are, in fact, most wise."

"I don't feel like it," she said, and turned her neck to stretch her aching muscles. "I don't think I'd make a good Vulcan. I feel very . . . sad."

"Why?"

She looked at him, but her mind's eye conjured up billions of faces she didn't know, could now never know.

"There really is no justice here, Tuvok," she said. "Too many people are dead to satisfy justice."

"Captain, the battle *is* ended," Tuvok said. "Those who have done wrong have paid for their crimes."

The captain shook her head. "No, Tuvok . . . debt remains. And in that . . . there is only a shallow victory."

He paused. Vulcans rarely touched others to lend them support, but in his voice she *heard* his hand on her shoulder. "Perhaps. But your words reached Lekket, and he might very well change the future."

Janeway lowered herself into her chair and swiveled to see out the window. She watched as the top of a beautiful blue-green planet spun slowly on its axis.

"Maybe," she agreed. "We'll have to have faith in that, I guess."

"No, Captain," Tuvok said, his voice smooth and quiet. "Not faith but confidence. Based on the evidence that you, and I, and those like us *may* struggle to find civilization in the chaos—but we do indeed find it. Within ourselves, and in others throughout the galaxy. You said it yourself. If one can think logically enough to conquer space, one can grasp the reason of liberty as well."

"Why must they grasp it so late? Why must innocent people die?" She wasn't asking him. She was lamenting reality.

"The answer is complex," he said.

She smiled up at him. He'd managed to break through her tension, just a little, and she smiled because the universe didn't look all that glum anymore. And tomorrow would be better, she knew. "You're a good friend, Tuvok. But the question was rhetorical."

He cocked his head slightly and looked a bit puzzled.

"Thank you. I was not attempting to be amusing or friendly. I was merely—"

"Mr. Tuvok?"

"Yes, Captain?"

She stood, her data padd in hand, and walked toward the door. "Sometimes it's okay just to nod when someone asks a rhetorical question."

The door opened and she stepped out, motioning for him to join her.

"I fail to understand," he began, "how you can maintain such a rational philosophy, and then indulge in something as irrational as a rhetorical question. If you do not wish the question answered, why ask it?"

Janeway strode to her command chair, and lowered herself easily into the soft but strong lines of the center seat.

Standing to one side, Tuvok looked at his captain a moment, as she tried very hard not to look him in the eyes. Finally, he spoke.

"Captain, did you hear me?"

"Yes, Mr. Tuvok . . . but I thought your question was rhetorical."

Tuvok pressed his lips into a thin line—the equivalent of a Vulcan sigh—and retired to his station.

On the forward viewscreen, the Edesian homeworld sparkled up at her. Lights brilliantly showed through the darkness of an Edesian night. Cities, filled with people who didn't die. Somewhere on that planet . . . a child was laughing, a family was eating dinner. People were playing games and were happy.

Somewhere below her someone was giving birth. Someone was dying naturally. It was raining somewhere on that planet. And somewhere else a small animal was rolling on the ground enjoying the sunshine.

She pushed away her dark thoughts . . . because the universe still held just too much light.

"Maybe I will beam down," she said, mostly to herself. "Just to feel their earth, if not my own, under my feet."

Look for STAR TREK Fiction from Pocket Books

Star Trek®: The Original Series

Star Trek: The Motion Picture • Gene Roddenberry
Star Trek II: The Wrath of Khan • Vonda N. McIntyre
Star Trek III: The Search for Spock • Vonda N. McIntyre
Star Trek IV: The Voyage Home • Vonda N. McIntyre
Star Trek V: The Final Frontier • J. M. Dillard
Star Trek VI: The Undiscovered Country • J. M. Dillard
Star Trek VII: Generations • J. M. Dillard
Star Trek VIII: First Contact • J. M. Dillard
Star Trek IX: Insurrection • J. M. Dillard
Enterprise: The First Adventure • Vonda N. McIntyre
Final Frontier • Diane Carey
Strangers from the Sky • Margaret Wander Bonanno
Spock's World • Diane Duane
The Lost Years • J. M. Dillard
Probe • Margaret Wander Bonanno
Prime Directive • Judith and Garfield Reeves-Stevens
Best Destiny • Diane Carey
Shadows on the Sun • Michael Jan Friedman
Sarek • A. C. Crispin
Federation • Judith and Garfield Reeves-Stevens
The Ashes of Eden • William Shatner & Judith and Garfield
    Reeves-Stevens
The Return • William Shatner & Judith and Garfield Reeves-
    Stevens
Star Trek: Starfleet Academy • Diane Carey
Vulcan's Forge • Josepha Sherman & Susan Shwartz
Avenger • William Shatner & Judith and Garfield Reeves-Stevens
Star Trek: Odyssey • William Shatner & Judith and Garfield
    Reeves-Stevens
Spectre • William Shatner

#1 *Star Trek: The Motion Picture* • Gene Roddenberry
#2 *The Entropy Effect* • Vonda N. McIntyre
#3 *The Klingon Gambit* • Robert E. Vardeman
#4 *The Covenant of the Crown* • Howard Weinstein
#5 *The Prometheus Design* • Sondra Marshak & Myrna
    Culbreath

#6 *The Abode of Life* • Lee Correy
#7 *Star Trek II: The Wrath of Khan* • Vonda N. McIntyre
#8 *Black Fire* • Sonni Cooper
#9 *Triangle* • Sondra Marshak & Myrna Culbreath
#10 *Web of the Romulans* • M. S. Murdock
#11 *Yesterday's Son* • A. C. Crispin
#12 *Mutiny on the Enterprise* • Robert E. Vardeman
#13 *The Wounded Sky* • Diane Duane
#14 *The Trellisane Confrontation* • David Dvorkin
#15 *Corona* • Greg Bear
#16 *The Final Reflection* • John M. Ford
#17 *Star Trek III: The Search for Spock* • Vonda N. McIntyre
#18 *My Enemy, My Ally* • Diane Duane
#19 *The Tears of the Singers* • Melinda Snodgrass
#20 *The Vulcan Academy Murders* • Jean Lorrah
#21 *Uhura's Song* • Janet Kagan
#22 *Shadow Lord* • Laurence Yep
#23 *Ishmael* • Barbara Hambly
#24 *Killing Time* • Della Van Hise
#25 *Dwellers in the Crucible* • Margaret Wander Bonanno
#26 *Pawns and Symbols* • Majiliss Larson
#27 *Mindshadow* • J. M. Dillard
#28 *Crisis on Centaurus* • Brad Ferguson
#29 *Dreadnought!* • Diane Carey
#30 *Demons* • J. M. Dillard
#31 *Battlestations!* • Diane Carey
#32 *Chain of Attack* • Gene DeWeese
#33 *Deep Domain* • Howard Weinstein
#34 *Dreams of the Raven* • Carmen Carter
#35 *The Romulan Way* • Diane Duane & Peter Morwood
#36 *How Much for Just the Planet?* • John M. Ford
#37 *Bloodthirst* • J. M. Dillard
#38 *The IDIC Epidemic* • Jean Lorrah
#39 *Time for Yesterday* • A. C. Crispin
#40 *Timetrap* • David Dvorkin
#41 *The Three-Minute Universe* • Barbara Paul
#42 *Memory Prime* • Judith and Garfield Reeves-Stevens
#43 *The Final Nexus* • Gene DeWeese
#44 *Vulcan's Glory* • D. C. Fontana
#45 *Double, Double* • Michael Jan Friedman
#46 *The Cry of the Onlies* • Judy Klass
#47 *The Kobayashi Maru* • Julia Ecklar

#48 *Rules of Engagement* • Peter Morwood
#49 *The Pandora Principle* • Carolyn Clowes
#50 *Doctor's Orders* • Diane Duane
#51 *Enemy Unseen* • V. E. Mitchell
#52 *Home Is the Hunter* • Dana Kramer Rolls
#53 *Ghost-Walker* • Barbara Hambly
#54 *A Flag Full of Stars* • Brad Ferguson
#55 *Renegade* • Gene DeWeese
#56 *Legacy* • Michael Jan Friedman
#57 *The Rift* • Peter David
#58 *Face of Fire* • Michael Jan Friedman
#59 *The Disinherited* • Peter David
#60 *Ice Trap* • L. A. Graf
#61 *Sanctuary* • John Vornholt
#62 *Death Count* • L. A. Graf
#63 *Shell Game* • Melissa Crandall
#64 *The Starship Trap* • Mel Gilden
#65 *Windows on a Lost World* • V. E. Mitchell
#66 *From the Depths* • Victor Milan
#67 *The Great Starship Race* • Diane Carey
#68 *Firestorm* • L. A. Graf
#69 *The Patrian Transgression* • Simon Hawke
#70 *Traitor Winds* • L. A. Graf
#71 *Crossroad* • Barbara Hambly
#72 *The Better Man* • Howard Weinstein
#73 *Recovery* • J. M. Dillard
#74 *The Fearful Summons* • Denny Martin Flynn
#75 *First Frontier* • Diane Carey & Dr. James I. Kìrkland
#76 *The Captain's Daughter* • Peter David
#77 *Twilight's End* • Jerry Oltion
#78 *The Rings of Tautee* • Dean W. Smith & Kristine K. Rusch
#79 *Invasion #1: First Strike* • Diane Carey
#80 *The Joy Machine* • James Gunn
#81 *Mudd in Your Eye* • Jerry Oltion
#82 *Mind Meld* • John Vornholt
#83 *Heart of the Sun* • Pamela Sargent & George Zebrowski
#84 *Assignment: Eternity* • Greg Cox

Star Trek: The Next Generation®

Encounter at Farpoint • David Gerrold
Unification • Jeri Taylor
Relics • Michael Jan Friedman
Descent • Diane Carey
All Good Things • Michael Jan Friedman
Star Trek: Klingon • Dean W. Smith & Kristine K. Rusch
Star Trek VII: Generations • J. M. Dillard
Metamorphosis • Jean Lorrah
Vendetta • Peter David
Reunion • Michael Jan Friedman
Imzadi • Peter David
The Devil's Heart • Carmen Carter
Dark Mirror • Diane Duane
Q-Squared • Peter David
Crossover • Michael Jan Friedman
Kahless • Michael Jan Friedman
Star Trek: First Contact • J. M. Dillard
The Best and the Brightest • Susan Wright
Planet X • Michael Jan Friedman
Ship of the Line • Diane Carey

#1 *Ghost Ship* • Diane Carey
#2 *The Peacekeepers* • Gene DeWeese
#3 *The Children of Hamlin* • Carmen Carter
#4 *Survivors* • Jean Lorrah
#5 *Strike Zone* • Peter David
#6 *Power Hungry* • Howard Weinstein
#7 *Masks* • John Vornholt
#8 *The Captains' Honor* • David and Daniel Dvorkin
#9 *A Call to Darkness* • Michael Jan Friedman
#10 *A Rock and a Hard Place* • Peter David
#11 *Gulliver's Fugitives* • Keith Sharee
#12 *Doomsday World* • David, Carter, Friedman & Greenberg
#13 *The Eyes of the Beholders* • A. C. Crispin
#14 *Exiles* • Howard Weinstein
#15 *Fortune's Light* • Michael Jan Friedman
#16 *Contamination* • John Vornholt
#17 *Boogeymen* • Mel Gilden
#18 *Q-in-Law* • Peter David

#19 *Perchance to Dream* • Howard Weinstein
#20 *Spartacus* • T. L. Mancour
#21 *Chains of Command* • W. A. McCay & E. L. Flood
#22 *Imbalance* • V. E. Mitchell
#23 *War Drums* • John Vornholt
#24 *Nightshade* • Laurell K. Hamilton
#25 *Grounded* • David Bischoff
#26 *The Romulan Prize* • Simon Hawke
#27 *Guises of the Mind* • Rebecca Neason
#28 *Here There Be Dragons* • John Peel
#29 *Sins of Commission* • Susan Wright
#30 *Debtors' Planet* • W. R. Thompson
#31 *Foreign Foes* • David Galanter & Greg Brodeur
#32 *Requiem* • Michael Jan Friedman & Kevin Ryan
#33 *Balance of Power* • Dafydd ab Hugh
#34 *Blaze of Glory* • Simon Hawke
#35 *The Romulan Stratagem* • Robert Greenberger
#36 *Into the Nebula* • Gene DeWeese
#37 *The Last Stand* • Brad Ferguson
#38 *Dragon's Honor* • Kij Johnson & Greg Cox
#39 *Rogue Saucer* • John Vornholt
#40 *Possession* • J. M. Dillard & Kathleen O'Malley
#41 *Invasion #2: The Soldiers of Fear* • Dean W. Smith &
     Kristine K. Rusch
#42 *Infiltrator* • W. R. Thompson
#43 *A Fury Scorned* • Pam Sargent & George Zebrowski
#44 *The Death of Princes* • John Peel
#45 *Intellivore* • Diane Duane
#46 *To Storm Heaven* • Esther Friesner
#47 *Q Continuum #1: Q-Space* • Greg Cox
#48 *Q Continuum #2: Q-Zone* • Greg Cox
#49 *Q Continuum #3: Q-Strike* • Greg Cox
#50 *Dyson Sphere* • Charles Pellegrino & George Zebrowski

Star Trek: Deep Space Nine®

The Search • Diane Carey
Warped • K. W. Jeter
The Way of the Warrior • Diane Carey
Star Trek: Klingon • Dean W. Smith & Kristine K. Rusch
Trials and Tribble-ations • Diane Carey
Far Beyond the Stars • Steve Barnes
The 34th Rule • Armin Shimmerman & David George

#1 *Emissary* • J. M. Dillard
#2 *The Siege* • Peter David
#3 *Bloodletter* • K. W. Jeter
#4 *The Big Game* • Sandy Schofield
#5 *Fallen Heroes* • Dafydd ab Hugh
#6 *Betrayal* • Lois Tilton
#7 *Warchild* • Esther Friesner
#8 *Antimatter* • John Vornholt
#9 *Proud Helios* • Melissa Scott
#10 *Valhalla* • Nathan Archer
#11 *Devil in the Sky* • Greg Cox & John Greggory Betancourt
#12 *The Laertian Gamble* • Robert Sheckley
#13 *Station Rage* • Diane Carey
#14 *The Long Night* • Dean W. Smith & Kristine K. Rusch
#15 *Objective: Bajor* • John Peel
#16 *Invasion #3: Time's Enemy* • L. A. Graf
#17 *The Heart of the Warrior* • John Greggory Betancourt
#18 *Saratoga* • Michael Jan Friedman
#19 *The Tempest* • Susan Wright
#20 *Wrath of the Prophets* • P. David, M. J. Friedman,
     R. Greenberger
#21 *Trial by Error* • Mark Garland
#22 *Vengeance* • Dafydd ab Hugh
#23 *Rebels Book 1* • Dafydd ab Hugh
#24 *Rebels Book 2* • Dafydd ab Hugh
#25 *Rebels Book 3* • Dafydd ab Hugh

Star Trek®: Voyager™

Flashback • Diane Carey
The Black Shore • Greg Cox
Mosaic • Jeri Taylor

#1 *Caretaker* • L. A. Graf
#2 *The Escape* • Dean W. Smith & Kristine K. Rusch
#3 *Ragnarok* • Nathan Archer
#4 *Violations* • Susan Wright
#5 *Incident at Arbuk* • John Greggory Betancourt
#6 *The Murdered Sun* • Christie Golden
#7 *Ghost of a Chance* • Mark A. Garland & Charles G. McGraw
#8 *Cybersong* • S. N. Lewitt
#9 *Invasion #4: The Final Fury* • Dafydd ab Hugh
#10 *Bless the Beasts* • Karen Haber
#11 *The Garden* • Melissa Scott
#12 *Chrysalis* • David Niall Wilson
#13 *The Black Shore* • Greg Cox
#14 *Marooned* • Christie Golden
#15 *Echoes* • Dean W. Smith & Kristine K. Rusch
#16 *Seven of Nine* • Christie Golden
#17 *Death of a Neutron Star* • Eric Kotani
#18 *Battle Lines* • Dave Galanter & Greg Brodeur

Star Trek®: New Frontier

#1 *House of Cards* • Peter David
#2 *Into the Void* • Peter David
#3 *The Two-Front War* • Peter David
#4 *End Game* • Peter David
#5 *Martyr* • Peter David
#6 *Fire on High* • Peter David

Star Trek®: Day of Honor

Book One: *Ancient Blood* • Diane Carey
Book Two: *Armageddon Sky* • L. A. Graf
Book Three: *Her Klingon Soul* • Michael Jan Friedman
Book Four: *Treaty's Law* • Dean W. Smith & Kristine K. Rusch

Star Trek®: The Captain's Table

Book One: *War Dragons* • L. A. Graf
Book Two: *Dujonian's Hoard* • Michael Jan Friedman
Book Three: *The Mist* • Dean W. Smith & Kristine K. Rusch
Book Four: *Fire Ship* • Diane Carey
Book Five: *Once Burned* • Peter David
Book Six: *Where Sea Meets Sky* • Jerry Oltion

Star Trek®: The Dominion War

Book 1: *Behind Enemy Lines* • John Vornholt
Book 2: *Call to Arms . . .* • Diane Carey
Book 3: *A Tunnel Through the Stars* • John Vornholt
Book 4: *. . . Sacrifice of Angels* • John Carey

Star Trek®: My Brother's Keeper

Book One: *Republic* • Michael Jan Friedman
Book Two: *Constitution* • Michael Jan Friedman
Book Three: *Enterprise* • Michael Jan Friedman